M000080951

Like
Happiness

Like Happiness

Ursula Villarreal-Moura

CELADON
BOOKS
NEW YORK

This is a work of fiction. All of the characters, organizations, and events portrayed in this novel are either products of the author's imagination or are used fictitiously.

www.celadonbooks.com

Designed by Michelle McMillian

Library of Congress Cataloging-in-Publication Data

Names: Villarreal-Moura, Ursula, author.
Title: Like happiness / Ursula Villarreal-Moura.
Description: First edition. | New York : Celadon Books, 2024.
Identifiers: LCCN 2023023342 | ISBN 9781250882837 (hardcover) |
    ISBN 9781250882844 (ebook)
Subjects: LCGFT: Queer fiction. | Novels.
Classification: LCC PS3622.I493986 L55 2024 | DDC 813/.6—dc23/
    eng/20230524
LC record available at https://lccn.loc.gov/2023023342

Our books may be purchased in bulk for promotional, educational, or business use. Please contact your local bookseller or the Macmillan Corporate and Premium Sales Department at 1-800-221-7945, extension 5442, or by email at MacmillanSpecialMarkets@macmillan.com.

First Edition: 2024

10 9 8 7 6 5 4 3 2 1

For women

Why would you want to be with someone if they didn't change your life? . . . Life only made sense if you found someone who would change it, who would destroy your life as you knew it.

—ALEJANDRO ZAMBRA, *BONSAI*

Like
Happiness

1.

The scene was this: I was seated on the 6 train, checking my mascara in a compact, when a trio of teenage boys deposited a large boom box near my suede boots. One leaned down to click PLAY, and within seconds they began break-dancing to "Billie Jean," launching themselves from metal poles and twirling on the floor of the sticky subway car. The oldest boy pointed to me whenever the song mentioned Billie Jean, clarifying to fellow commuters that I was not his lover. The repeated intrusion of a finger near my chest prevented me from stowing my compact or feigning aloofness.

Anyone other than you might incredulously wonder how I could recall this night so vividly. You, however, never doubted my photographic memory, perhaps because you realized how present I was with you at all times.

As "Billie Jean" faded, the teens collected donations and their stereo, then jangled off to an adjoining train car. While watching their backs recede, I noticed several passengers reading the January 2012 issue of *New York* magazine with your face on the cover. In a bold white font, THE RETURN OF A LEGEND overlaid your black wool turtleneck. The photo was flattering, but your aging, angular face exuded a zen serenity I knew to be counterfeit.

By this point, I'd become accustomed to seeing your face and name everywhere I turned—in newspapers, on trains, in bookstores, on TV, and forget the internet. Your web hits ranked in the 8.5 million range.

Days before, you'd emailed me that you were reading at NYU and asked if I was interested in a reserved seat. You suggested a date afterward at a martini bar. To mark the occasion, beneath my black down coat I was dressed in an ox-blood wrap dress, houndstooth hosiery, and black boots. Five of my pulse points were dabbed with ylang-ylang perfume, and physically I'd never felt more radiant. When my reflection jagged across a smudged train window, I was agog over the newfound energy in my eyes, the emotional possibilities of my mouth. It seemed that finally my dream would be deferred no longer, that we were on the brink of happening. The tectonic plates of our relationship were shifting that night, but I had miscalculated the direction.

At the 33rd Street station, a sequined mariachi quartet bustled onto the train. They positioned themselves far from where I sat and began strumming "De Colores," a song my grandmother and I had sung at night when we shared a bedroom. I wasn't accustomed to hearing Mexican folk songs in this pocket of the city, and the lyrics evoked the dried-rose scent of my grandmother's dusting powder.

After the last chord dissipated, my focus wandered back to your magazine cover. Your face, I figured, would end up between my legs by the end of the evening. The thrill dampened my underwear, forcing me to adjust my posture.

For the past several months, my imagination had successfully obscured my role in the fantasies I concocted of us. But the probability that we would be intimate that night was high. For the thirty hours leading up to that train ride, I'd been unable to focus on much else. It had been a while since I'd locked lips with anyone, so I reminded myself that I'd have to tilt my head and keep my tongue engaged.

As the train dropped down the grid from 23rd Street to 14th Street–Union Square, I inspected myself one final time in the circular compact, admiring the lava hue of my lipstick. I lifted my arms away from my torso to allow my perspiration to dry while searching through my phone for your last email.

The halogen platform lights vanished, and the train thundered down the track toward Astor Place.

CHILE: 2015

IT WAS A HUSHED SUNDAY AFTERNOON in Santiago. Fog rolled in outside my southward window. Bossa nova filled the living room, and my Siamese cat napped on the rug. I lay on the couch, and between lulling lyrics, my eyelids kissed closed. I had nowhere to be, so I intended to let myself drift.

As the vinyl record serenely spun on the credenza, a sharp trilling interrupted the song. I assumed at first that I was dreaming of a disturbance. The menacing noise continued until I realized it originated in another room. Soon I was upright and padding toward the kitchen island.

My head swayed with heaviness as I placed the phone to my ear. "Buenas tardes," I mumbled.

On the other end, someone exhaled asthmatically but hesitated. "Uh, he-hello?" a man's voice finally stammered.

My neck tensed. Who was calling from the United States?

"Is this Tatum Vega? My name is Jamal O'Dalingo. I'm an investigative journalist for *The New York Times*."

Despite embracing the expat life, I still subscribed to the *Times* and read it nearly every morning. I couldn't imagine why the US paper of record was contacting me, but I was now less inclined to hang up. This stranger also had a Mississippi or Alabama drawl, a charm I'd forgotten about while living below the equator.

"Go on," I said. The sternness of my voice in English startled me.

"I'm contacting you because I'm looking into allegations against the writer M. Domínguez, a friend of yours—"

"You must be confused," I interjected. "He and I aren't even in touch, much less friends."

"Maybe not anymore, but there's plenty of photographic evidence online showing that you two were in contact for years."

My gaze tumbled down the length of my gray lounge pants. My socked feet curled against the wood floor, and again I considered hanging up.

"What's this about? Why are you contacting me?" I asked.

"A young woman has come forward with sexual abuse claims against M. Since she isn't requesting anonymity, I can share with you that her name is María Luz Guerrero."

"Oh," I breathed, rattled by this information.

"I'm curious if you'd be willing to answer some questions."

"I don't think I even know this woman. I mean, surely I don't," I replied, still drowsy and ruffled to be having such a serious conversation in a language I had almost completely retired in South America.

My eyes wandered into my living room. My Siamese, the most noble of my three cats, now stood like a soldier facing me. The vinyl record abruptly reached its end. The needle lifted.

"I promise I won't take much of your time. Just a few questions. What do you say, Ms. Vega?"

In that moment, the only thought I had wasn't an answer at all. It was that I had a history of not liking myself in English. I had made so many mistakes in the language. What if I lapsed back into that version of myself?

2.

You're likely wondering what all this is about—my aim in contacting you. It's been three years since rain flicked our glasses as we stood inches apart and I stared at your quivering upper lip, which always reminded me of the tilde: ~.

Last week, a journalist contacted me. Since I appeared in a number of online photos with you, it wasn't long before the media identified me. I learned that a young woman in Upstate New York named María Luz has leveled serious accusations against you. She claims you two met years ago at a library reading you gave in Albany. Obviously, I don't know María Luz like you do, but I believe her. You weren't that person with me, not exactly, but the fingerprints of our stories are strikingly similar.

Answering the journalist's questions brought you back into my lens. For years, it's perturbed me how things ended between us—rashly but with the finality of a guillotine. Even as we stood on that street corner, my heartbeat deafening the roar of city traffic, I knew I had so much to tell you, but the words remained unformed, timid syllables under my tongue.

It's taken me all this time to come to terms with what happened between us. We spent so many years of our lives traveling together and sharing secrets, yet we were purposely oblivious to certain aspects of each other. I'm writing to you because so much of my life was spent fixated on you. And while I told myself for years that you viewed me with the same intensity, it's doubtful you ever really saw all of me. I finally see all of you, the parts I admired and the parts I denied existed. And now I need you to do the same. So, Mateo, here is an account from me to you.

Despite the fact that you were my best friend for a decade, there's a lot you never knew about me. It's important that you understand who I was before you. Your first book shaped my life, but my fascination with fiction and authors preceded you.

When I was a child, reading was a struggle because my brain refused to learn phonics. In second grade, I started memorizing words out of necessity and piecing them together in chains. After much repetition, comprehension kicked in and sentences began to excite me. Then one day when I was nine, I fell in love with Judy Blume's *Just as Long as We're Together*.

My mother claims that she and my father were sound asleep in the middle of the night when I shuffled into their bedroom in my pajamas.

"What's wrong, mija?" she asked.

I was nearly crying. I held my hand over my mouth as if to prevent a sob from escaping.

"What? Tell me!" she pleaded.

"I'm worried Rachel's going to be left out," I said. "What if Stephanie and Alison ignore her?" I hovered over my mother's prostrate body and continued sharing my anxieties.

My mother had never heard me speak of girls named Rachel, Stephanie, or Alison, so her mind scrambled to place them. "Nena," she whispered, "where'd you meet these girls? Do I know their moms?"

"No," I said, annoyed that I had to explain what I felt was so obvious. "Only I know these girls. They're in *Just as Long as We're Together*."

"What?"

"The book's gonna end the wrong way," I said. "Don't you understand? Do something!"

Looking back at my childhood, I can see that my subconscious had solved an important riddle—how to counter the loneliness and boredom of being an only child.

Inside books I found quietude, a marvelous oasis. I could read stories with such ease that I was reduced to a pulsating mind. Nothing mattered but the stories, my understanding of them, how the stories affected me, and the dreams the stories ignited.

3.

The problem was that I never fell out of love with reading, or more specifically, with other people's imaginations. In high school, I realized that nearly every writer I admired was from Massachusetts. Sylvia Plath was the first, followed by Emily Dickinson, then Robert Lowell, Susanna Kaysen, and Anne Sexton. In each of their works, I identified with the suffocating sense of malaise, and in the case of Dickinson, with her isolation and misanthropy. It was a sign, I thought, that all these writers hailed from the same area. The logical choice for college was to situate myself near Boston, that fault line of literary genius.

This daydream of mine included finding a like-minded friend who'd be interested in making the pilgrimage with me to McLean to visit the legendary psychiatric hospital where my heroes had recuperated from their mental breakdowns. Together we would eat tuna fish sandwiches and split a thermos of hot coffee, just like Esther Greenwood did in *The Bell Jar*. Our lives would imitate art, or so I'd hoped.

In my first semester at Williams College, I realized the literary canon was an exclusive club of white, predominantly well-to-do Americans and Brits. You might want to take credit for my awakening, but the credit doesn't belong to you. I reached this conclusion before I read your book or had ever heard of you.

What became undeniable for me as an English and art history dual-degree student was that syllabi at Williams were homogenous. My diet consisted of the Brontës, Thomas Hardy, Ford Madox Ford, Jane Austen, Charles Dickens, and occasionally Henry James or Oscar Wilde.

In art history, the term "fine arts" meant work created by fair-skinned Europeans. Nearly every art movement chronicled in my textbooks had roots in the United States or Western Europe. Initially, the Clark Institute, a museum in walking distance from campus, had tantalized me. After a few visits, though, its silverware collection and ancient paintings almost convinced me that art spaces were only for the affluent. The Harlem Renaissance painter Jacob Lawrence was the only Black artist I learned about in depth. I didn't learn about Latino artists at all. The Mexican painter Diego Rivera's impressive murals were highlighted in a Latin American section of our textbook that my professor chose to skip.

I hungered for writers and painters to teach me something I didn't know about desire or consciousness. For fun, I read *Prozac Nation* by Elizabeth Wurtzel, *Wasted* by Marya Hornbacher, and the somewhat risqué *Oranges Are Not the Only Fruit* by Jeanette Winterson. I lived in Sawyer Library, thumbing through shelves, searching for art books containing work by Basquiat or Leonora Carrington.

My first two years of college, I wanted to be brought into

the fold so badly that I took a number of risks. Sophomore year, I showed up uninvited to a couple of parties only to quickly learn my lesson. To my disappointment, the like-minded friend of mine—the one who would accompany me to McLean—never materialized. She or he was supposed to be the right ratio of similar to me versus different from me. But true to my inner Emily Dickinson, I preferred the hemisphere of my thoughts, and in my last two years, I made little to no effort to befriend peers.

You could say reaching out to you was another limb I crawled out on in hopes of a best-case scenario. Had I developed healthy friendships at Williams, I doubt I would have sought out a relationship with you.

It was hard to pinpoint what exactly I was learning in class, but I trusted the price tag of my education. Almost 100 percent of the novels I was assigned dealt with Europeans experiencing romantic strife or ennui because they were bored with tea parties, or they disliked a neighbor or family member. Sometimes they were strapped for money or depressed while servants waited on them. This was literature with a capital L and an ascot. This was what English majors like me were supposed to discuss for hours upon hours— books about English people and their "universal" problems.

Since I usually took two or three English courses a semester, I sometimes confused the assignments. So many novels had parallel structures and conflicts. But I liked these books because they engaged my curiosity about the United Kingdom, an area of the world that remained a gigantic question mark for me. Or the novels addressed religious fervor, a topic that piqued my interest as a lapsed Catholic. Still some books were tedious, requiring the reader to know and care about boat life, horses, or Victorian dance etiquette.

It was hardly surprising, then, that I ended up in a D. H. Lawrence spring seminar my junior year. The novella *St. Mawr* had been a breeze to read, though not terribly pleasurable. It seemed to me that Lawrence regarded all his characters with disdain, from the rich American Mrs. Witt and her daughter Lou to the British society women and men, down to the servants. Lawrence referred to servants as savages and showed how lacking in substance the society people were with their frivolous banter. The one thing that made me perk up while reading it was when the main characters traveled through San Antonio, my hometown, on their journey through the Southwest. Never before had I read a mention of San Antonio in a novel for class. As much as I had yearned to flee my hometown as a teen, I now considered it a type of geographical mirror, and I craved a bit of it in New England.

I'm not going to bore you with a blow-by-blow of each of my junior- or senior-year courses, but you should know about this D. H. Lawrence seminar. If it hadn't been for this experience, perhaps your book wouldn't have resonated so deeply with me when I picked it up a few months later.

As I entered the seminar classroom, I wondered how the professor would begin the discussion, what angle he would take on the author's attitudes toward society.

I took the seat around the oval conference table closest to the door. A handful of faces around the table were familiar to me from my bakery job in town. On the weekends, I worked all day making sandwiches and often had to scrawl my classmates' names on their food orders. This is to say, I knew their hangover faces and their tipping habits.

Professor Hatch, a man in his sixties with Brillo pad hair and tortoiseshell bifocals, waltzed into class with a smirk. He tossed his paperback of *St. Mawr* on the conference table, draped his coat around his chair, and took a seat.

"It's two twenty-eight p.m.," he said, eyeing the clock. "We'll wait a couple more minutes." Hatch looked across the room before asking, "Does anyone have spring break plans yet?"

Several students shared about upcoming trips to the Hamptons, while a couple of others chattered about Miami. A reedy boy with pimply skin stumbled in and plopped himself into the only empty seat around the table. All of us had our copies of the book out, and some opened spiral notebooks for note-taking.

"It looks like we're all here," Professor Hatch said as he pushed his glasses up the bridge of his nose. "General thoughts about *St. Mawr*?"

"There's not much resolution at the end," someone offered.

"Well, okay. But backing up, what's the book about?" Hatch asked as he stood from the table and began circling the classroom.

It is a narrative about a rich family, a horse, masculinity, and the idea that women sometimes can't find what they're looking for in men, so they look elsewhere. It's about boredom and searching, concepts with which I could identify then. I didn't speak up, but eventually someone did, and she summarized it similarly.

"All the women in the book are awful," one of the Hamptons guys announced.

"How so?" asked Hatch. His stride brought him close to my chair.

It was tempting to say that all the characters, not just the women, were insufferable, but I merely listened.

"They basically want to castrate the men," the Hamptons guy continued.

"Do others agree with that?" Hatch asked.

"Well, you can tell that Lawrence hates dumb people," a guy in a North Face pullover said with a chuckle.

"I don't disagree, Marshall. But how can you tell that? Show me in the text," Hatch said.

As Marshall started flipping through pages to find an example, another voice piped up, "Look at all his descriptions of the Mexican and the Welsh characters who tend to St. Mawr."

Professor Hatch ran his fingers through his white hair and nodded before asking, "And what do we make of the Mexican?"

"Phoenix?" a girl in a dainty sweater set offered.

My breath tightened in my chest as if I were trapped in quicksand. I wanted to say that the character of Mexican and Native ancestry in the novella was named Geronimo Trujillo but called Phoenix because the white ladies refused to adopt his Spanish name. It was no different from when Kunta Kinte in *Roots* was renamed Toby. This racist act of renaming a person of color for a white person's convenience had not registered with my classmates. And clearly neither had the notion that these unfavorable characterizations were offensive.

"Lawrence introduces him on page seven by referring to him as 'an odd piece of debris,'" another student added, snorting at the phrase.

"Throughout the novel, Phoenix is described as savage . . . ,"

Professor Hatch began, but I missed the rest of his sentence. Instead, I found myself averting my eyes to the lap of my black trousers. Did anyone know my ethnicity? Did I look Mexican? Since freshman year, I'd been mistaken for Filipina or Polynesian, and once for Turkish. Never had I denied my heritage, but until that seminar, I'd also never had to sit through such an offensive discussion of it. Above all, I was outnumbered by people who hadn't objected to the language in the text and who treated the discussion as cold, critical analysis. My presence in the room didn't register or matter to them.

I angled my Swatch toward me and noticed a fresh scratch across the face. We still had over an hour left of class. Surely you can recall a time in your life when each minute represented a debilitating unit of torture.

Hatch continued, "Turn to page forty-two. Lawrence says, 'Phoenix was not good at understanding continuous, logical statement. Logical connexion in speech seemed to stupefy him, make him stupid.'"

I glanced up momentarily to see my classmates nodding at the passage being read. Their silent agreement reminded me of the days when I still attended mass with my family, and everyone but me seemed to believe whatever hyperbolic tale was being read from the Bible. My chest heaved, drowning my thoughts and the voices in the room.

My copy of *St. Mawr* remained untouched on the table. While my classmates listened intently to the various passages, I furiously picked at my cuticles. I focused on the skin above my right thumbnail as if my flesh could surrender what I needed. The world fell away and only my raw hands existed, one working on the other until a fat droplet of blood appeared. A gush erupted so quickly that I reached for my copy of *St. Mawr* and plunged my bleeding thumb between the dry pages.

"And on page one thirty-seven, Phoenix is described as 'a sexual rat.'"

Pages flipped to the quoted text. Professor Hatch read more quotes until he was interrupted by a blonde wearing pearls who added, "Phoenix has skills but is disposable."

Others in the class voiced agreement with her assessment. Not one person pointed out the blatant objectification or racism in Lawrence's characterization of Geronimo.

With my hand inside the book, I neither jotted notes nor actively listened. Instead, my body buzzed with adrenaline. My heart pounded as if I were running a marathon from my chair. I swallowed the sour taste in my mouth, and after a near eternity, I heard mention of the next assignment.

"For next week, read *The Rainbow*. I think you will all have lots to say about Ursula Brangwen," Professor Hatch announced with an air of satisfaction.

When class was dismissed, I kept my hand wedged inside the book. Putting on my coat was a challenge, but I succeeded with my one free hand. It helped that no one was looking at me.

As I exited the building, I tried to recall the times I'd made eye contact with anyone in that seminar, or even with Professor Hatch, but the longer I thought about it, I realized I never had.

On the walk to my dorm, I saw Jamie smoking a cigarette in front of the computer labs. Jamie and I had met during my sophomore year, when he struck up a conversation with me in the library. He was half Cuban and, as luck would have it, like me he was from Texas. He was one of two people I considered friends on campus. My other friend was Julissa. Remember her? The hippie chica you met in New York?

Jamie's immaculate posture and faux eyelashes made him one of the more notable characters on an otherwise uniform campus.

When I was only a few feet away, he waved me over. Snowflakes clung to his lashes, rendering him otherworldly. "Hey, girl!" he hollered. One of his hands remained hidden in his coat pocket while his gloved smoking hand welcomed me.

I stopped near him, careful to stand away from his trail of smoke. "Hey," I replied.

"Where are you coming from?" Jamie asked. "Your job?"

"No. From class," I said with defeat.

"Oh no! You say something stupid?"

It was becoming obvious to me that I should have said something, but what was the point of spotlighting problematic language in the book when I was so horribly outnumbered? The last thing I wanted was all eyes on me, or to be a bumbling spokesperson for my ethnicity.

I shook my head. "Nah, it's not worth rehashing."

With his boot, he extinguished the last of his cigarette. "What are you doing later tonight?" Jamie asked. "Wanna go to Onota Lake with me and Adam?"

"Who's Adam?"

"You know Adam! German guy in my year. Blond, tall, square jaw, blue eyes."

"Last name?" I asked.

Jamie pronounced a name I'd never heard.

"What are you doing down at the lake? Isn't it still frozen?"

"Yeah, it's frozen. You wanna go?"

I shrugged. "Yeah, I'll go. What time? Who's driving?"

Jamie flipped the metal top of his Zippo back and forth, mesmerized by the mindlessness of it. I chanced a look at my thumb. Dried blood caked the skin, so I feigned coldness, crossed my arms over my chest, and hid my hands in my armpits.

"Adam has a car. We'll go around eight. We'll stop by your room," Jamie said.

"I'm gonna take a nap. My last class gave me a headache."

For a second, I considered telling Jamie what had happened in seminar, but instead we parted with unenthused waves.

It was snowing again. Dozens of flakes pinpricked my face. In those days, I never complained about New England winters. I was too terrified to admit I'd miscalculated my fit at Williams, too proud to say that perhaps Massachusetts—home of Plath and Sexton—wasn't for me.

In my dorm, I extracted the D. H. Lawrence book from my backpack as if it were a biohazard, my fingertips gingerly pinching a corner of the bloodied paperback. I swung it into the trash can under my desk. If I had to write a final paper on it, I'd consult a copy from the library. I never wanted to think about that book again.

———— ❦ ————

At eight o'clock, I sat on my bed, admiring a print of Egon Schiele's *Sitting Woman with Legs Drawn Up* hanging over my desk. In total, I had prints of two Egon Schieles, two

Jean-Michel Basquiats, two Georgia O'Keeffes, an Andy Warhol, and a Franz Kline on my walls.

Much of the art I wanted as wall décor didn't seem to exist in print form. After exhausting the internet for the umpteenth time, looking for Florine Stettheimer's lighthearted, jubilant prints, I shut down my desktop. Even international websites with euro prices had nothing of hers for sale. It was as if the art establishment allowed only a few token women artists to be printed. O'Keeffe was the American token. It pleased me that Frida Kahlo was the representative of Latin American women artists, but I wanted more choices.

A double knock interrupted my ponderings about Stettheimer. When I opened the door, I found Jamie and an attractive blond standing there shoulder to shoulder.

"Ready?" Jamie asked.

Both men were bundled in coats and knit beanies.

"Hi," I said to Adam. "I'm Tatum."

"Heeyyy," he said slyly, training his eyes on me.

Given the glee in Adam's voice, it seemed he found me as attractive as I found him. Were we going to kiss by the end of the night? It seemed possible, even likely.

"Put on your coat and let's go, Tatum," Jamie said with an impatient spin down the hall.

I grabbed my belongings, locked the room, and hurried behind them.

—⋗⋇⋖—

Adam parked his Volvo at the edge of the lake, and we explored the area on foot in the dark. The lake was frozen, as we'd known it would be, but the woods surrounding it were a tranquil evergreen that reminded me of Nordic fairy tales.

Normally such darkness would've frightened me, but Jamie and Adam had a contagious sense of adventure.

Since lakes in Texas never froze, until this jaunt, my only experience with the phenomenon was via *The Catcher in the Rye*, when Holden wonders what happens to the Central Park ducks during winter. Sharing that reference struck me as naïve, especially because both Adam and Jamie were treating our night like it was old hat, so I kept it to myself.

Adam was the first to slide over the lake in his sneakers. He navigated the surface like a hockey player, pushing his heels out as he slid forward with determination.

"C'mon!" he hollered.

Jamie clung to my coat sleeve. "So," he asked, "is Adam a hottie or what?"

I chuckled. "He's not ugly. Are y'all cool? He doesn't strike me as someone with tons of gay friends."

"Oh, Tatum," Jamie said, tugging my arm. "He isn't going to hook up with *me*."

"Are you two gonna whisper to each other all night, or join me on the ice?" Adam shouted. His hands were cupped over his mouth like a cone, causing his voice to echo.

"We're coming," I said as I coaxed my feet forward.

Because I couldn't swim, I was deathly afraid of tempting bodies of water. But I tried to slide over the lake as if it were the most natural action in the world. As if I belonged on a frozen lake in Massachusetts with these two men.

On the drive back, Jamie dared Adam to drive with his headlights off for half a minute. We all knew the act might result in our deaths, but Adam smiled and accepted the challenge.

Internally I panicked as Adam flicked off the lights and we barreled down pitch-black roads, invisible to animals and other cars.

"Are you timing this, Jamie?" I asked as I double-checked my seat belt in the back seat and closed my eyes. "You better be timing this!"

"Jesus! We'll be fine. Only fifteen seconds left."

Until Jamie called time, I didn't breathe, only prayed, asking a benevolent universe to protect us.

Finally, Adam flooded the road with headlights, announcing, "Dare completed!"

"Nice," Jamie said, laughing.

"That was fun. The lake," I managed to say after my heart rate settled.

"When we reach campus, can you drop me off first?" Jamie asked.

I glanced up to the rearview mirror, where I found Adam's eyes waiting for mine. Was Jamie trying to set us up? What was happening? Had Adam asked Jamie to invite me?

Adam inserted a CD, and for the remainder of the drive we listened to an ambient Brian Eno album.

As Jamie requested, we pulled up to his dorm first. Even before Adam stepped on the brake, Jamie was unbuckling his seat belt.

"Good night, kids," Jamie announced as he leaped out and slammed the car door.

Adam and I watched him shuffle off in the snow toward the entrance of his building. The night was an inky black mirror dotted only with dorm lights.

"Wanna have a drink in my room first before I take you home?" Adam asked.

I worked the opening shift at the bakery the next morning, which meant I had to be up in seven hours. But this type of thing rarely happened to me. Adam was traditionally East Coast beautiful. His skin was smooth, blemish-free, and even while sitting he towered over me with his good health and strong genes. I was intrigued.

"Sure. Let's do that."

Are you wondering why I'm telling you this particular story, Mateo? Since this is my account, I decide what to reveal, even if what I share makes you uncomfortable.

Adam and I parked in a plowed lot and hurried toward his dorm. I knew what this was about, and I was about it too. Since his dorm had no elevators, we raced up the stairs two at a time as if a fire clipped our heels.

On the fourth floor, out of breath and gleaming with sweat, Adam unlocked a single room and we fell on his bed as if we had just escaped a Jack London–type disaster. Wasting no time, Adam cupped my face and began passionately kissing me. Up until this night, I'd kissed only two guys in my life, neither of whom kissed as well as he did. Not by a long shot. Immediately I realized I never wanted to stop kissing Adam. We continued, surfacing only momentarily for air or to miss each other's mouths for a second before resuming.

"Are you German?" I murmured during our third break.

Adam grinned. "Yeah, my parents met in Bonn. My brother and I were born in New York, though. Do you know my brother, Max?"

I shook my head, but once he'd mentioned it, I realized I had seen someone on campus who resembled Adam.

"Do you have siblings?" he asked.

Instead of answering, I resumed kissing Adam. This time, his hands groped my breasts, and I released my blouse and unhooked my bra. We kissed until eventually Adam removed his shirt.

When we finally unlocked mouths, I said, "I'm an only child."

I'd repeated such words hundreds of times, but this night the statement struck me as a sad, lonely fact to pity.

"Oh," Adam said. "Where is your family from?"

"Texas," I replied. "We've been in Texas for hundreds of years. Since it was Mexico, actually."

Adam's mouth met mine again and we kissed so deeply that I could almost imagine us kissing every night like this until he graduated. It could be our secret. We could even keep it from Jamie, who would undoubtedly have been proud of my score.

After several minutes, Adam unbuckled his pants, then mine. His erection pushed through his boxers onto my thigh. Our mouths meandered down each other's necks, chests, and stomachs.

"Do you speak Spanish?" Adam asked. His voice was buried near the crook of my neck.

"I do," I answered. I asked him in Spanish if he did too.

"Yeah. When we were growing up, our maid spoke Spanish. She taught it to Max and me. My parents still use her."

Something like strychnine filled my veins and our kissing stopped. I backed away and leaned against the window framing his bed. My mind became dizzy with bits of conversation from the D. H. Lawrence seminar. *What's the purpose of Mexicans? Use her. Sexual rat.*

A chill from the windowpane crept over my naked skin.

For a beat, the Catholic notion of sin felt real again, and I wore it like a heavy necklace. Your writing deals with being seen or caught with the shame of one's own actions. Well, at that moment in Adam's room, I was being seen by the moon, by a creator, by an attractive racist, and by everyone who spoke or taught Spanish to a child. I grabbed my blouse off Adam's floor and stuffed my bra into my coat pocket.

"What happened?" Adam asked. "Should we have that drink now?" he said, and laughed.

As I buttoned my blouse, I noticed his walls were bare except for a rectangular water painting of a Parisian café. *What kind of personality does that reveal?* I wondered. An utterly boring one. He was boring. It was just making out. I could find a better mouth elsewhere.

4.

When I returned home for the summer, my parents' two-story house was exactly as I remembered it: messy. Since both of them worked long hours, I didn't entirely fault them, but its disarray caused me endless anxiety. I fought a compulsion to dust every surface, then hide in my room with the air conditioner on arctic blast.

When I could, I tried to keep conversation with my parents topical. Their future planning always involved God. It bothered me that they were totally fine with the idea that God had us all on marionette strings.

One of my first nights back home, I wandered downstairs to brew a cup of peppermint tea. I found my father dicing an avocado on a cutting board in the kitchen.

"That's a beautiful fruit," I said.

"I know how to pick 'em. Avocados and watermelons. Must be in my DNA," my father bragged with an arch in his eyebrow.

"Must be," I said as I filled a kettle with water and placed it on the stove top.

"You're getting a job, right?" he continued.

"I'll have one by the end of the week."

Having a job was paramount to my father, and he took great pride in the fact that I'd been continuously employed since the age of sixteen. You'll learn more about my father later, when it counts, because he saw you more accurately than I did.

"I'll ask God to give you the right job," my father said. "Are you planning to see any of your friends while you're back in San Antonio?"

In many respects, I had shaped my father as much as he'd shaped me. In eighth grade, I'd called my parents to pick me up from a house party where everyone was doing drugs. At the time, I didn't know the difference between marijuana and mushrooms versus crack and heroin, and I was terrified someone would have a horrific reaction and stab themselves or me. I'd heard shocking stories of hallucinating people nose-diving off balconies or carving their own faces up like jack-o'-lanterns. All I knew then was that I had to leave the party.

After I hung up with my parents, I waited outside on the curb like an orphan. After fifteen excruciatingly long minutes, my parents' 1980 brown Toyota Corolla stopped in the cul-de-sac. Although they told me they were proud of me for calling them and "doing the right thing," months later my father began to worry that I was utterly friendless. Ever since, it was as if he'd internalized me as that thirteen-year-old girl standing outside in the pitch-black night, perpetually waiting for her parents to rescue her.

"I don't know," I replied. "Maybe I'll call Patty and let her know I'm back."

Patty was a chubby white girl who was two-faced. In high school, she'd ostracized me on and off for reading through lunchtime, and twice she'd ridiculed my family's dire financial situation to up her own popularity within certain cliques. My parents didn't know about the gossip she spread about us. Both Patty's dad and my dad had been drafted into the Vietnam War, so my parents liked the idea that I was friends with her. What I appreciated about Patty was that she never initiated any hangouts. If I ignored her, she ignored me back.

———— ❖ ————

As I had promised my father, within the week I got hired as a waitress at a restaurant downtown. During the interview, the manager, Debbie—a butch Chicana with spiky black hair—explained that we worked from seven-thirty to three-thirty, serving breakfast and lunch to the downtown business crowd. "After we clean up and close, we hit up happy hour next door at Lulu's Icehouse."

"Is that part of the job?" I asked.

"Pues no, but we're looking for someone who likes to decompress with us."

Happy hour was not my scene. My style was to go home and study art books, read, or zone out listening to music on my headphones. Drinking beer and shooting the breeze with strangers struck me as a ridiculous waste of time.

I stared at Debbie's frown, the oversized mole near her left nostril.

"Okay," I said. "I want the job."

Debbie ushered me into the kitchen, where I met Oscar, a fortysomething-year-old cook with a bushy detective's mustache and thick black glasses. An army-green bandanna covered his head, and on his husky frame hung a faded Santana T-shirt, dark Levi's, and black combat boots. It was a given that somewhere in his home he had a Che Guevara poster.

"Whassup," he said when I approached. He tilted his head back, showing me his chin, as was common for vatos in San Antonio.

"Sup," I involuntarily replied.

Scrubbing dishes over the sink was Jesse, who I learned was nineteen and about to be a dad. His arms were tattooed with snarling dogs, barbed stars, and names without vowels. His body art and T-shirt bore matching Gothic lettering.

I introduced myself to Oscar and Jesse before Debbie finished the tour of the restaurant, and the next day I started taking orders, earning tips, and going to happy hour with my coworkers.

Lulu's Icehouse next door consisted of two dark rooms, one with a pool table and barstools against the wall, the other containing an air hockey table, rickety wooden tops, and plastic chairs. From four to six, Lone Star beers were a dollar. I wasn't a beer enthusiast, so I usually nursed one drink while Oscar and Debbie put them away like champs. Jesse tagged walls downtown and didn't like dulling his talent, as he called it, so he knocked back only one or two before peacing out.

Since Jesse's fake ID was laughable, Debbie and Oscar ordered our drinks and distributed them before pairing off to play pool. Their favorite pastime was fantasizing about winning the lottery.

"Mama's gonna get herself a purple Corvette," Debbie said, pointing her fingers like pistols in the air. Debbie happened to be a purple queen, forever decked out in plum lipstick and electric lilac nails. Blocks away at Rivercenter Mall was a shop called Primarily Purple. It was easy to imagine her there, cradling purple stuffed animals and restocking her supply of purple gel ink pens.

"I'd donate a quarter of my lotto winnings to the Boys and Girls Club. That way mijo and all the chamacos in his class would be okay. For life, man. You know?" Oscar added.

Within a couple of days, Jesse became eager to get the dirt on me. Their last waitress had gotten pregnant and vanished, so his first question was whether I was with child.

"No," I answered. It was tempting to explain that I was a totally dependable nerd.

"Where did you work before here?" Jesse asked while we were playing ice hockey.

"At a bakery," I replied.

"I can't imagine you selling pan dulce. Which bakery?" he asked as he steered the plastic puck straight toward my goal.

I blocked his shot and shook my head. "I've never sold pan dulce," I said, laughing. "Though props to pan dulce, 'cause I love me some empanadas."

"So then, where did you work?" Jesse said. "Nadler's?"

It was clear that he assumed my entire life was based in San Antonio.

"You don't know the bakery. It's in Massachusetts," I said before scoring on him.

Debbie's and Oscar's laughter roared through the icehouse.

They were likely on their fourth beers, and we could hear them yapping in Spanglish about a much-anticipated boxing match.

Jesse stood upright and held the puck in his hand. "I thought you were from around here. Why were you working in Massachusetts? Are you on the run, chica?"

While he studied me, I took a swig from my beer and chortled. Even though Jesse was running me through his own version of Twenty Questions, an ease existed between us. I already liked him better than most of my college peers.

"Put the puck back on the table, güey," I said. "My college is in Massachusetts."

"So you're not running from nothing?" Jesse asked before placing the plastic disk back on the table. "Like, the law or a bad boyfriend?"

"Thus far, I don't have a record or much of a past," I said before scoring on him again.

"*Thus far*—" Jesse laughed. "*Thus far* . . . What does *thus* even fucking mean, yo?"

⚜

On the weekends, I rode the bus to one of three places: the public library, Borders, or a museum. Sometimes I ventured to the McNay to gaze upon Kirchner's *Portrait of Hans Frisch*, which endlessly fascinated me. In the painting, the subject is reclining on a love seat, his face a contemplative mélange of mustard, plant-green, and navy hues. Other times I made my way to the San Antonio Museum of Art, where I scared myself shitless with the Oceania exhibits. All the old vessels contained spiritual echoes of erased tribes. Standing in a room with recovered artifacts—war tools and masks with exaggerated eyes and preserved hair—made me feel vulnerable and haunted, so I preferred being around books.

With books, meaning was hidden. It had to be excavated, whereas with art pieces the excavation process felt complete. It was also cheaper to go to bookstores and libraries. I could while away hours reading random chapters or admiring dozens of book jackets.

At first glance, *Happiness* looked misplaced on a table at Borders among the classics. A diamond-studded Puerto Rico constellation graced a black vellum cover with your name—M. Domínguez—in the lower right-hand corner. I picked it up and flipped it over to read the synopsis. It was a short story collection about the lives of Latin Americans in Florida, New York, and Puerto Rico. Half a dozen blurbs trailed on the back cover, all praising the lyrical prose and multicultural themes. Above the ISBN and barcode was a black-and-white author photo that struck me as nondescript. But I'd already made up my mind that your book had to be mine.

In middle school, I stumbled across a young adult book titled *Say Goodnight, Gracie*. It was about a defining friendship that abruptly ends. I had never lost a best friend, but the book spoke so deeply to me that I taught myself to read it in a single sitting. I started planning my reading of *Say Goodnight, Gracie* as if it were an event. Thursday nights, I'd prepare by washing and freezing a ziplock bag of grapes for my Friday-night reading of it. The book became my friend, and together we'd welcome twilight on my bed.

Eating frozen grapes while reading on a Friday night

was my first reading ritual, and I carried it into high school. It was no surprise then that I took a ziplock bag of frozen grapes with me upstairs when I started *Happiness*. I expected to read one or two stories that night and then crash. But after reading "La Mónica," I felt like I'd received a Greek oracle. You understood the psyche of a young woman and wrote from her perspective with stunning clarity. Part of me ached to be Mónica, funny and resilient even while living with her alcoholic grandmother and enduring long workdays at a video arcade.

I lost track of time in an immersive way that rarely happened with college syllabi novels. In high school, I had loved discovering work by Vonnegut and Salinger because I'd never heard voices like theirs before. But reading *Happiness* was like being in my own brain—the mix of English and Spanish, a vernacular I'd never read before in a book. It so closely mirrored my own thought processes and speech patterns that it was hard to believe it existed, that it was sold prominently at Borders on a front table display. I wasn't sure if *Happiness* was considered literature, but I hoped so.

After reading five of the ten stories, my eyelids began sagging with fatigue. The alarm clock next to my bed informed me it was one forty-five. I rarely stayed up past midnight, but as sleep overtook me, I wondered about the writer behind these words. Your narrative voice whirled in my head so naturally that my last thought was that I knew you from somewhere. I wandered into the cavern of my memory, trying to place you until eventually sleep kidnapped me.

In the morning, I found *Happiness* forked open on the floor by my bed. I grabbed the book by the spine and studied your author photo. You have to admit your first author photo was untraditional. In fact, I could only vaguely make out that you were Latino, with wiry glasses and unruly black hair. It struck me that you were dressed in a short-sleeve polo shirt and pants that were likely Dockers. It seemed so working class, so unpretentious. Minus the glasses, you could have been an older Jesse or any dude I rode the bus with in San Antonio. Your short bio revealed only that you were born in San Juan, Puerto Rico, and had published stories in *The Paris Review*.

As I dressed for work, I repeated the word "happiness" unconsciously, a worm in my brain. A similar obsession had sprouted when I first learned about Umberto Boccioni's sculpture *Development of a Bottle in Space*, a bronze futurist work that teemed with dynamism and sexual possibility. For the first time in years, my mind felt electrified, as if in communion with other imaginations.

On the bus to work, it occurred to me that M. Domínguez—you—the author of *Happiness*, was alive. Cognitively I knew plenty of writers were alive, like Sandra Cisneros, Amy Bloom, and Susanna Kaysen, whose books I liked, but it was exhilarating knowing you were paying bills or buying antacids like the rest of us.

My skin felt dangerous and nervous at the prospect of attending one of your future readings. I made up my mind to meet you. Your book had cast a spell over me the previous night. What better way to stay spellbound than to orbit the magician?

———※———

I had become accustomed to happy hour with the work gang, but I desperately wanted to skip it after I started *Happiness*.

All I could think of was fast-forwarding time so that I could rush home and be with the book in my bedroom. The hours dragged at work, and I disliked that your voice was becoming a distant echolocation inside me.

Naturally, I was distracted as my coworkers clinked their beers in a toast when we finally made it to the icehouse, minutes after four. I'd opted for a Coke that day and only half-heartedly raised my can to meet their drinks.

"Are you on a diet?" Debbie sneered.

"Nah, but I gotta do something when I get home. A project," I said.

"You know, Tatum pretends to be like us, but she's in college," Jesse blurted.

I shot him a death stare. He offered his hands up as if to ask what the big deal was.

"I went to college," Debbie stated as she peered at me.

Debbie's moods shifted from happy-go-lucky to disgruntled so fast that I came to consider her more of a troublesome tía than my boss.

"Did you get a scholarship?" Oscar asked me.

"Two," I replied, sipping my soda. "But I also have loans."

"Is that really gonna be worth it? The debt?" Debbie asked. "That's why I stopped going. It was getting fucking expensive."

"Everything's a risk, right?"

"What's the name of your college? Harvard?" Oscar said, slapping Jesse's shoulder with an exaggerated laugh.

"No." I shook my head. It was tempting to admit both were in Massachusetts, but instead I said, "It's called Williams."

"William? Like the prince in England?" Oscar probed.

"No, Williamzzz. Like lots of vatos named William," I replied.

"I got it now. You go to a school named Guillermos!" Jesse hollered.

"Yeah, like that," I said, rolling my eyes.

"Why you going to school in another time zone?" Oscar asked. "You got beef with your fam?"

All three of them turned to hear my answer. Someone like you would've understood why I left Texas, but they didn't.

"I've always wanted to live somewhere else, so now I do." I shrugged, hoping the Q & A session was over.

In truth, while I preferred my coworkers to people at Williams, I still preferred books to people. I kept an eye on the time. At five-thirty, I stood and stretched like I was about to start the evening anew. Half of *Happiness* remained unread, so in a sense the most thrilling part of the day still awaited me.

CHILE: 2015

AS WAS MY CUSTOM, I SPENT MY lunch break outdoors, admiring the topiaries as I strolled the museum grounds. The weekend fog had been replaced with a blustering wind that rustled leaves on spherical bushes and popsicle-shaped trees. With my free hand, I tossed my floral pashmina over my shoulder and made a mental note to reread *Wuthering Heights* soon. *Different weather but similar mood*, I thought.

When I rounded the corner, I caught a glimpse into my office. It always felt so furtive to spy on my private space, to see it from the outside. It was an expansive rectangular room with a long desk, five metal filing cabinets, a blue velvet couch, oversized framed art prints adorning the walls, and a Nespresso machine resting on an end table.

Inside my trouser pocket, I fingered a scrap of paper containing the contact information for the reporter—Jamal. My mind was still reeling from the unexpected Sunday call, largely because I hadn't been able to give him an answer as to whether I'd be open to an interview. In the moment, something akin to paralysis had constricted my vocal cords. When Jamal realized our impasse, he offered me his phone number and email address, both of which I'd jotted down. He ended the call by telling me he hoped I would think it over.

A conspicuous suction noise caused me to turn my head. Replete in one of his standard tweed suits, my colleague Rodrigo exited through the rear sliding door of his office, leaving it wide-open as he wandered outside. The museum was temperature controlled to preserve the art, yet the ease with which Rodrigo glided out signaled to me that this was not his first transgression. How had he not tripped a security alarm? With the sliding door still open, Rodrigo shoved a cigarette in his mouth under his bristly mustache, inhaled, and waved at me. Smoking on museum property was also prohibited, yet Rodrigo exhibited absolutely no shame in flaunting his delinquent behaviors.

Although I'd never seen him exit via his back door before, I had witnessed him puffing away on a green box of luxury cigarettes on museum grounds. For Christ's sake, was he also smoking *inside* his office? Had he disabled the smoke detector along that corridor? Despite finding Rodrigo's behavior morally egregious, I had never uttered a word about his smoking, not to a soul at the museum or in private to my partner, Vera. Despite his arrogance or maybe because of it, he'd managed to buy my silence.

Rodrigo waved in my direction again, assuming I'd missed his first salutation. Instead of waving back, I dug the scrap of paper out of my pocket. The letters and numbers appeared wavy, as if I had scribbled them in the midst of an earthquake.

Turning my back to Rodrigo, I made my decision.

WHEN I ARRIVED HOME, Vera was rinsing green beans in the sink. Her long peroxide-blond hair was knotted at the top of her head as usual. A Camila Moreno album spun on the credenza as Vera swayed.

"Hola, mi amor," I greeted her as I dropped my bag on the floor and landed a kiss on her neck.

She responded by singing the lyrics of the song filling the room. Despite glimpsing only a few sandwich ingredients, I knew Vera was preparing chacareros for once.

As I headed toward the bedroom to change into sweatpants, I stopped to rub the petals of our succulents. With their waxy texture, they served as worry stones for me. While my day spooled through my nerves, Vera looped her arm around my waist.

"¿Qué te pasa, calabaza?" I asked, grateful for the affection.

In Spanish, she erupted into a monologue about her day. As an audiologist, she typically worked with six to ten patients daily, but her practice had absorbed clients from a clinic that had recently closed.

When it was my time to share, my shoulders tensed. An image of Rodrigo flashed through my mind. Until today, I hadn't fully allowed myself to dislike him, but now I practically tasted it. What audacity and selfishness, to say nothing of the injustice to the institution that employed us, to art, to the works we were charged with protecting and preserving for posterity.

Vera and I meandered from the hallway to our bedroom, where we sat on our neatly made bed.

"I can't stand Rodrigo," I blurted out in English.

Her head tilted as my words hung in the air; her eyebrows puckered in curiosity. "Your colleague? Why did you say it in English?" she asked.

I rolled my shoulders back and tried to formulate an answer. "It's more than just Rodrigo. On Sunday when you were at the nursery buying soil, a journalist called me from New York. His name is Jamal, and he works, or claims to work, for *The New York Times*," I said.

The story, which I'd kept to myself until then, tumbled out. My initial reluctance to talk about M., my perpetual desire for anonymity, and how Rodrigo's smugness was the final straw. I had grown weary of merely being a quiet observer in the shadows. It was time for me to use my voice.

Relief washed over me as I relayed my decision to Vera, but I wondered if she'd fight me on this choice. So much of our life together hinged on my ability to start anew in Santiago, to leave my New York misery behind.

Vera observed me as I blinked and turned my eyes up to the ceiling. "I'm proud of you, Tatum," she said finally with a gentle smile.

"What?" I asked, turning back to face her. "Why?"

"This experience will prove to be good medicine," she said.

"What if it backfires?" I said, allowing the pessimist in me to catastrophize. "Mateo still has power."

"Think of all the women in history who refused to be hampered by self-doubt."

It was a lofty sentiment, but it probably applied to Harriet Tubman and Dolores Huerta more than to me.

Still, I craved the chance to identify my feelings, organize them, and set them aside with clarity and peace. The opportunity Jamal was offering me felt like an invitation for closure.

5.

In August, I returned to Williams. Between juggling class time, homework for four courses, and working twenty hours a week at the bakery, I read *Happiness* three more times cover to cover during the fall term. It was my new *Say Goodnight, Gracie* in that I planned its reading days in advance, as if I were arranging aspects of a date.

I made sure my favorite gray cardigan, black Patti Smith T-shirt, and oversized Gap sweatpants were clean. I froze grapes in advance, and right before opening the book, I unplugged my landline and lit several bergamot candles. The book deserved my undivided attention, so I inserted foam earplugs to block out the shouting imbeciles in my dormitory. People my age were drinking beer most nights, knocking on wrong doors, and barfing in the hallways. I couldn't be bothered by Massholes. *Happiness* allowed me to return to my favorite state, that of a pulsing mind.

Sometimes after finishing the book, I gazed at your author photo for long stretches. Your face reminded me of a metal spoon, smooth and malleable. Your eyewear resembled Sigmund Freud's diminutive spectacles. I reasoned that surely you must've updated your glasses since the time of the author photo; otherwise, I wasn't sure how you could properly see a computer screen. Your hair was a terrific black wave of personality. It was so daring and wild that I tried to imagine its texture on my fingertips. The idea of sharing personal space with you sent shivers through me.

A question I asked myself several times a day was whether I'd recognize you on the street, buying a newspaper or stuffing a bagel into your mouth. You were still the M. of my fantasies and not yet a person in the flesh, so the answer was always no.

On campus, I was alone. Jamie had graduated, as had Adam, so Julissa was the only person with whom I had any sort of connection in Massachusetts. My friendship with her was troubled, but it had its own logic. I wanted someone to talk books with, and she needed to feel superior to other people. Since meeting in an American literature course our freshman year, we'd fallen into the habit of eating dinner together twice a week.

One snowy fall evening, Julissa and I were lounging on the second floor of the cafeteria. I watched her dab Burt's Bees balm in a quick arc over her lips. She had a strange habit of reapplying gloss between bites of food.

"Do you have a subscription to *The Paris Review* yet, or do you still read it in the library?" she asked.

"Library," I replied. "I read everything at the library: *The New Yorker, Story*—"

"You read more than most people in my writing work-shops. Are you sure you don't want to be a writer? It's freak-ish how you've memorized parts of books."

Her comment stung. She had a knack for portraying me as damaged and delayed. The truth was, I'd written nu-merous short stories I considered passable, but given my background in English and art history, I figured I was guar-anteed more career luck working in a museum or teaching. Plus, unlike my peers, I wasn't going to be spending the next year backpacking through Europe with four paperbacks and a French press coffeemaker. Julissa wouldn't be backpacking either. She was determined to succeed as a writer and con-sidered herself the second coming of Ann Beattie.

I often felt intimidated by Julissa, although she was four inches shorter with bland Modigliani features. The day we met, she outlined for me all she planned to accomplish in her life, and I got the distinct impression she was sharing this information with me because I could serve as a good witness to her success.

Will it come as any surprise to you that whenever I tried to attach a face to my ideal person, my mind re-turned to your author photo on the back of *Happiness*? I certainly had parts of the book memorized. Still, I didn't think that qualified as freakish. It was the only book you'd written, but according to the internet, you were "at work on a novel," just as every short story writer I admired seemed to be.

"I'm assuming you read *The Paris Review* interview with M. Domínguez?" I asked.

Midway through a sip of lemonade, Julissa nodded. "Yeah," she said, setting down her glass. "I thought of you while I was reading it. What a coincidence that you're both Spanish, right? Anyway, it was really good."

"It was excellent," I said, leaving it at that.

I didn't have it in me to clarify that I was of Mexican descent while you were Puerto Rican. Neither did I have it in me to inform her that after dinner I planned to write you a fan letter. In fact, once we bused our trays, I was heading to the bookstore to purchase an envelope and a stamp to mail said letter. It was doubtful my letter would leave an indelible mark upon you, but the mere idea of you holding the same paper as I had upturned my lips in pure delight.

"Have you started looking for jobs yet?" Julissa asked.

My jovial attitude disappeared with her question. "Jobs?" I asked, immediately thinking about my work at the bakery. "Oh, you mean after graduation?"

Julissa nodded once more. A strand of blond hair attached itself to her newly glossed lips. "Are you going to the career fair next month?" she asked as she readjusted her turquoise frames and unstuck the errant hair.

Although I was eager to be done with college, I wasn't looking forward to entering the workforce. Student loan debt dictated that I should find a job immediately, but graduation seemed eons away. It meant finding a place of my own, supporting myself, and facing the reality that I was single with no prospects of romance or even a secure friendship.

"Nah," I replied. "I resent the notion that college grads have to start their 401(k)s immediately after graduating. It feels like a poisonous prospect."

The dinner crowd was dispersing and only a boisterous table of jocks chugging Mountain Dew from clear plastic cups remained.

"I'm looking into jobs at publishing houses in New York," she offered, indifferent to my remarks. "I'm also considering working for a major magazine. Job stability and contributing to an industry I believe in are my two main goals."

Julissa's ability to articulate her career objectives thoroughly nauseated me. I was positive she would find several jobs at the fair. Employers loved people like her.

With my art history major, it made sense for me to look for positions at museums. If I'd been able to stomach Massachusetts for a few more years, I'd have applied to MASS MoCA. It was alluring and near my college, but I was dying to be set free. Still I couldn't decide where I wanted to live—back in Texas, or start fresh somewhere else. Truthfully, I had zero leads, ideas, plans, or even an unbiased voice of reason to serve as a sounding board. For months, my mother had been mailing me job postings for ESL teaching positions within the Catholic diocese in San Antonio. Naturally, I wanted nothing to do with the pyramid scheme known as religion.

"Are you, like, not getting a job after college?" Julissa asked. A distinctive *ch* punctuated the end of her question, the indisputable sound of mocking disbelief.

"I'll get a job," I scoffed, and started to stand. "Relax, Mom."

Julissa and I had reached our limit with each other. It was time to branch out.

Alone in my dorm, I broke into a cold sweat. After parting ways with Julissa, I'd purchased a couple of envelopes—in case I committed an egregious handwriting mistake on the first—and two stamps—in case I affixed a stamp onto an envelope with an egregious handwriting mistake. I decided to listen to "Stan," Eminem's song about an obsessed fan who writes to his favorite rapper. Although I wasn't obsessed with you, I needed a push from an external source.

Once the song's rainy introduction began, I climbed into bed, rested my back against the wall, and pulled my knees up to my chest. Under my heel, I felt the rectangular shape of *Happiness*. Over the past couple of months, gazing at the cover had become a meditative exercise for me. I rotated the book in my hand as the desperation in the Eminem song intensified. I focused on the fact that in the song, Stan receives a reply.

Before the song ended, I found myself ruffling through my desk drawer. I brushed aside highlighters, sticky notes, an old sketchpad with designs from a cartography course. In the bottom drawer, I found a ream of printer paper. It was almost empty, but I only needed a few sheets.

You can draft different versions of the letter, I reminded myself. This idea liberated me a bit and my shoulders slackened. I exhaled, scooted my chair closer to the desk, and began.

December 12, 2000

Dear M.,

First off, ***scream***

I'm sure you receive many letters each week, but please know this is the first fan letter I've ever written. To be as authentic as possible, I'll allow myself the belief that what I'm writing to you is unique and consequential.

Your book Happiness *has been a lifeline for me. I'm currently a senior at Williams College and often I'm the*

*only minority in my classes. As unbelievable as this may
sound, I honestly think I'm the only Latina on campus.
Although I'm Chicana, not Boricua like you or your characters, I identify with the Latino culture in your work and
have found your book to be affirming. It's not often that
I see myself reflected in literature, TV, or music; for that
reason, your book continues to resonate with me even after
multiple reads.*

*Sometimes in class I find that I'm silencing myself
while others openly share their ideas and opinions. My
rational side understands this is senseless and absolutely
counter to who I am elsewhere, but this is why I find your
book so indispensable. Your work legitimizes Latino culture and quietly celebrates it. I apologize for placing so
much responsibility upon your writing. My intention
isn't to overwhelm you, but to thank you. You truly are
my favorite writer.*

*I know your book has received critical praise but be-
lieve me when I say you're going to be huge. Huger than
you are now, like translated into Icelandic huge—maybe
into Gujarati! Anyway, you get my drift. I look forward
to your future libros.*

un abrazo,
Tatum

*p.s. Since we'll never meet, I'm gonna be so bold as to say
I love your author photo. You look exceedingly serious but
intelligent.*

I capped my pen and averted my gaze from what I'd
written. The following day, I planned to review it with fresh

eyes and decide whether it was okay to mail or whether a re-write was in order. In the meantime, I searched the internet for your work address at Columbia University.

The next morning, I proofread the letter before breakfast. It accomplished what I'd set out to do, so I folded it into thirds and shoved it into an envelope. Before sealing it, I retrieved it and read several paragraphs out of order, check-ing that the tone mixed humor with gravitas and that the voice mimicked the frenetic energy of your fiction as much as my own personality. I hoped you would like the parts of yourself I mirrored back. That's the beauty of human nature.

6.

In early February, I found a razor-thin envelope in my
student mailbox. By then, I'd abandoned hope of hearing back from you. When I'd written you, it was romantic, peacoat weather. Now the sun was setting at ten past
four, and I was bundled in thermal layers. The interim weeks
had embittered and aged me. Nothing had materialized on
the job front, because I was still sorting and recycling the
clippings my mother sent me. In fact, I automatically assumed the letter in my box was from her.

But as I slid the envelope out and stared at the wayward
slant of my name and address, I saw that it was not her
handwriting. Each letter was elongated into delicate filigree.
It took several seconds for my eyes to drift up to the return
address. It wasn't your work address at Columbia University. It was a residential address in the city, complete with
an apartment number. My hands began to tremble, and my
throat constricted. You'd written *Happiness* for the entire
world, but what I held was specifically for me.

Using my index finger, I ripped open the envelope and read the following:

Querida Tatum,

A trillion thanks for your letter. I don't know if you're a writer, but we writers toil in the dark, often doubting the power of our words and ideas. I'm glad my stories have had an impact on you and served as a mirror.

Enough about me—let's talk about you. What's your major? I imagine English, but if you say physics, that's cool too. What are your postgraduation plans?

Your favorite writer,
M. Domínguez

Your signature, composed of two reclining capital letters with a squiggle following the *D*, resembled Salvador Dalí's. Do you recall your postscript? It was your personal email address, a hotmail account.

The week before, while Julissa and I gushed over a back issue of *Ploughshares*, I'd considered coming clean about the fan letter but couldn't. I'd seen no point in bringing to light my pathetic and ignored efforts. But now those insecurities felt remote and childish.

When I arrived at her dorm, Julissa was reformatting her résumé. She hardly looked up when I flapped the letter in her face.

"From M. Domínguez! I wrote him a fan letter weeks ago. Check it out—I got a reply today."

Julissa held the letter like it was a subpoena, taking shallow breaths as she continued down the page. "Oh my God. He even sent you his freaking email address! This is way cooler than my response from Ann M. Martin when I was ten."

"Can you believe my luck?"

Although I had initially doubted you would respond, I now envisioned us becoming inseparable. Unlike guys my age, you were established, remarkably intelligent, and on course to becoming part of the literary canon. If we fell in love, I wouldn't fight it. I had yet to discover my true talent or purpose in life, but your keen eye would help me identify it and share it with the world.

"This is the coolest thing that's happened to you since we met, so I'll forgive you for not telling me you wrote him a fan letter. But listen—you can't write him back tonight or tomorrow! It took him weeks to reply, so show some self-restraint."

The following three days, I attended class on autopilot, unable to concentrate on anything except my burgeoning future with you. In the evenings, I listened to "How Soon Is Now?" by the Smiths on repeat while examining your author photo with profound focus.

My name was on the verge of becoming meaningful to you. A pattern of syllables you'd pronounce for years to come. Each time I imagined your eyes meeting mine, I erupted in chills. Being in contact with you was sure to do a number on my central nervous system, but I welcomed the discomfort.

On the fourth day, I emailed you.

Whether you saved our letters and emails or sent them into actual or cyber trash cans, I'll likely never know. Nevertheless, I myself saved quite a few. What I didn't tell you before is that I photocopied the first letter I mailed to you. Why? On the off chance that you didn't respond, I still wanted the opportunity to hold on to my words and feelings in that moment.

Our first emails were dulce to the *n*th degree:

> Dear M.,
>
> Thanks for replying to my letter and for sharing your email address with me.
>
> I'm in an English and art history dual-degree program. As for what I'm doing after I graduate, I'm not certain yet. I know I don't want to stay in MA. Snow sucks!
>
> How's New York? Do you have any new stories coming out soon? What are you reading?
>
> Un abrazo,
> Tatum

I still remember sending that email from a library computer. Then I immediately opened my sent messages to make sure our correspondence was really happening. Nothing in me doubted that you would respond; it was a given, and less than thirty-six hours later, I found your reply in my inbox:

> Tatum,
>
> Two majors! What a workhorse you are, little one!
>
> New York is chill. No new stories yet. I'll let you know.
>
> Rereading Paulo Freire's Pedagogy of the Oppressed and The Fire Next Time by Baldwin. Whatcha reading in MA?
>
> Abrazos,
> M.

Little one? With those two words, you made me feel like I was yours. But was *little* really code for "insignificant"? I refused to count characters, but your reply looked slightly shorter than my email to you.

I waited three days to reply. During that time, I did dozens of push-ups on my dorm floor and hooked my feet under my metal bed while doing sit-ups to Björk songs. It had been months since I exercised, but suddenly it seemed important that I make myself as lithe as possible for you.

> Dear M.,
>   *I'm reading* Everything That Rises Must Converge *by F. O'Connor. I love her. I'm also rereading* Ceremony *by Leslie Marmon Silko. Been listening to Björk albums and* Bueninvento *by Julieta Venegas. She's Mexican. Do you know her? What do you listen to?*
>   *Un abrazo,*
>   *Tatum*

Your replies began appearing almost daily, so, without realizing it, I stopped questioning whether you were just being polite. It was never-ending, the ease of successive questions, more replies, the daisy chain of our friendship. Nothing in my life had come this naturally to me before. The like-minded friend I had yearned for—well, you existed after all.

When you suggested we move our correspondence to the teléfono, I was game.

The first few times you and I spoke over the phone, I was sure I was having an out-of-body experience. I almost refused to believe that the man on the other end of the line, this man of slow speech and a thousand sighs, was my favorite writer.

I lived in fear of saying something unforgivably corny or immature. You were only eight years older, but the fact remained that I was still an undergraduate and you were a professor.

"Tell me about your favorite things," you said one evening into my ear.

It was hard to think of three things I cherished more than *Happiness*. The truth was that your book was leagues above all else.

"I don't know—I like tamarindo and chamoy candies. Also being inside when it snows," I said, immediately feeling self-conscious for mentioning junk food.

"Just kidding," I interjected, although it was all true. "I know it's totally random, but I collect old library card catalog slips. Like, from the backs of books, but they have to be important books to me."

I was lying on my bed squinting at a Basquiat print on my wall. My stomach was full of Israeli couscous, and in an effort to avoid uncomfortable silences, I considered asking you what you'd eaten for dinner.

"Which cards are you looking to add to your collection?"

"Oh," I replied, unprepared for a follow-up question. "Anything by Oscar Wilde, Flannery O'Connor, Sandra Cisneros, or Haruki Murakami."

"Whaat? La Sandra's work shaped me," you retorted, causing a huff of static on my end. "And I'm a huge Murakami-head. We were on a panel together in Australia last year."

I elbowed my way into a sitting position and laughed in astonishment. It was my turn to ask you something personal.

"Tell me something no one else knows about you," I nearly whispered.

You sighed, then made me promise that I'd not tell

anyone, because you wanted zero fanfare. My curiosity was piqued, so I agreed.

"On Saturday mornings, I volunteer at a church near Times Square. I bag food for the homeless and help distribute it," you finally said with another sigh.

In my mind, I awarded you my heart.

—◆—

It was surreal answering my ringing phone to find you on the other end. The first few times it happened, I thought back to when I first laid eyes on *Happiness* in a San Antonio Borders. Finally, my existence felt like art.

"Have you even told me what you're studying?" you asked one night.

In a previous email, I'd answered this question. You had a lousy memory, I learned early on, so I tried not to take it personally.

"I'm in an English and art history dual-degree program," I replied.

"And when do you graduate, darling?"

On the wall in front of me hung a pink Andy Warhol print with the quote THE IDEA OF WAITING FOR SOMETHING MAKES IT MORE EXCITING.

"May," I said. "Don't ask me again what I plan to do after graduation. No sé."

You were quiet on the other end. I couldn't tell if you were listening intently, or if you were distracted and possibly thumbing through papers on your desk. It seemed wise for me to fill the lull.

"Eventually, I'd like to work in a museum. Curate collections. Or I'd be happy analyzing artwork for tour groups. I just don't want to do that in Massachusetts."

"Why? Why didn't you transfer colleges if you hate it?"

"I'm loyal to a fault," I admitted. "Even about stupid things. I think I'm the only Mexican American woman from Texas here, so I feel obligated to stick it out. To prove that I belong.

"Where did you go to college?" I asked you, because though I had scoured the internet for everything about you, your educational past was nowhere to be found. It was like you were born in San Juan ready to start publishing stories in *The Paris Review*.

"I went to City College," you offered. "Then I did my MFA at Brown, but that was a lifetime ago."

"Didja like your schools?"

"I had lots of friends at City College, and my eyes were opened to all sorts of writing, so I can't really complain. Brown was something else. But I expected it to be different. It's probably like Williams, though I can't say for sure."

"Probably," I said, because I needed our paths to converge somewhere.

Minutes after we hung up, I found an email in my inbox from you. Surely you have forgotten by now this first act of cowardice. The subject was *P.S.*

Tatum, I keep meaning to ask you if you have a novio.
If so, what does he think of our friendship? Is he
Latino?

  Mad curious,
  M.

This email seemed like a test in that I already knew how I was expected to answer. Either I could say yes, I have a boyfriend and he's insanely jealous, or I could reply that I didn't have a boyfriend. The latter was the truth. I stared at the screen until my vision blurred.

I clicked REPLY, typed LOL, and hit SEND. Who knew I had it in me to be so coy? If you wanted to know about my love life, you were going to have to ask me over the phone because even though your book was my talisman, I was initially intent on making you work for my affections.

———————

After a month of emails and phone calls, you suggested we meet. This you must remember. You were giving a reading for the New York Public Library at the Barnes & Noble in Union Square on a Friday night. Afraid to brave New York City alone, I asked Julissa if she'd be interested in taking a bus to Manhattan and sharing a hotel room with me for the night. Julissa had never read your book, but she jumped at the connection to literati. She'd been laboring away on her first novel for over a year. Though I hadn't read a word of it, I figured she was probably a wunderkind.

"Oooh, do you think his agent will be there? Or Lorrie Moore?" she asked.

I stifled the impulse to roll my eyes. After all, a piece of me knew I was chasing you as much as Julissa was hounding personal fame.

We were in the laundry room of her dorm. A dryer full of her jeans and overalls clacked loudly as it spun.

"It's New York." I shrugged. "Toni fucking Morrison could be in the audience."

"I don't know what to think anymore," Julissa said.

"What do you mean?" I asked.

"Well, so a famed author of a wildly successful book wants to meet you. I mean, you're cool, but you're a college student in Massachusetts. Like, what's the rub?"

Julissa tilted her head and began braiding a section of her hair. Her question burned. She had no clue what you and I had exchanged via email and phone. She couldn't fathom the bond we'd created in a matter of weeks. Whatever she fostered with her boyfriend had taken years, and even still it remained simplistic. You and I, on the other hand, our minds pulsated together.

"The rub is that he expressed an interest in my coming to New York. The rub is that this is *his* idea, not mine—therefore, I'm trusting it as sincere."

The dryer whined to a stop and we stared at each other, hardly blinking. Julissa's plain face showed no affect. It was a skill she had, looking unperturbed while juggling distressing thoughts. In a matter of days, we'd possibly have to share a hotel bed. Neither one of us wanted to sabotage such a potentially significant trip, so I forced myself to produce the semblance of a smile.

DAYS LATER, I ESCAPED AT LUNCH TO Casa Esperanza, a nearby coffee shop that had always served as a reading oasis for me. Thankfully it wasn't crowded with tourists that afternoon. Although I was prepared to talk, I first needed to verify the journalist's identity and legitimacy. I opened my laptop and googled Jamal O'Dalingo. He was a handsome thirtysomething-year-old Black man with hazel eyes and a close-lipped smile. His journalistic beat focused on labor unions and women's rights.

Quickly, I skimmed an article he'd written about a pay discrimination case in New Jersey. Jamal's writing style was intelligent and engaging. He struck me as the opposite of cavalier, and deep in my gut, I wanted to trust him.

I popped a handful of walnuts into my mouth and chewed while my gaze wandered the café. An older woman whom I always assumed to be Esperanza herself arranged quiches inside a refrigerated case. I logged in to my email account and began typing:

> Hi Jamal,
>
> I've had time to consider your call. Yes, I'm willing to talk with you. Even though I'm reaching out via email, I'm open to another phone call, preferably on the weekend. Sunday, coincidentally, works best. I'll be up front and tell you right now that I did not have the experiences with M. that María Luz did. If that disclosure means you're no longer interested in interviewing me, I understand.
>
> Respectfully,
> Tatum

Much like when I emailed M. for the first time as an undergraduate, I knew a reply was only hours away. I had the feeling of once again setting events in motion.

Writing to Jamal short-circuited my nerves, and my hands were left trembling. I approached the counter where Esperanza stood and pointed to a decadent piece of tiramisú. I couldn't stomach quiche or a sandwich, but I knew I could easily inhale cake.

At my table, I pulled out a Buddhist book I was reading about mental formations and sank the metal fork into the dessert.

ON THE WALK HOME from work, my phone vibrated in my cardigan pocket. I had two new emails, one from the public library and a reply from Jamal. My breathing hooked in my chest as my thumbs fumbled to open his message.

> Hi Tatum,
>   I was delighted to see your name in my inbox. While I appreciate your disclosure about abuse, I remain interested in talking with you. Your experiences could still shed light on this ongoing investigation. I know the woman who came forward with the allegations would appreciate your participation as well.
>   If you're available this Sunday, I'll call at the same time as last week.
>   Looking forward,
>   Jamal

Even though I was mere blocks from home, I detoured and sat on a bench outside an upscale bar. Office employees were letting loose post-work, their raucous hollers spilling out the door. Ordinarily, the sounds of unleashed freedom would have boosted my spirits. Instead, my head swam in panic with second thoughts about sharing my story. It would be easier to make no waves, to continue living my quiet, unassuming existence in Santiago. Why was I stubbornly determined to dredge up the past, to give voice to the tangled feelings inside me? My stomach growled as if weighing in. I now regretted the impulsive choice to skip lunch for dessert.

A woman in a blue wool dress teetered out of the loud bar on silver heels. She pushed her red curls out of her eyes and grinned at me.

"¿Eres Carla? La prima de Gustavo, po?" she asked, as I learned the party inside was waiting for a coworker's cousin to arrive.

I shook my head. I was never the type to swagger into bars, swing back a few drinks, and enjoy the random company of strangers.

The woman in the blue wool dress shrugged as if to indicate what a pity it was that I wasn't the expected guest. Balancing herself on the doorframe, she climbed back inside as if vanishing into a black hole.

While skeptical of astrology, tarot cards, and the power of crystals, I once put a bit of stock in personality tests. In New York, I took a test that labeled me an INTJ, an introverted, intuitive, thinking, judging person. It's supposedly a rare personality type. When I learned that only 0.5 percent of women have this combination of traits, I reveled in a wave of satisfaction. Here was the data to prove that I was almost one of a kind.

7.

On Friday morning, Julissa and I boarded a bus to New York. Five hours and multiple stops later, we entered a colossal Barnes & Noble and ascended the escalator to the third floor. A sea of chairs facing a podium stretched out before us. At least eighty people had already gathered for your reading.

During our last phone conversation, when it became clear that you were not going to ask about my appearance, I volunteered a basic description of myself: shoulder-length black hair, anime-sized cheeks, and retro eyewear. After a brief pause, you admitted your interest was piqued, and I could hear you smiling on the other end of the line.

Prior to the reading, you emailed me instructions to proceed to the first row, where I would find two reserved seats. I instantly became a VIP.

"These are ours," I announced proudly in the first row, dropping the reserved signs under my chair.

"There're a lot of people here," Julissa observed. "Some

book groupies with their fingers crossed that M.'ll be free after the reading."

Such a possibility hadn't occurred to me, but craning my neck back I noticed a disproportionate number of young women in tight dresses and impractical heels. I had naïvely failed to factor in the competitiveness of other women.

My gaze returned to my own attire—a black peacoat, a wool scarf, a cream-colored waffle sweater, black jeans, and broken-in Doc Martens. On my left wrist, I wore two black jelly bracelets looped together in an X, and on my right wrist, my vintage Swatch. Hours before, I'd spritzed myself with a magnolia perfume, but the notes had faded.

"You bikini-waxed, right?" Julissa asked.

I ignored her question. I hadn't waxed anything—bikini area, upper lip, or eyebrows. Of course, I wanted you to find me attractive, but what I sought couldn't be traded in one month, much less one night.

Inhaling sharply, I turned to face the vacant podium. The reading would start in fifteen minutes, but I couldn't imagine sitting in front of you. The Andy Warhol quote about how waiting for something makes it more exciting had taken on a whole new significance. Over the past few weeks, our communication had intensified, and in some respects, I already felt closer to you than I did to Julissa. Recently, you'd told me about your mediocre credit score and how your last girlfriend dumped you for a taller Wall Street guy.

I pushed a strand of straightened hair behind my ear and adjusted my maroon cat-eye glasses. Julissa snapped a photo of me that night, which I still have among my letters, so I know exactly how I looked: dewy, innocent, expectant of the future. If I could turn back time today, would I warn myself not to meet you? Either way, it would have made no difference because I was on a mission. We were star-crossed, which made all the events that followed inevitable.

I rotated my gaze from Julissa back to the podium, and that's when I saw you. You were standing ten feet from the microphone stand, reviewing a few printed pages in your hands, mouthing words to yourself. Your tan skin was as sleek as an antelope's. Your author photo had been a static stamp, but in the flesh, your unruly black hair dipped down your forehead into a widow's peak, and your profile was shaded by a dark beard circling your mouth and trailing your jawline. A thin pair of black glasses slipped down your aquiline nose, which you quickly pushed back up. In that moment, you turned, and our eyes met. An elated smile transformed your face as you waved to me. While I was waving back, every cell in my body dilated with excitement, and a surprising possessiveness overcame me. Instantly, I regretted bringing Julissa along.

Following a florid introduction by a Barnes & Noble moderator, you approached the podium nonchalantly and adjusted the microphone.

"Good evening, everyone. Thanks for coming out on this cold New York night, and thanks to the NYPL and Barnes and Noble for having me," you said modestly, then paused. "I'm going to read from a story titled 'Listening.'"

Within seconds, you launched into my favorite story from your collection, about a high school girl who turns down an Ivy League scholarship to become a nun in Puerto Rico. In one of our earliest emails, I'd praised your ability to write a young Latina's interiority so convincingly, so I wondered if you'd selected "Listening" especially for me, a private wink.

Once the reading ended, the bookstore moderator announced that you would remain on hand to sign books. Stacks of *Happiness* covered a table.

Given the proximity of our reserved seats, Julissa and I were the first people to arrive at the autograph station.

"Hey," I said as you took a seat. "You were amazing!"

"Coooñoo, you made it! Thanks for coming all this way," you said.

It's embarrassing to admit this now, but I had never known any Puerto Ricans before you, and I had no idea what *coño* meant. I hoped you weren't expressing anger, but your glazed grin assured me that you weren't.

As you rolled up your sleeves to sign Julissa's copy of *Happiness*, I knew you had to be assessing my attractiveness, pairing the pitch of my phone voice to the heart-shaped face before you.

"It's such an honor to meet you," Julissa blurted out, even though she'd not read a single story in your collection.

After you asked her name and scribbled it inside her book, you turned to me. "You wanna grab coffee afterward? Once the crowd leaves?" you asked, semi-shrugging, passing the book nonchalantly back to Julissa.

I felt my face flush with the certainty that you wanted to be alone with me, not the chic women waiting in line behind me. Regardless of what happened that night, I was not removing my sweater. Surely I'd left armpit stains on the T-shirt underneath.

"Um," I said, "yeah, I'd love to. Should I meet you here or somewhere else?"

You rubbed your chin, then said, "Let's meet here in an hour, then go somewhere else."

Julissa awkwardly wedged herself between us, expecting you to extend the invitation to her as well. Instead, you turned to the next fan in line.

A chuckle formed in my throat at this absurdly perfect scenario. I'd deliberately left my copy of your book in my bag, but you hadn't seemed to notice. Would you ask me about it over coffee? In fact, you did not. You were never as observant of me as I was of you.

——❖——

At nine o'clock, I returned to Barnes & Noble alone. I had a room key and, depending on how the night unfolded, enough money for roughly two taxi rides.

Approaching the escalator, I tried to keep my expectations in check. The last guy I'd made out with was from my Art Through Time seminar. We'd both been tipsy on Purple Jesus punch at a party and hadn't acknowledged each other since.

"Mi vida," you said, walking toward me. "You came back. I was afraid the crowds scared you off." You grinned, then stuffed your hands into your jean pockets. Your puffy black down jacket was unzipped, revealing a faded gray Henley.

Déjà vu engulfed me. My fantasies repeatedly conjured this exact scenario: me, you, a bookstore late at night. If my hearing could be trusted, you'd just called me "mi vida," which sounded much more electrifying in person than it had over the phone. I touched my earlobes—a nervous habit I had when I doubted a situation—to check that I hadn't lost an earring along the way.

A taxi ride later, we stood on the corner of 124th Street

and Lexington. We strolled under bright streetlights, passing housing projects and hostels. Sirens disrupted the indigo night, and my head flicked as an ambulance approached us.

"Relax, querida. I know this area. You're safe with me," you said, embracing me against your puffy jacket.

Your initiation of physical contact surprised me, but I leaned into your chest and tried to act natural. My forehead aligned with your lips, and I found my shoulder slipped easily under your arm, though you didn't kiss my head. It was more of a casual grazing of your lips near my temple. This intimate contact was what I wanted, but it was hard for me to breathe naturally. We were so close I was sure I was going to stumble over your suede sneakers.

At the end of the block, we entered a Mexican café. In one of our previous phone conversations, I mentioned that it had been too long since I'd eaten pan dulce and that I'd commit a crime for an authentic empanada.

An elderly man behind the counter hunched over a newspaper, whispering dates to himself. Seeing him standing there made me feel like you'd transported me back to San Antonio.

You and I scooted into a booth and perused the laminated menus.

"¿Qué tú quieres?" you asked as you considered the options.

We'd only ever communicated in English or Spanglish, but there it was—a full question in Spanish, absent of our standard crutches. Your phonology, truncated and brusque, was devoid of the musicality I had expected.

"Empanadas de camote," I replied, now acutely aware that the same language exiting my mouth likely sounded like a rococo curl with no end, unnecessarily long and full of extraneous syllables.

When the elderly man approached our table, you ordered us a basket of sweet potato empanadas and two decafs. It pleased me that you had conformed your tastes to mine.

"Before I ask you about your night, let me say this—now that we've met, you can't call me M. anymore. It's Mateo from here on out, okay?"

"Okay," I agreed with a pert nod.

Strangely enough, I had never speculated what the M in your name stood for before this moment. But asking me to call you Mateo felt incredibly intimate.

"Also, I've been meaning to ask you, Tatum, if you're an immigrant? You know I came to the mainland as a kid, right?"

"Yeah, I read that in an author bio or an interview," I replied, immediately embarrassed. "Anyhow, no, I was born in San Antonio. Soy Tejana. Why do you ask?"

You shrugged as your eyes drifted across our booth. "Not sure why, but I got the vibe that you were born en México."

What you meant was that my socioeconomic status was equivalent to that of an immigrant. The judgment was subtle, presented as an innocent observation, but reading between the lines was second nature to me.

"So, how's Gotham treating you? Did you and your friend do something fun after the reading?"

I tried remembering the timeline of the night, but I could only focus on the present moment, the lone eyelash clinging to the lens of your glasses. It made me smirk that I'd been correct in assuming you'd updated your eyewear since your author photo.

The elderly man arrived with our order, nodded, then returned to his newspaper.

I considered mentioning the gaggle of girls at the reading, but every statement I formulated in my head sounded accusatory. As I watched you, I decided you weren't yet mine, but you would be one day. What we had in that moment was platonic, unhurried, and I savored every breath.

"Why me?" I asked, surprised that my inner monologue had become public. "Why did you write me back?"

You inhaled deeply. "Why are we friends? Do you want nothing to do with me now? People expect me to be significantly taller—"

"I like you," I announced too loudly. "I mean, I like knowing you and sitting here with you. Why are you hanging out with me, though, and not, like, Nathan Englander?"

"I see you *don't* have a communication problem," you teased. "I can't be friends with competition." You chortled. "I mean, I can and I *am* friendly with my colleagues at work, but I don't know—I love that you don't want to be a writer. . . . I just trusted you from the moment I read your letter. You seemed sincere and chill. It drew me to you."

You sipped coffee, then continued, "Also, you seem very aware for a young person. Like your bullshit meter detects flaws in the system."

My skin buzzed with validation and humiliation. I broke off a corner of my empanada and chewed it with mechanical detachment, wondering if my only talent in life was being friends with more accomplished people.

"Why did you want to be my friend?" you asked.

"I dunno," I lied while shaking my head. I wasn't ready to

discuss my motivations, so I spouted the most aloof phrase that came to mind. "Why not?"

You half laughed, but I feared I'd offended you, so I focused on the fan letter. "I know it's going to sound juvenile, but I read your book and I felt it's okay that I don't have everything figured out yet. In a lot of ways, your book gave me permission to just be me. . . ." I paused as I gazed at the shiny black manicure I'd hastily given myself after your reading. "I know so much has been written about *Happiness*, but most reviewers overlook the theme of sacrifice. Like, in every story, people give up pieces of themselves for others, but in the end, it turns out to be worth it."

My spontaneous confession made me blush. Staring down at my plate, I was deathly afraid of your judgment of me and hoped you wouldn't argue my interpretation.

You leaned over the table and grabbed my hand. "Sometimes I don't believe anyone's praises, but I believe yours," you said. "We're tied together for life, Tatum."

On the bus ride back to Williams, Julissa stared at me, expecting the scoop. I'd returned to the hotel at midnight. After coffee, you and I had wandered around Harlem Meer before hailing a taxi to my hotel. In the lobby, we hugged goodbye in a non-romantic wintry way that made me feel like your niece or goddaughter.

"Well?" Julissa asked.

"We didn't kiss," I said as I searched for a paperback in my satchel.

"Laaaame."

The depth of our relationship was probably beyond Julissa's realm of comprehension, but I was grateful and relieved that you had acted respectfully. The few moments, over the course of the night, when you had pulled me in closer struck me as meaningful.

Before saying goodbye, you handed me a white legal envelope but made me promise not to open it until the ride back. As the bus sluggishly departed Port Authority, I used a metal barrette to snag it open.

Inside were two slips from the backs of library books: *A Good Man Is Hard to Find* by Flannery O'Connor and *The Importance of Being Earnest* by Oscar Wilde. Each card was speckled with something akin to Christmas tinsel and stamped with dates preceding my birth. The fact that you surreptitiously stole the cards from a library specifically for me was almost too preposterous for me to fathom. Reality was proving itself grander than my fantasies.

"Are you glad we came? Is he at least nice?" Julissa asked.

Her long blond hair hung crimped against her cheeks, a remnant of her braids from the previous day. She fished for her bag under our seats, and I knew she was either about to apply lip balm or unwrap a candy.

"Nice?" I paused, gawking at the question. "Whether he's nice is irrelevant, 'cause he's brilliant and self-actualized. I think he genuinely needs a friend, at least more than he needs another fan."

Julissa rattled a box of lemon drops before crunching one between her molars. "Except you *are* a fan, silly. That's how you met, remember?"

8.

Three weeks before graduation, I interviewed for a summer house-sitting job in Hyannis. I felt both romanced by and excluded from Cape Cod's culture and mythology—its lighthouses, lobster rolls, the Kennedys.

When I accepted the job, I didn't know if you would still be promoting your book. Over the phone, I could feel myself becoming emboldened and reckless with ideas of us.

"You should totally come to the Cape with me—" I began to suggest. I had meant to invite you for only a few days, but once the idea was out in the open, you interrupted me.

"Mi vida, it's a no-brainer. I'm there with you already." And with that, something like happiness took possession of us because you ended up staying much longer than I expected.

I arrived alone at the beach house midday. The house key was hidden under a bronze rabbit statue to the left of the front door. When I walked inside, I was left breathless by the grand spiral staircase leading to the second floor. Its massive redwood stairs immediately brought to mind deforestation. But that doom was quickly replaced by a clean scent that filled my nostrils in the atrium. It took me a moment to identify it: fresh linen.

I plopped my suitcase by the door and began exploring the first floor. I passed a spacious dining room with a long slate table surrounded by six white leather chairs. On the wall hung an abstract painting of a fluorescent orange sphere. I stared at it for a full minute before shrugging in confusion.

The kitchen was open concept, with stainless steel appliances, a marble island, and copper pans hanging from ceiling hooks. *What a way to get a concussion*, I thought, though I wasn't tall enough to worry about that possibility. Floor-to-ceiling windows completed the kitchen's layout, and once I pulled back the drapes, I found myself mesmerized by the lushness of the rolling green backyard. The expanse of grass reminded me of *Brideshead Revisited*, and to no one I announced, "Damn, I bet people play croquet here."

You likely remember the second floor well, because that's where we spent most of our time that summer, lolling about watching television or sleeping in because we had nowhere to be. I remember the moment your car pulled up the driveway and our summer together began.

Our first evening together, we found ourselves driving out to Kalmus Beach in your rented Audi A6. It was your dream car, and this entire scenario, us together in a luxury car in New England, was straight out of my daydreams.

In the car, we listened to *Aquemini*, the OutKast album. This detail I'll never forget, because it was the proof that you were hip and not too old for me.

"If *Amores Perros* is playing in town, we should watch it

this week. It might help me with my novel. I'm stuck and I'm hoping to steal from a better story," you announced.

Something about your statement bothered me, although I couldn't quite place it. A chalk flavor clung to my tongue.

"How are you stuck?" I finally asked.

You looked behind me and extended your arm across the back of my seat before merging into another lane. It was how my father often drove when next to my mother.

"Well, in my writing classes, I'm always encouraging students to give their characters lives outside of the main plot. I remind them that good characters don't exist solely for their manipulation. They have outside interests, motives, family, et cetera. But now I'm up against the same crap."

"You have a character with no outside interests?" I asked.

You nodded, then lowered the music. "Yeah, my protagonist right now exists solely for the plot of this novel. She doesn't even belong to herself."

Obviously, I wanted to read what you'd drafted, but I was too nervous to ask for a sneak peek, particularly if you felt what you had wasn't working. I made a mental note to ask for a draft when you were feeling more optimistic about your progress.

"How many pages do you have of the novel so far?"

Reflected in the passenger's side window, I witnessed my head tilt with deference and admiration. I tried to dilute my excitement, to sound like a friend more than a fangirl, but you had to have known you were still my favorite writer.

"I dunno," you said, shaking your head. "Probably about seventy pages, seventy-five, around there. I have the premise down, but the writing itself isn't there yet. The tone and cadence don't yet match the story."

I had no idea what you meant, but I offered a half nod as reassurance. I didn't want you to realize how mismatched we were.

—————— ✳ ——————

Before arriving at the Cape, another fear I had was that the time you and I spent together would blur into indistinct memories. As we approached the beach, pink sunrays bisected the windshield, suggesting I was wrong, that life surpassed the limits of my own imagination.

The beach was almost entirely deserted when we arrived. The sun, an hour from setting, had begun to stain the sky with swaths of aqua and periwinkle. A low bouncing figure appeared near the coastline, which I presumed to be a dog or a beach ball buoyed by the wind.

We snapped photos of ourselves and eventually I announced with a smile, "We have so many more days like this one ahead of us."

I twirled in a circle like a five-year-old, free of my own judgment, my feet stomping an uneven pattern into the sand. As I spun, your face flickered into focus for a nanosecond, then disappeared. As soon as I missed you, you reappeared, then vanished, reappeared, vanished, reappeared, vanished, ad infinitum.

Without warning, you wrapped your arms around me, and I spun to a stop, face-to-face with you. The logical continuation was for us to kiss. My breathing was labored and our mouths mere centimeters apart.

For a lifetime, we stood frozen in an embrace of your making. Then you slowly loosened your grip and we separated, both of us cautious of the mood we'd created. You

must have read the disappointment on my face. When you
failed to kiss me, I consoled myself with thoughts that I
was sacred to you in ways I couldn't fully understand. My
eyes dropped toward our bare feet while you focused on the
burnt-orange horizon.

"It's definitely a good summer," you finally offered. A
sense of satisfaction relaxed your facial muscles. "You're
right—we have a summer of glorious days. I don't know why
I'm always focused on the future when this, here, is fantastic."

I nodded, though you were speaking more to the sea than
to me.

"After this vacation, I have to go to Spain for a writing
fellowship, but right now I'm here and it's good."

Spain? I hadn't heard a word about this until now. I assumed you were going alone, but it was pure speculation on
my part. That you'd even applied or had been nominated for
a fellowship—and won—was news to me.

"¿España?" I asked.

The sun inched farther down, outlining our standing
bodies in twilight.

You relaxed into a cross-legged sitting position in the
sand. The current rushed up but stopped several inches from
us. I followed your lead and sat as well.

"Yeah, I'm going to Madrid to try to work on my fucking
novel."

Within reach was a patch of wet algae. You poked it with
your index finger as you continued to explain the fellowship. "I'll be gone for two months, but that's good because
it might take me a while to get back into the groove of the
story I'm trying to tell."

Unsure of what to say, I babbled, "I've always wanted to go to Madrid."

Immediately I regretted making myself vulnerable. It sounded like I was begging to be invited, which had not been my intention.

"Well, enjoy Spain and your writing time," I flippantly added.

The sun vanished entirely, and we sat surrounded by a navy-blue vibration.

"Have you been to Europe?" you asked.

I shook my head. I'd been to Mexico and Canada, but I'd never left North America. My limited travel experience made me self-conscious, especially because I knew you often circled the globe for literary events. I might as well have confessed I was prepubescent.

"You didn't study abroad?" you asked incredulously.

You tried to remove judgment from your tone, and for the most part, you succeeded. But I knew you too well and sensed an undercurrent of disapproval. Hadn't we already established my socioeconomic standing?

Again, I shook my head.

"I'd have thought you would want to see all the pieces of art you study up close and personal. At the Louvre or Sistine Chapel."

You were right to conclude that the vast majority of the art I studied was housed in international museums. Yet I squirmed at the hooks in your questions.

"Maybe you haven't noticed, but I'm poor. A foundation or arts organization is flying you to Spain to write, but I haven't won anything ever," I said, digging my heels into the sand.

You extended your legs in front of you. The side of your foot brushed against mine, and it felt like you were debating whether to pull me into an embrace. When you didn't reply or initiate more contact, I continued.

"I'm not sure if you deduced this from the first letter I sent you, but I had a hell of a solitary experience at Williams. I had virtually no friends and few acquaintances. The possibility of having to learn a new culture abroad *and* make friends was too overwhelming. I could barely make it in Massachusetts, much less Milan."

The words streamed out of my mouth with a coherence that surprised me. Studying abroad never struck me as an opportunity for people like myself. If anything, I'd mentally shoved the topic aside and moved on. But here in my brain was a perfectly composed explanation as to why.

You readjusted your legs and listened as I continued.

"The thing that baffles me," I said with irritation, "is that you write about disadvantaged people with language barriers who are discriminated against because of their ethnicity or poverty, yet I *am* that person. I'm your protagonist—that's why your book spoke to me. I'm a bit surprised that I have to explain this to you."

Did the razor's edge in my voice unsettle you? Your eyes flickered as if I'd disturbed you or seen you too clearly.

After a minute of quiet contemplation, you replied, "You're right."

You bowed your head and rubbed your scalp with your palms as if in mild frustration. It's hurtful knowing that none of these moments changed the course of what was to come.

"I'm sorry," you said. Your voice rippled through the solar blue blanket surrounding us. "I'm sorry," you repeated. The second time, your sentiment rang with more sobriety and remorse.

I believed you and accepted your apology, but I also hated myself for painting such a clear picture, for stupidly attaching tripwires to my hardships and solitude. Somehow, you'd obscured our differences or managed to befriend me despite them. You were my only true friend, yet I couldn't let our relationship be. Something had compelled me to booby-trap the precarious bridge between us, or maybe it was a test to see if you'd stick around.

<hr />

Our second night together in Hyannis, we grilled swordfish in the backyard and polished off a bottle and a half of white wine while blasting Wu-Tang Clan.

Despite being fortressed inside a posh estate, I couldn't ignore the fact that I still needed a real job once summer ended. You made no secret of the fact that you struggled to manage all your reading engagements and travel itineraries, so I wondered if it would make sense for me to become your personal assistant. While we threw back glass after glass of pinot grigio, I brainstormed ways to broach the subject. But the more the scenario played out in my mind, the more I realized it was an asshat idea. Working for you would endanger the dynamic we'd created, so it was out of the question.

While we loafed on lounge chairs, I tried to divert my attention from your tan biceps. My drunken gaze wandered down to the yawning between your legs, where your boxers peeked out through your shorts.

"Why don't you have a boyfriend, mi vida?" you asked as you wiped your glasses with a corner of your shirt.

I tossed my head back and a loud throaty laugh escaped. In that moment, I barely recognized myself, this version that was flirty and unrestrained.

"What's your new novel about?" I asked from my Adirondack chair, inches from you.

The opening beats of "Protect Ya Neck," my favorite Wu song, floated toward us.

"I'm not really writing much these days," you said matter-of-factly. "I'd rather chill with you."

An inadvertent giggle escaped my throat as I stood and stumbled over to your chair. The heat of your torso through your T-shirt hushed me as I balanced myself on your lap. I wasted no time pressing my forehead to yours and stared into your serious face. Your hand cupped my back, but your lips didn't part. *Are we going to get married one day?* I thought as our foreheads touched.

"Do you know what I'm thinking?" I slurred.

You nodded, then twisted your lips into a wavy smile.

The album ended, and our breathing became audible.

"What's your answer?" I whispered.

"Of course, mi vida," you said, biting my ear, then planting a kiss above my eye.

The few kisses you'd given me up to this point had been aimed at my forehead, so you were slowly making your way down my face.

"Is that all you have in you?" I scoffed, teetering on your lap, more than a little tipsy.

Speaking so cavalierly to a man was new to me, but I was an unapologetic flame.

You stood and scooped me in your arms. The movement caused my flimsy poplin dress to shift, exposing the cups of my black bra. I squirmed, pretending the contact tickled, but really I was embarrassed to be exposed.

You kneeled and placed me on the ground. The cloudless sky and your wounded expression spun above me in kaleidoscopic quarters. I expected you to kiss me, but instead you hesitated, your body in a partial plank over mine.

"Do something you mean," I dared.

Quietly you considered my taunt before elbowing your way into a sitting position. Brushing grass from your shorts, you stood and entered the house. I remained motionless with my back pressed to the ground, marveling at the speed at which the earth spun. I knew it was a trick of the alcohol, but I stayed fingering the blades of grass beneath me until the sky bruised itself into black.

———— ✸ ————

You know where this is going. Neither one of us could forget the next part.

Climbing the stairs to the second floor, I heard what sounded like a televised baseball game drifting from one of the bedrooms. You and I hadn't discussed sleeping arrangements. The night before, you had passed out on a gigantic sofa while watching TV near the dry bar.

To my surprise, I found you splayed out in my bed now. You'd peeled back half the duvet and were resting on the cool bedsheet. The action on the screen appeared to have semi-hypnotized you, and your black widow's peak had matted itself onto your sweaty forehead.

"Hey," I said from the doorway.

"My boy Jorge Posada is up at bat," you announced with glee. You patted the mattress, motioning for me to join you.

I circled the bed and kneeled on top of the bunched-up duvet. "Do you know him, like, personally?"

"Mi vida," you said with a laugh. "My God, you're so cute sometimes. It's an expression. Posada is Boricua. He's Nuyorican familia."

You hadn't meant to chastise me, but as the alcohol wore off, my mind kept reminding me that I was interacting with a powerful literary figure, an Ivy League professor, no less.

"Okay, maestro. I get your drift," I said while cozying up against your arm.

Hours later, I woke under the duvet and found myself pressed against your chest. Your arms enveloped me in a possessive lock, one that I welcomed. Instinctually my mouth hungrily wandered up your neck to your mouth.

In my fantasies, we were always asking each other questions, talking out our pent-up tension. In the flesh, though, we acted without speaking. Your fingers rushed through my tousled hair before cupping my face. We kissed deeply for a long spell, my legs straddling your waist. Clasped against each other, we writhed until I guided you inside me.

Unexpectedly, the running ticker in my mind started repeating my favorite lines from *Happiness*. It was hard to believe that the man who had written "Listening" was inside me. When I quieted my thoughts and focused on being present, the physicality was thrilling but somehow insultingly base. Only when my mind wandered back to your book was I able to engage with sustained vigor. If you're offended, know that I'm merely being honest about my connection to you.

Throughout the night we woke each other to continue. My hunger for you multiplied to the point where I expected to articulate a confession, a statement involving love or *Happiness*, but neither of us uttered a word. I pulled the duvet over my nose and found your smell enmeshed in the fabric. Since our first embrace, your scent had been consistent, but now I could pinpoint it: ripe figs.

I assumed this night would set the tone for the rest of the trip, but we were never physically intimate again that summer. Back then, I had no way of knowing that, so I quietly waited for a romance that never materialized.

For years, I knew exactly how many days we spent together at the Cape. Now I can only recall that it was in the ballpark of a month. On your last day, we were driving back from Kalmus Beach when you lowered the Daddy Yankee song blasting at us from the car speakers.

"Tatum," you said as we approached the house, "we need to talk."

Even though I was naïve, I knew where this was headed. I watched as the speedometer dropped from forty-five miles per hour down to thirty.

"I didn't expect us to get physical on this trip," you said. "And you probably know this already, but I really love you."

"What?" I blurted out.

Sensing this was not a conversation to have while driving, you pulled over onto the shoulder of the road. No one was behind us, the town surrounding us quiet and quaint.

"Don't play coy. You know how I feel about you. You're the only person I actually trust. I love you, which is why we shouldn't have sex anymore."

You'd said it twice—you loved me. I was sure a ridiculous smile was plastered on my face. I wondered if this was the right time to tell you that I loved you too.

"Why?" I asked. I was afraid of what you might say, but I needed to know.

"Mi vida, you're young and beautiful. I'm old and fucked-up. I'm not generally good to women, but I'm not going to ruin shit with you. I'll *never* forgive myself if I do something stupid like give you a disease or hurt you."

It was clear that you didn't like what you were saying. Your face scrunched in aggravation and you looked like, depending on my reaction, you might bang your head on the dashboard. I solemnly nodded, but internally I was falling apart.

Are you ashamed that you asked a young woman to constantly protect your feelings? Back then, I refused to see the ways you subordinated me.

"Okay. But I have two questions," I said, peering at you from the corner of my eyewear.

"Sure. Ask," you said.

"Was I bad? It wasn't my first time, but was I bad?" Several tears rolled down my chin as I waited for your answer.

You dropped your head, making it impossible for me to read you. "No," you said. I didn't believe your answer, but you continued, "That's not it."

"Will you let me know if you change your mind? I mean, aren't we going to know each other forever?"

You smiled and grabbed my left hand. "Yeah. I promise."

"All right," I said, though I was feeling cheated and demoralized. Why had you toyed with me and asked if I had a boyfriend? This conversation convinced me that you were out of my league, that I was an idiot for thinking you'd want anything amorous with me.

When we reached the house, I watered the plants while you finished packing your belongings. You must have noticed that I'd turned into a mannequin, that I'd stopped talking altogether. What had happened in the car felt too much like a breakup to me.

Not long afterward, we were standing in the pebbled driveway. Despite my attempts to appear collected, I was shaking from the idea of us parting. You noticed my nervousness, my bodily tremor.

"Mi vida, I love you. Don't worry. This isn't the end," you said.

Even though it was the exact thing I needed to hear, I didn't know whether to believe you. But I noticed that you still called me mi vida.

"Really?" I asked, trying to rein in my quivering lips, my jitteriness.

My adoration of you was a given, but here you were reassuring me that you loved me back. The clingy romantic in me wanted to ask when we'd see each other again, but I knew that if you loved me, we would see each other again. It was just a matter of time.

CHILE: 2015

HALF AN HOUR BEFORE SUNDAY AFTERNOON'S CALL with Jamal, I ran a comb through my wavy black hair in the bathroom. For the first time in months, I examined my hollowing cheeks in the mirror, cognizant of the fact that I was aging. Until four years ago, bartenders routinely carded me, inspecting my ID as if it were potentially fake. But no one mistook me for a young woman anymore, a fact that stung.

Resting in a ceramic dish were an array of Vera's trinkets: an eyelash curler, two jade bangles, and her gold UFO barrettes. I smiled at the barrettes and considered applying a nude lipstick left on the bathroom counter. For decades, societal conditioning had ensured that I beautified myself for men, but this time I opted against the lipstick.

In the living room, I found my tabby, Lispector, perched on the ottoman in a praying position. The cat's paws moved in a circular motion as if massaging the air with holy requests.

"Perdono tus pecados," I said to Lispector, absolving her of her misdeeds.

As the cat continued praying, I brewed tea. In the living room, I lit a cedar candle and arranged myself on the couch with my phone at my thigh.

At 2:01 p.m., the phone buzzed.

"Buenas—" I said out of habit before catching myself and switching to English.

"Hi, Ms. Vega. It's Jamal. Does this time still work for you?"

I nodded, then said, "Yes. Sorry I didn't confirm via email."

"No worries," he said before continuing. "I have questions for you, Ms. Vega, but feel free to tell me anything you want. This is an opportunity for you to tell your story. At your request, I can stop the recording at any time, and you can share information off the record."

I didn't know exactly what that meant from a legal standpoint, but instead of asking for clarification, I murmured okay. My story was destined to be the outlier. My relationship with Mateo had been of the intellectual variety.

Mentally I tried to recall the various times I'd strolled past the New York Times Building in midtown Manhattan with its silvery windows and classic logo in Gothic script. Now I imagined the journalist reclining in an ergonomic chair inside that imposing structure.

"How did you and M. Domínguez meet?" Jamal started.

"We met in New York City at one of his readings, but we'd been in touch before that," I explained.

"Go on," Jamal murmured.

For forty minutes, I relayed the early weeks and months of my relationship with M., the excitement and intensity of our emails and phone calls.

"Would you say you trusted him?" Jamal inquired.

"Definitely," I offered, "particularly at the beginning. He instantly became my best friend."

"What was the nature of your relationship with Mr. Domínguez?"

"What do you mean?" I asked.

"Was he a mentor to you? Was it a platonic friendship? Was the relationship romantic?"

"Oh," I stammered. "It was a friendship."

"So, you were strictly friends?" he asked, parroting back my statement.

"Mm-hmm," I uttered faintly.

"Did he speak about women he was dating or seeing?" Jamal asked.

"Yes. He never hid his girlfriends from me. We didn't keep those types of secrets from each other," I replied.

I expected Jamal to follow up with a question asking about the kinds of secrets we did keep, but instead he was curious if I could recall the names of any of these former girlfriends. From there, he asked me to clarify a few timelines.

My memory has always been strong, but it shocked me how many details immediately flooded back—full names, months as well as years, names of restaurants where we ate and hung out. All the information was preserved inside me as though I had lived it not years ago but yesterday.

9.

After Cape Cod, I had no alternative but to move back to San Antonio and live with my parents. I had successfully procrastinated on the job front, and though I'd saved a few hundred dollars from housesitting, I knew it would evaporate quickly if I failed to line up more work.

My parents expressed ambivalence about my moving home to regroup. Both were perplexed about my reluctance to teach English to international priests—a position they kept pushing me to take.

During dinner one evening, my parents again raised the subject because I'd returned to my old waitressing job, a position my mother considered beneath me, now that I had two college degrees.

"I don't want to work for the Catholic Church," I stated with finality.

"You're qualified, and they pay so well," she reasoned.

My refusal to capitalize on my college education angered her.

The story of how my mother had worked to put my father through college while securing a managerial position of her own was a family legend. Since she was never able to complete college, my mother considered my education our only true gold.

"This is all just temporary," I explained through bites of chicken salad. "I won't be a Texas resident for life. Te lo juro. *You* believe me, don't you, Papa?"

My father, with heavy bags under his eyes, sighed with resignation. He had always been less critical, but the choices of his only child were clearly starting to peeve him.

The prospect of living long-term in Texas was an ice pick to my soul. Moving to New York was my dream, because it would allow me to be in your vicinity and start my real life. If I stayed more than six months in San Antonio, my trajectory would be wrecked and I'd be furiously backpedaling. Six months was the imaginary deadline I imposed on myself but shared with no one, least of all you.

⁘

During our time in Cape Cod, I never saw you write, and I don't think you were hiding work from me. In reality, you probably had nothing to show for the past several months. I figured you were likely brainstorming ideas, juggling a myriad of narrative possibilities. It was easier to give you the benefit of the doubt than it was to cut myself slack. What I was doing was procrastinating. What you were doing was percolating brilliance. My reasons for wanting you to finish your novel were selfish. As a bona fide fan of your work,

I almost couldn't contain my eagerness to read your new book, and now that we were periodically connected at the hip, I knew book sales equaled more meals in restaurants, more leisure for us, more happiness.

Perhaps you recall that we communicated often while you were in Spain. You started the chain of email correspondence, which I was happy to receive because I told myself that I'd let you be, let you write your novel.

Your first email was short:

> *mi vida, how goes it in America? Madrid is gloomy*
> *today. Wrote two pages. Thinking of you in Tejas.*
> *x mateo*

Usually, I waited between an hour and a day to respond. Even though we were separated by seven time zones, your emails arrived during my normal waking hours. It was oddly comforting knowing you were thinking of me and writing to me during the same span of hours that I was going about my business of waitressing and reading.

Within a matter of weeks, the tone of your messages turned somber. Missing from all your desperate emails was my name. Each time I received one, I imagined it being eked out of an orb of self-hate.

> *i haven't written in three days. tell me i'm not worthless*
> *because i'm convinced i am. do you miss me?*

Upon receiving the first of these curt pleas, I became nervous and certain I was too immature to respond with the right amount of empathy.

Mateo, you're far from worthless. Of course I miss you.
I flip through our pictures from Kalmus Beach all the
time.

Sorry to hear you've been struggling with your
novel. You wrote the best book of all time, so I'm sure
whatever is forming in your imagination requires time
and patience. I have more faith in you than I do in
anyone.

con cariño y abrazos,
Tatum

For weeks, I responded punctually, with heart, wondering how many times I could comfort you without sounding trite or repetitive. Occasionally you thanked me or asked about my new routine, but mostly we addressed your emotional state.

i should've brought you to madrid. maybe being with
you at the Prado would've inspired me. imagine us
splitting a plato of papas bravas at a hole in the wall.
we will next time! i'm deficient when alone. emptier
than you can imagine, mi vida.

The frequency of our communication increased, so that your malaise became the backdrop of my days. According to the internet, 5,161 miles separated us, but your misery was as palpable to me as my own clothes. I could almost feel your breath on my shoulder. Your brusque Spanish echoed in my dreams, and when I awoke I cursed myself for not staying under. Sleep was my favorite spell in San Antonio.

Mateo, I'm there with you in spirit. Always. xoxo Tatum

To what extent we talked about my employment and how that shaped me, I'm not sure. I know we treated work differently. You had the luxury of not forcing yourself to write or teach for a semester if you didn't feel like it, but for me, work meant that I could afford to live. In retrospect, I wonder how creative a person can be if she's always at work. Don't tell me that Octavia Butler or Franz Kafka juggled both well, because one drove herself to a premature death and the other was a sexually dysfunctional man who remained single. So back in Texas, I waitressed all day as I hatched an escape plan.

"It's good to have our little waitressita back," Oscar said at happy hour.

Being with Oscar, Jesse, and Debbie at the icehouse initially brought a cozy comfort. They were family, my work family. In many ways, it was as if I'd never left—only I had. Now I technically had two college degrees and was building something with you.

"Are you paying back those pinche loans yet?" Debbie asked over one-dollar Lone Star beers.

"Nah," I said. "I have six months, I think, until I'm responsible for them."

"(Hey Baby) Que Pasó" started rocking out of the speakers overhead. Everything around me was part of a romantic Tejano dream, a quiet lull extending its hand toward mine. I knew how easy it would be to stay in San Antonio and live a complacent life full of rummage sales, happy hours, and Spurs games.

"You better get a real job pronto, chica. One that's worth your education," Debbie said before adding an "uh-huh."

"Déjala," Jesse said. Becoming a dad had softened him up, made him protective of others. "She's fine. She's got a job. Don't judge, Debbie. Only God can judge."

Every time Jesse trotted out God language, I thought about my dad, but also Tupac. Tupac and Nas lyrics sometimes mirrored my parents' creepy religious talk, yet hip-hop made it sound delectable and deep.

During the day, I waited tables, and in the evenings, I researched ways to return to the East Coast. But this time, it wouldn't be to Massachusetts. I had begun associating New York City with self-realization. It was, after all, where I'd met you and where you lived. Since your reading in Union Square, I'd come to view the city as a playground where dreams go to actualize.

It was no coincidence that many of my favorite books—*A Tree Grows in Brooklyn*, *Invisible Man*, *The Bonfire of the Vanities*, *Motherless Brooklyn*—were set in New York. Living in New York would also situate me closer to the museum scene: the Met, MoMA, Guggenheim, Whitney. And closer to you.

———— ◆ ————

Nighttime at home was isolating. Both my parents retired to their bedroom by nine-thirty. My mother's job was across town, so she woke early to eat and begin her commute before rush hour traffic. My father's sleep apnea required him to stay connected to a CPAP machine.

While they slept, I showered in the bathroom down the hall. On my bed, I whiled away hours detangling my hair and reading until either my hair dried naturally or my eyes shut.

A few times I searched the internet for songs with "mi vida" in the title. Unfortunately, there were almost no matches. I wanted symphonic reminders that I was, if not your life, at least a part of it. When I was growing up, one of my grandmothers had called me "mis ojos," her eyes. Both terms of affection, hers and yours, made me feel adored.

In the library one Saturday afternoon, I wandered into the memoir section. It was not my standard scene, but I found *Down These Mean Streets* by Piri Thomas, which I checked out and read over the weekend.

The Piri Thomas book shared more than a few significant similarities with *Happiness*. Before *Down These Mean Streets*, I believed *Happiness* to be the first book of its kind to examine Latino culture so honestly and viscerally, but here I was, faced with a precursor that had accomplished the same thing thirty years earlier. *Down These Mean Streets* was my quagmire—an unignorable object blooming in my head that demanded acknowledgment. It felt safe to say that you must have read Piri Thomas's book.

I mentioned it in an email:

Mateo,

How's Spain? Has time been going fast or slow for you as you write?

Things are fairly well here. I'm saving money and my book diet has been steady. In fact, I recently read Down These Mean Streets *by Piri Thomas. Are you familiar with it? Parts of it reminded me of* Happiness . . .

Next, I plan to read Bad Behavior *by Mary Gaitskill*

and The Voyage Out *by Virginia Woolf. I've seen both on the shelves at the library and they've mos def piqued my interest. My experience with Woolf up until now has been mixed since I couldn't quite grasp* To the Lighthouse *as an undergrad. The orderly, linear side of me fought the narrative and lost.*

I'm still looking into finding housing in New York. Last week, I met with the priest at my parents' parish. I need a reference letter so that I can possibly live at a boardinghouse run by nuns in New York. I know how this sounds! It's all so freaking absurd, but I'm less thrilled about the prospect of moving in with a total stranger. At the nunnery, I have the option of paying monthly for a single room—no roommate. This is ideal for me, though the rent is mega-steep. Anyhow, the priest, who I'm positive is gay, asked me a bunch of questions about my spiritual life and worldviews. It was whatever. I think I passed, for lack of a better term. He said he'd provide a reference letter and for me to call his office in a week to check if it's ready for pickup. I'm one step closer to moving out of San Antonio! The only thing I'll miss, besides my parents, is the breakfast tacos.

Please tell me what you're reading and how the writing is going. Are you spending most days indoors? Is it jeans weather?

un abrazo fuerte,
Tatum

The trick was to make it sound like I wasn't stuck in Texas, even when paralyzed. People are drawn to optimism, so I projected hope as often as possible since that's what we both needed. The chance existed that you would fall for my cheery outlook, and if that happened, then we'd both be borderline happy.

An internal voice, though, kept kicking me to my knees. Last I'd heard, Julissa had enrolled in the Radcliffe Publishing Course and was on her way to greatness. According to an alumni bulletin, Jamie had won a Fulbright to Scotland.

I had been educated at a prestigious college and—just as Debbie had predicted—all I had to show for it was massive student loan debt. No career had fallen into my lap. Sure, I hadn't pursued one, but I wasn't even certain of my options. A haze of discontent followed me like an electrically charged cloud. It not only clung to me, it murmured discouraging comments: *What if I never make it to New York? If I fail to move, will my friendship with Mateo fade out? What if I was only accepted to Williams because of affirmative action, as my white high school counselor bitterly suggested?* These questions suffocated me inside my own private bell jar.

My parents had been retired for hours one night when I slipped into the bathroom down the hall. In the mirror, I inspected my gums before brushing my teeth for the second time in two hours. Although I had not eaten between brushings, it felt productive to cleanse my mouth, to freshen the taste on my tongue.

"I don't love you," I said to my reflection once I'd placed my toothbrush inside the cup on the counter. The declaration startled me. I heard it again and witnessed my mouth moving in the mirror.

"I don't love you."

I narrowed my eyes and wondered if I was addressing myself. My impulse was to counter, asking why, but I was too stunned, too disconnected to make sense of what was happening. Maybe, I figured, I was addressing my parents. Immediately I dismissed the notion that I didn't love my family. It was easier to accept that I was speaking to myself than to them or to you. Something toxic had taken up residence inside me, but I couldn't name it.

In your emails, you sometimes responded to only half my questions, which made me feel dismissed and insignificant. You were a cafeteria-style friend, serving yourself only small plates of me. Still, I had to get to New York.

In the hall, I bumped into my father. The tubing of the CPAP mask had left indentations on his forehead and above his lip.

"You scared me," he mumbled. "Who were you talking to in there?"

My heart plummeted as if being shoved off a ledge. "I was singing," I said, sliding past him.

"What?" He half shrugged, groggy and unconvinced.

"Good night," I said, and disappeared into my room.

On my bed, I ran my palms over my stomach, thighs, and biceps. Waitressing had strengthened my skinny arms. I wondered what I hated about myself.

I closed my eyes and transported myself back to May, when you and I had spent a string of unstructured days on the beach, sitting on dunes together, snapping photos of each other, admiring the sea. Walking side by side for hours with no rush in the world, the strength of the wind our only concern. Our relationship seemed to morph from something as substantial and purposeful as a steel ship to an object as fragile and replaceable as a light bulb. What we shared was impossible to categorize, to define, to hold.

I buried myself under two blankets and masturbated to memorized passages from *Happiness*.

The following day you replied to my last email:

> *Of course I've read the Piri Thomas book. He was writing the Latino-Caribbean story back when no one wanted to know the truth. Sadly, he was a one-hit wonder. Never wrote anything else equal to the memoir. But I'm glad you got a Boricua education of sorts. You're growing your Latina wings, mi vida.*
>
> *Currently, I'm not reading anything. Trying to keep influences and other voices/styles away from my novel. But when I can read again, I want to read* Infinite Jest. *I've met DFW. Complicated guy but really beautiful spirit.*
>
> *Keep me posted on your move to NYC.*
>
> *x mateo*

Your email sent me to the internet. What you'd said wasn't entirely true. Piri Thomas had written other books, and while none had been as successful at *Down These Mean Streets*, your words didn't quite sit right with me. I should've sensed something was amiss in how dismissive you were of his oeuvre. It was too early then to know how David Foster Wallace's legacy would play out, how problematic he would become with time.

10.

The nunnery that became my first home in New York was much more Dickensian than I could have imagined. Upon arriving in midtown Manhattan, I paid rent for the month of October. Once I handed over my signed check, Sister Cristina, a petite woman in a gray habit, gave me a tour.

The ground floor consisted of a cluster of offices, guest rooms, and a chapel. The second and third floors were designated for women residents, with a mix of twenty single and double rooms, a communal kitchen area, and bathrooms at the end of each hallway.

Sister Cristina explained the features of the communal kitchen before yanking open the refrigerator. All food items were tagged with masking tape. Women's names scrawled in purple and teal declared the owners of cottage cheese, cartons of orange juice, pouches of salami, containers of chocolate puddings, and other perishables.

Under no circumstances, the nun stressed, were men or

nonresidents allowed upstairs into the individual rooms. You weren't officially my plus one, but this news made me frown.

"Also, there is a daily curfew. You must be back by eleven o'clock. We close the doors at that hour, and they don't re-open until six in the morning. If you decide to stay out for the night, you must sign Sister Magdalena's log. She keeps track of our residents."

"What's on the fourth floor?" I asked once the nun led me back to my room.

"We live on the fourth floor," Sister Cristina said. "But the girls are forbidden there. In fact, the main elevator won't stop. It'll take you only as far as the third floor."

I had no desire to see where these strict Sisters of Mary Immaculate lived. I only cared about my room on the third floor, which I'd tried to imagine for weeks while still in Texas. Given the steep price of rent, I was aghast to find the twin bed mattress deformed and discolored and my room narrower than a shopping aisle.

"We're happy you've arrived. You'll be able to help with our Spanish mass," Sister Cristina stated. "Very few of our residents speak Spanish. We've been praying a long time for someone like you."

I had been in New York all of three hours, and already I could feel myself being masterfully manipulated. Now defi-nitely wasn't the moment to announce my agnosticism.

"Good night," I said abruptly, leaving Sister Cristina in the hall.

After unpacking my suitcase, I turned off the lights and gazed across the street at a Verizon Wireless parking lot full of reception towers and vans. I bet you don't remember where you were that day, but I do. You were giving a reading

in Vancouver and were away for three days. You and I hadn't
made any concrete plans, and I sat there in the shadows, trying to convince myself that I hadn't made a colossal mistake
by moving and blowing a hefty chunk of my savings. Books
had long kept me company, but I'd only had space to pack a
few, too few to feel their warmth.

As I stared out at the reception towers and a hideous fleet
of vans, I reminded myself that this was one pocket of Manhattan, but there were other parts waiting to be explored. I had
to make my way, even if time kept magnifying my solitude.

⁕

In the morning, I awoke to a medley of women's voices in
the hallway outside my room. Drifts of conversation—in
Italian, English, French, Spanish, and what I assumed was
Tagalog—broadcast my hallmates' productivity. From my
bed, I caught notes of an opera blaring from a stereo.

As an only child, I found it somewhat unsettling to now
be living with more than sixty people. The night before, I'd
had a nightmare in which I was riding the subway alone
with an agitated jaguar. The train was headed straight into
the Hudson River via the rowdiest boroughs. Since deciding
to move to New York City, I'd been plagued with nightmares
involving doomed trains traveling at unstoppable speeds.

That first morning, I was still half asleep in an oversized
Spurs T-shirt and panties, but I welcomed my hallmates'
proximity. The women asked one another for advice. *Heels
or flats? Tights or bare legs?* An upbeat voice inches from my
door called out a happy hour location for later.

Hurriedly, they bade one another goodbye, their voices
scattering, fading into partial vowels, final footsteps. I

pressed my warm body against the door and listened as the noise dissipated into a hush. There were so many women from all over the world living on my hall that it was inevitable I'd make friends, but I wanted to choose carefully.

My third night at the nunnery, I was in bed reading when I heard a knock at my door. A woman with wavy black hair leaned against the doorjamb. I estimated her to be thirty-one, almost a full decade older than me. Around the woman's neck was a silver cross on a shiny chain. She smiled, revealing blocky teeth that reminded me of white computer keys.

"My name is Valeria. Where are you from?" she asked in Spanish.

"Texas."

"I'm from Peru," Valeria said. "I've been in New York a long time, though. I work as a nanny."

I peered down the hall at the ladder of closed doors. Someone on the third floor was watching a game show at maximum volume.

"You make friends yet?"

Valeria's question struck me as intrusive. "Not yet," I answered honestly while retreating to my bed.

Despite my abject loneliness, I'd decided not to contact you. You knew I'd moved to New York, so I was waiting for you to reach out to me.

Valeria shoved her hands into the pockets of her dark-rinse jeans. Her eyelids shimmered with body glitter, a trend I had long forgotten about until I started writing this account to you.

"Hey, what is that?" Valeria said, pointing to a plastic statue on my windowsill. It was a glow-in-the-dark Infant Jesus of Prague. For me, it was merely a kitschy item that reminded me of my grandparents and San Antonio. It held no religious significance whatsoever.

"It keeps you company late at night when you're fearful about being alone in this new city," Valeria volunteered with a firm nod. "I understand."

Back in Texas, I knew a host of women like Valeria: submissive, overly religious, almost childlike, with bedrooms filled with Bibles, inspirational quotes, and ten thousand saint cards tacked to their walls.

"Do you want to listen to music in my room?" Valeria offered. "We could paint each other's nails and listen to Juanes."

The only people I had spoken to since my arrival days before were cashiers at delis and the Strand, where I'd purchased several paperbacks.

"Um, okay," I said reluctantly.

The walls of Valeria's room were covered in Winnie-the-Pooh posters, deflated Mylar Donald Duck and Mickey Mouse balloons, and crosses and crucifixes constructed of various woods and metals.

"Sit on my bed," Valeria said as she gestured toward it.

Spread over the mattress was a faded Elmo sleeping bag. I eyed it incredulously as if it were a prop on the set of a Todd Solondz film. But then it struck me. This new life in New York provided me with the opportunity to reinvent myself and the right to say no to people who didn't interest me.

"You know what?" I said, rubbing my neck. "I don't feel well. My throat hurts, and I'm starting to get a headache. We should probably hang out another time."

Valeria's eyebrows turned down in an expression I had only seen on Precious Moments figurines at Hallmark shops. The resemblance was so unnerving I had to look away.

"Lo siento," I apologized as I brushed past Valeria into the hall.

As I turned to go back to my room, a tall Japanese girl with a blond mohawk exited her room and connected eyes with me. Her full face and neon-green glasses instantly captivated me.

I smiled, but the punk girl seemed unfazed by my openness.

"I'm new here," I managed to courageously announce as she passed me. I made note of her pink-and-black-striped overalls, the fishnet socks covering her lean feet.

"Oh, hey," the girl said as she continued down the hall toward the bathroom.

A newfound animalistic urge excited me. My balance felt uncertain, as if the floor were tilting. My palms began sweating profusely and I found myself breathless. I couldn't tell if I wanted to *be* this cool hallmate of mine or if I wanted to *date* her. I'd come to New York in part to be in a relationship, but up until that moment, it hadn't occurred to me that it might not be with you.

I floated toward my room in a daze. Every door I passed, Eucharistic white with brass doorknobs and black calligraphic numbers, seemed to judge me. In my room, I lay on my bed, lost in reverie. That girl had to be the hippest person I'd seen in years, and we were floormates. Her androgyny was electrifying, so confident and unapologetic.

Several minutes later, a firm knock interrupted my trance. It was Sister Cristina.

"Spanish mass starts at seven a.m. tomorrow. Do you prefer to read from the Old Testament or the Gospels?"

I studied the nun's starched gray habit, the oily creases of her eyelids.

"I won't be available at that time tomorrow."

"Oh?" the nun said. "I thought you would be free, seeing as how you're still unemployed. You know, all the sisters are praying for your success in New York."

"I appreciate that, Sister Cristina," I replied.

I shut the door behind me and retreated to the window. For several minutes, I tried to conjure the face of the punk girl in the hallway. I kissed my pillow, imagining a romp in my room, the fun inherent in being known.

———

The next afternoon I was hunched inside the communal refrigerator, searching for my carton of banana yogurt when I felt a light tap on my shoulder. At first, I assumed I'd brushed against the frame of the refrigerator, but then I felt the tap again.

Over my shoulder, I saw a patch of red fabric. It was the Japanese girl with the blond mohawk from the night before. She was dressed in a coral-red sweatshirt with the words TRY ME glimmering in rhinestones. From the waist down, she sported purple leopard-print leggings and jelly sandals. Her flamboyance was authentic, which I loved.

"Heeyyyy," I said, unable to hide my surprise. Had she taken an interest in me? My mind raced for something witty to say. Finally, I managed my own name.

The punk girl introduced herself as Mayumi.

"I think I'm going crazy," I said. "I bought yogurt yesterday and put it on the second shelf. Today I can't find it anywhere."

Mayumi nodded knowingly. "Naomi eats everyone's food. She's from Singapore and terribly homesick."

I stood in the draft of the refrigerator, trying to downplay how thrilled I was about this chance encounter.

"Are you a dancer?" Mayumi asked.

"I'm not," I replied. "I'd be happy to talk to you about my job when I actually have one."

Mayumi chuckled. "Well, I'm a dancer, and if you want a stage job, let me know. I get a bonus for each successful referral."

It unnerved me that everyone from the nuns to my hallmates had an angle to play. When I didn't immediately respond, she added, "Anyway, I heard you like to read a lot."

I nodded. It stunned me that this woman knew anything about me. Obviously, I'd failed to recognize that a rumor mill is a natural by-product of boardinghouse life.

"Do you know the Kinokuniya bookstore?" Mayumi asked, shifting her weight from one leg to the other.

I realized I was making too much eye contact. Was she making a pass at me or simply being friendly? I shook my head to indicate I didn't know the bookstore.

"It's not far from here," Mayumi said with a wink. "If you're free right now, we should go."

Half an hour later, we stood in Kinokuniya, browsing the section lined with beginner's guides to Japanese. Mayumi grabbed a thick turquoise workbook from the shelf.

"You want to learn?" she asked, cocking an eyebrow.

Until that moment, the idea of learning Japanese had

never occurred to me. Mayumi's offer sounded too casual to be genuine. I busily scanned the rows of manuals and guides with slender businessmen and demure nurses on the covers.

"I'll teach you Japanese, if you're really interested . . . if you study."

Less than a day before, I'd been secretly freaking out over Valeria's corny taste in room décor and music. I was uncertain how the Fates had changed their minds about me, but I was grateful, so very indebted and relieved.

"Yes," I said, nodding. "I'll most definitely learn it."

As we exited Kinokuniya with a plastic bag full of books, I felt giddy and overwhelmed. I wasn't sure what I'd agreed to, but it sounded much more exciting than reciting Scripture in mass or searching for a job.

———— ✦ ————

Every evening, I had a Japanese lesson with Mayumi. Learning a new alphabet and wearing contacts were the only things I knew for certain I wanted to commit to, so I devoted myself to practicing hiragana and making it through the day with silicone disks on my eyes.

The details of gaining employment continued to elude me. I remained undecided about what type of job I wanted. Whenever a nun, Valeria, or my parents inquired about my job search, I responded with conviction that I was "working on it," though honestly, my money was running out and I was beginning to panic.

It took you four days to contact me after you returned from Vancouver. Four. Each one of those days, I wondered if Mayumi was my new you. The term "lipstick lesbian," a phrase I'd first heard years ago on a *Real World* episode, became my mental Rubik's Cube. Was Mayumi a lesbian? Was I bisexual? Ultimately, it was a blessing that you ignored me because it forced me to be social and open to new experiences, which had been one of my reasons for moving to New York.

The day before you contacted me, "Decades," your first published short story in almost a year, appeared in *The New Yorker*. Back then, my morning routine involved getting a one-dollar coffee from a food truck and browsing magazines at a news kiosk by the nunnery. Between sips of coffee, I opened *The New Yorker* to see who had contributed fiction, and much to my surprise, my eyes landed on your name. My stomach sank with the realization that you hadn't told me about it ahead of time. Instead, you let it drop without notice, leaving me to find out about it like a stranger. I was so incredibly hurt that for hours I thought about returning to Texas and cutting my losses.

"Decades" was one of your trademark stories, sprinkled with Boricua slang and set in a gritty urban landscape. Although it contained a couple of laugh-out-loud funny lines, I didn't love this story of a fifteen-year-old Bronx boy being bullied in high school. Never would the criticism leave my mouth, but I found the writing to be a little sloppy on the sentence level. I sincerely hoped "Decades" was merely an aberration, but I will admit to wondering if *Happiness* had been a stroke of luck.

The next day, you finally called and invited me to hang out. You wanted to celebrate my move and the publication of your latest story. You kept the invitation unspecific, but I accepted. The New York life I had envisioned for myself was finally getting back on track. As I moisturized my face and brushed my hair, I reminded myself of our last in-person exchanges in Cape Cod. You made it clear that we were strictly friends, so I applied lipstick and dolled myself up to make you regret the boundary you'd established.

When Mayumi asked where I was going, I smiled and answered, "Out." She smirked at my coyness before telling me to behave myself.

This part you're sure to remember: You picked me up outside the nunnery on a Saturday evening. Unsure of the dress code anywhere, I'd decided on a cream blouse, black jeans, black flats, and silver nail polish. I hadn't yet received the memo that New Yorkers were notorious for their dark wardrobes, but you arrived in a black guayabera, black jeans, and black New Balances. We hugged for a record-long time and you planted kisses on my forehead and cheeks. Your kisses came with a soundtrack as you said "muah, muah, muah" with each one.

"Mi vida, I can't believe you live here," you said with pure joy.

I nodded, my body relieved to be greeted with such authentic excitement. You'd been busy in Vancouver, you explained. Meanwhile, I had begun a whole new life that you knew nothing about.

"Let's celebrate all the good news. How about Madame X?"

Again I nodded but had no clue what, or where, anything was in the city except for a few bookstores. You were taking me to a bar in SoHo, but I wouldn't know that until we arrived at its door.

The fastest route to the bar, you explained, involved taking the N/R to Prince Street from Times Square. Before this jaunt with you, I'd ventured by myself to Times Square in the evening only once. On that occasion, I became instantly intoxicated with the claustrophobia of a million lights, street performers, huddled skyscrapers, and the indiscernible funnel of dialogue. Heading south on 7th Avenue, I loved being greeted by the Cup Noodles figure poised atop the most central building in Times Square, illusionary steam rising from the lip of the container into the sky.

As we hurried down Broadway, the aroma of honey-roasted peanuts wafted from street vendors hawking nuts by the bag. The blare of honking taxis wallpapered the space around us.

"Mi vida, down here," you said while guiding me into a subway entrance.

I purchased a MetroCard from an automated machine and together we swiped through the turnstile. The platform was densely packed with twentysomethings in neon club gear and Day-Glo face paint.

"You probably haven't been in the city long enough, but do you know what people call this line?"

My focus remained fixed on the cast of outlandish personalities before me. Two had neon-pink antennae protruding from their heads, and another sported a furry gold tail. Your question didn't even make sense to me. Did I know what people called this line—what line? No one was standing in any particular type of formation, much less in a line.

I shook my head and returned my gaze to your familiar profile. You had shaved, and if I leaned in close enough, your fig scent hung like an invisible curtain between us. As much as I wanted to inhale you, our safest mode was platonic. The vibes you gave off were mostly nonsexual, so I returned the same energy in equal measure. This was a game, right?

Hot air rippled through the train station followed by the

arrival of the N train. You and I approached a set of doors, waited for passengers to disembark, then slid in. We found an unoccupied orange bench and sat while a pigeon fluttered around the car in panic.

"As I was saying, this line—the N—is referred to as 'the Never' because it almost never runs on time. The R is 'the Rarely' because it's marginally better. The W is 'the Whatever' because hace lo que le da la gana."

"Thanks for the tutorial," I said with a nod.

The trapped pigeon pecked the laces of your black sneakers. We said nothing as you kicked your leg out, causing the pigeon to sputter backward.

Although I outwardly presented myself as blasé, it elated me to be out in public with you. Our bond was proving to be everlasting, and I trusted you to steer the relationship. Despite the obstacles of your reading schedule, the difference in our ages and occupations, and a thousand other potential points of contention, we were sitting next to each other on the N train headed to SoHo. Finding a job would eventually become a priority, but on this night, I refused to acknowledge my own financial pickle. Technically, I could afford rent at the nunnery for six more weeks, but after that if I came up empty-handed on the employment front, I'd have to return to Texas. This knowledge had the power to poison me, but that subway ride was not the moment to share those concerns with you.

"So, is the place we're headed to one of your favorite bars?" I asked.

You nodded, then drew your legs back beneath you. "Yeah, Madame X has a vibe. I'm curious to see what you think."

I had no idea what to expect, but I prayed it wouldn't be so loud we'd have to shout.

At the Prince Street stop, we resurfaced to ground level. The evening unleashed a gust of wind that greeted us as we turned the corner onto Houston. I hadn't anticipated such a dramatic temperature change and realized I was terribly underdressed and the night was only getting colder. My teeth chattered as I hugged my shoulders with my hands.

"Usually I have a hoodie, mi vida," you said as an apology.

"Don't worry about it," I said. "I was pendeja for not bringing a sweater as backup."

I couldn't believe I'd pulled such an amateur white girl move. Endlessly throughout college, I'd witnessed white girls flock to parties in the snow, wearing tank tops and miniskirts. In the privacy of my mind, I'd tsked them for being so hungry for attention, so available at their own expense. Now I was tsking myself for wanting to be seen and admired.

The interior of Madame X resembled a chic red blood cell. The bar was awash in red mood lighting, and puffy scarlet furniture—couches, ottomans, and Queen Anne chairs— lent the place a mature, historic air.

When I later mentioned Madame X to Mayumi, she replied, "The bordello?"

"Oh, I'm certain that's just the vibe, not the purpose of the place," I explained to her.

Although the venue was crowded with people lounging languidly on red furniture, we found an unoccupied red velvet couch. You remained standing as I sat.

"What do you feel like drinking?"

This question always flustered me. Whenever I found myself in bars, I made a mental note to learn more about cocktails, to educate myself so that I wouldn't be embarrassed in this type of situation. But I was so rarely in bars that the thought always slipped my mind, and I ended up ordering the same thing every time.

"Can you bring me a rum and Coke?" I asked with a shrug.

"Sure," you replied. "Any type of rum in particular?"

Was this a test? I hated that people assumed I was an adult.

"Surprise me," I said, then looked away to show I was bored with questions.

You returned with a rum and Coke for me and a whiskey sour for yourself. I only knew what you got because I asked. The few alcoholic beverages I could identify on sight were a glass of red wine served in a wineglass or a beer served in a beer bottle. Surely you didn't care that I was a baby in this area.

While drinking, we chatted for two hours about an out-of-print Nikki Giovanni poetry collection, and *The Driver's Seat*, an unnerving novella.

"Mi vida, what are you doing reading Muriel Spark?" you asked regarding the novella.

"Oh, I looooove Muriel Spark. She's one of my favoritas," I said, reclining into the velvet couch. "In eighth grade, I had an English teacher from the UK—Mrs. Glauser. She assigned *The Prime of Miss Jean Brodie* and played us Kate Bush albums. Since then, I've been a huge Spark fan."

"Interesting," you said. "I've only read *The Driver's Seat*. I'm curious to know what you loved about it."

At the time, I considered these literary conversations with you to be the backbone of our friendship. But looking back, I can't recall you ever actually offering original thoughts on the books we discussed. All your questions and replies were typical academic scaffoldings. Was this how you conducted class at Columbia?

In total, we each threw back three drinks, and when I eventually drew my wrist to my face to see if I was going to make curfew, my turquoise Swatch refused to come into focus. The arms twitched forward and backward in a repetitious tango. Either the battery was kaput, or I was beyond drunk.

"It's past your bedtime, mi vida," you said, swinging your arm around my shoulders. We hadn't moved much on the couch, and residing in a red blood cell seemed natural now. It would be strange not being under red lighting back at the nunnery, if I returned in time.

"I'm pretty sure the nuns have locked the doors for the night," I said in defeat.

My words performed gymnastics and I may have reversed the order of what I was attempting to say. Still, you understood and solemnly nodded.

"You know you can crash at my place," you said. A sense of well-being and a thrill of excitement spread through my body at the offer.

"Thank you." I nodded before standing up. "Ladies' room?"

You pointed an index finger in the direction of the bathrooms, and I made my way on unsteady feet. I'd been smart to wear flats. Had I opted for heels, I'd have eaten carpet in front of many bar patrons.

The women's lavatory was a humid room consisting of

two stalls and a sink. Using the wall for balance, I meandered into one of the stalls and locked the door. As I released
the contents of my bladder, I heard another woman enter
the bathroom in heels. The clicking rhythm of her shoes
abruptly stopped and I figured she was applying makeup. I
flushed and exited the stall to find a thirtysomething Latina
in a tight designer floral dress leaning against the sink. Her
curly copper hair appeared to be whispering secrets to itself.

The other stall was unoccupied, so it was clear she was
waiting for me.

"Excuse me," I said as I attempted to use the sink.

As I turned on the faucet, she idled over to my side and
stared at me in the mirror. In middle school, cholas had
started trouble with me, but I'd never had an adult confron-
tation.

"You're here with M., right?" she asked.

Whenever people referred to you as M., I assumed they
were anonymous fans. You shared your name with friends
and colleagues but remained an initial to the rest of the
world.

I let water rush over my hands long after the soap
rinsed off.

"It's okay," she said. "You're still a little girl," she continued. "I don't know if he told you he's your boyfriend, but
he's not."

The woman shook her medusa head. Her tense face
flickered like rapid snapshots before me.

"Just so you know," the woman said, "I slept with him a
couple of months ago." She held up her left hand, casually
displaying a diamond ring the size of a walnut. "Ssshh."

After this strange warning, she vanished. I turned off the

cold water and scrutinized the dirty mirror. It had contained the woman's reflection mere seconds before, the sharp slant of her cheekbones, her fuchsia lipstick. Until that moment, I hadn't realized I was wearing my glasses. Somehow, I'd forgotten to insert my contacts for this excursion. In my glasses, I certainly looked like nothing more than a dumb teenager. I hung my head over the sink, expecting to vomit, but all that exited my mouth were dry heaves.

As I walked back to the couch where you were sitting with our empty drinks, I decided not to say anything. Ours was a complex relationship. You never claimed to be my boy-friend and you were Mateo, not M. Had the woman in the bathroom recognized you from the back cover of *Happiness* and fabricated a story? I reminded myself that we had time, years ahead of us, the entirety of the future. I practiced smil-ing as I resumed my spot on the couch and nodded when you asked if I wanted a fourth rum and Coke.

<hr />

Around two o'clock, you hailed us a taxi to your Harlem apartment. The address was the same one scribbled nine months ago on your reply to my fan letter. Before this night, I'd relied on my imagination to re-create your home in my fantasies. The natural next step had been to insert myself into the landscape, lounging on the couch, sipping coffee from a ceramic cup in the kitchen, reading a book next to you in bed. Your place had featured so prominently in my daydreams that I worried I'd let out a gasp while standing inside your actual apartment.

As my veins swelled with alcohol, SoHo boutiques spooled by like dark Gothic cutouts. The streets were remarkably empty, and within minutes our driver merged onto FDR Drive headed toward Harlem.

"I have a T-shirt and boxers that you can sleep in," you said, grabbing my hand.

All I could think about was that I might have to wait until I returned to the nunnery to brush my teeth. The thought revolted me. No, I'd squeeze whatever toothpaste you had in your bathroom onto my index finger and clean my mouth that way, however ineffectively.

"Gracias," I murmured. It was impossible for me to discern if I was still slurring.

Night shadows morphed your features into unfamiliar exaggerations. Your brow became severe and judgmental, and your gaze darted out the window in a sinister manner. Bitter saliva coated my tongue and I carefully let go of your hand. It was suddenly disturbing to me that I trusted you—a relative stranger—with my well-being, that I spent time with you alone, closed my eyes and trusted that you would never harm me as I lay prostrate and helpless. A string of worst-case scenarios played out in my mind before I convinced myself that a famous author would not jeopardize his career for the thrill of killing me. My young life simply wasn't that valuable, a realization both reassuring and devastating. For the remainder of the drive, my heart thudded in my chest, and I deeply regretted staying out past curfew.

The taxi deposited us in front of your apartment complex on the corner of West 145th Street and Frederick Douglass Boulevard. The greenish glow of a 7-Eleven shone on the taxi windows as it sped off.

You unlocked the main entrance door to your building, and we slipped inside, both of us chilled by an autumnal gust. Under normal lighting, your features reverted to the ones I was accustomed to seeing. The malice that emanated from you in the taxi vanished. The swift transition unnerved me, but I reminded myself that I was still drunk.

We cut diagonally through the lobby to the elevator, which arrived seconds after you pressed the button. As soon as the elevator door shut, you scooted next to me.

In my intoxication, I knew there was no logical reason to be afraid. I struggled to pinpoint the doom I felt, then remembered the woman in the Madame X bathroom. My encounter with her had shrunk itself into a compact after-thought, a bolt of lightning that flashed for a millisecond over my psyche. She claimed to have slept with you a couple of months ago, but hadn't you been in Spain then?

Your apartment was spartan. The cream-hued walls were bare except for a framed poster of Frantz Fanon's *The Wretched of the Earth*. Pinstripe poplin curtains covered the windows, and the living room contained a wooden writing desk, a metal chair, three overstuffed bookcases, and nothing else. The floor was hardwood with a few errant strands of hair and lint clustered on the floorboards. Your bedroom contained a futon covered in black sheets and a black duvet. Haphazard stacks of books lined the walls, and a plastic alarm clock with neon numbers glowed at us like the eyes of a suspicious cat.

"This is my place," you said, sweeping your arm through the air. A few times I'd allowed myself to estimate your savings, what you earned from book events, your teaching salary. Having been raised in poverty, I had an instinct for recognizing when someone was on a budget, but now it seemed like your restraint was self-imposed, not a product of limited funds. I had expected more comfort, softness, yes, even a marble island in the kitchen. Instead, you lived in an abode that was practically dormlike. *Everything is in his head*, I thought. *He doesn't need things, because everything he needs, he creates with words.* Whereas before I had speculated about your genius, now I was certain that you were the most brilliant, monastic man alive, a literary Thich Nhat Hanh. It embarrassed me that I'd entertained the ludicrous possibility that you might murder me.

"I'm not scared of you," I whispered when you turned your back.

You relaxed on your futon and motioned for me to do the same. I sat, our kneecaps touching through our jeans. The inside of my mouth was bitter, and I feared breathing on you.

"You've been so quiet, mi vida," you said. "¿Tienes miedo?"

"I don't want to get into it," I started, "but a mujer at Madame X approached me in the bathroom."

Your eyes widened a couple of centimeters in anticipation of what I would say next. In the apartment below, someone suffered a vicious coughing fit. Seconds later, the neighbor directly above us began lifting and dropping heavy dumbbells.

"It doesn't matter what she said," I said, shaking my head.

That night, I convinced myself the Madame X woman was an opportunist, a pathological liar. It seemed preposterous to me then that a man residing in such humble digs could be living a sordid life. Manipulative men draped themselves in bling and collected Rolls-Royces. They didn't sleep on futons. "I'm tired and we can talk about it another time."

"Whatever you want, mi vida," you said. Exhaustion was starting to weigh down your eyelids and form creases around your mouth. I expected the same signs were beginning to show on my face as well.

"I'm going to the bathroom," I announced as I stood. "Can I get that T-shirt and pair of boxers?"

Before you could answer, I made my way to the bathroom and ran the faucet. A crumpled tube of Crest lay on the rim of the sink. With the water still running, I squeezed the white paste onto my finger and jammed it into my mouth. The tingle of mint was a welcome surprise, and I focused on the flavor as I arranged myself next to you on the futon, anticipating what would come next. You turned to me and for a moment I couldn't breathe. But you only kissed my forehead and shoulder, then turned to the wall and instantly dozed off.

Afraid to interrupt your rest, I listened to your quiet breathing, a spring of inhales and feathery exhales. When I was sure sleep had you locked inside another realm, I pressed my lips gently against your back and imagined what it would feel like for you to awaken and kiss me back. More than anything, I wanted to experience the thrill of your desire upon me. I'd had it in Cape Cod, and I wanted it again.

As I lay staring at your darkened ceiling, thoughts of the woman returned, swirling in my head. I wanted to question you about it, but I was the definition of powerless. If I'd pressed you, who knows how you would've explained yourself, or even what you owed me? What if we had argued and you'd kicked me onto the street? I couldn't risk that, so I ate my doubts, hoping they'd dissolve.

CHILE: 2015

BEFORE I SAW HER, I HEARD VERA park our Toyota 4Runner in the driveway. She'd insisted that I needed privacy with Jamal, so she and a friend had gone to the cinema to see a foreign film.

I was drinking a Shirley Temple in the kitchen when she slipped into the house.

"¿Qué tal todo?" she asked me with a smile.

The conversation with Jamal had gone well, but it'd left me depleted. My body felt more drained post-call than it did after my 15K runs.

"Me fue bien," I said before launching into a couple of details of the conversation and explaining that Jamal and I were planning to talk again the following Sunday.

Vera's eyebrow arched in surprise, and she asked me if I still felt comfortable cooperating. I sipped more of my mocktail and nodded.

Vera's childhood had been stained with abuse. An uncle broke her arm in a drunken rage when she was eleven.

Although the bone had healed, a few times a year she still cradled her elbow and complained of a deep-seated ache. Given her past, I sensed Vera wanted me to make certain Mateo was charged for his crime, but I wasn't sure my statements would help prove his guilt.

"We only covered basic information today. If this is going to be worth my while, I'll need to lead myself back into those hazy places that I avoid in my memories. There's so much from that time I haven't considered. At least not in years."

I slid my drink over to Vera, who gulped the rest.

"It's so weird to be talking in English again—with Jamal and even you. Is it weird for you? Is it strange for you to be responding to me in English? Does it make me seem like a different person?"

Vera laughed. "This is different, but it's good," she added with a shrug, rising and starting to mix herself a pisco sour. "It must be hard to hear that your friend abused a woman, no?"

I started to nod but caught myself lying to her. "Well, we actually haven't spoken about the victim yet, but I'm sure we will in the next call. As you know, Mateo was never inappropriate with me," I shared with a sense of pride.

"Consider yourself lucky then—because apparently Mateo had it in him the whole time," Vera quipped. "You were spared."

Shame raised my body temperature and I burned with regret. Vera vigorously shook the cocktail shaker, ice cubes clanking.

11.

A month into my stay at the nunnery, I was lying on my bed, rereading a book I had enjoyed in middle school—H. G. Wells's novel *The War of the Worlds*—when a nun knocked on my door. It was three in the afternoon, so most of my housemates were still at work.

"Hello, Sister," I said, puzzled by her visit.

Sister María de Jesús was a squat woman probably ten years my senior.

"Muchacha, do you have a job yet?" she asked point-blank.

"No, not yet," I mumbled.

A sheen of sweat covered Sister María de Jesús's forehead, and the strip of her gray habit above her eyebrows darkened with moisture. Instinctively, I ran a finger over my upper lip, the place where sweat accumulated on my face, but the skin was dry.

"You can't read all day. How many jobs have you applied to?" she asked.

Technically, I *could* read all day. Since my arrival, I had done exactly that, with breaks only to learn Japanese, buy more books, shower, eat, and venture out on a few walks so that I could claim to be "exploring the city."

Twice a week, my parents called, asking me where I'd applied to work. My mom suggested several nonprofits, all organizations with a Catholic bent to them. Living with nuns filled my religiosity quota, so I applied to none of the places she suggested.

My dream was still to work at a museum, but I was too intimidated to even inquire. Only one street and three avenues separated my new residency from MoMA, a place I'd long assumed was quasi-real and part mirage. To be in its vicinity was all my central nervous system could handle. I had no relevant work experience. Art history had been one of my majors, and I could identify art from a range of centuries, but thus far the knowledge had only served me when taking art history exams and while playing *Jeopardy!* in my parents' living room. It was hard for me to see myself transferring those skills into a career.

"I'll start looking for jobs tomorrow," I said, and inched the door closer to Sister María de Jesús. She took a few steps back, and though shame washed over me, I closed the door and returned to the novel I'd left forked open on my bed.

The problem with many books, I found, is that they disappoint. When the payoff of a book was mediocre or nonexistent, my respect for *Happiness* compounded. The emotional kick of your book, even after more than a dozen reads, produced a well-crafted tsunami. The characters had heft and humor, and the sum of the collection was an unforgettable wave of complicated emotions. For this reason and a thousand others, I was eager for you to finish your new novel. Many times, I stifled my own curiosity about the novel's title or plot. I had to wait until it was all definitive. I preferred to see the final product without the framework—a literary Eiffel Tower. Of course, I never hinted at this to you, because I respected your process too much to interfere.

This is all to say *The War of the Worlds* had let me down, so when Sister María de Jesús returned to my room the following day with a telephone book, I was defenseless.

"Go through the phone book. Apply to different places," she urged me.

The New York City phone book was a massive brick. Phone books reminded me of the times my grandparents had me look up the number for upholstery shops, discount tire stores, tarot card readers, and shoe repairmen. I associated the grimy pages with suffering and bureaucracy. The idea of finding a job via a phone book struck me as a 1950s construct, but I knew the nuns expected me to mine it for employment treasure. I took the hefty slab from Sister María de Jesús's hands.

"Thanks, I'll do my best," I said with no affect.

My response satisfied the nun, and she left full of expectation.

In the back of my mind, I entertained the idea of applying for a stage job with Mayumi's dance company. It likely required a minimum amount of effort to be hired, but I knew I could never last in that position.

I turned pages until I stumbled across the school section. Scores of boxes advertised K–6 or pre-K–8 education. Working at a school struck me as far less intimidating than gliding around a museum floor while posing as an expert.

My geographic knowledge of the city was still rudimentary, but I knew subways and buses connected any two points. I marked a handful of schools with a blue ballpoint pen. Defacing the nuns' phone book brought me a cheap thrill. I considered drawing inverted crosses next to school emblems but decided against it.

It was late November, so it'd be challenging to find a full-time job now, as the school year had already begun. For that reason, I sent email inquiries on the communal computer to various schools about after-school positions and tutoring opportunities. I figured it would be a way to get my foot in the door. Perhaps I could strike a balance by earning sufficient money without being fully committed to an adult job. That was my thinking at the time.

Within hours of faxing my résumé to several private schools, I received two interview offers. One was for an after-school tutoring position in the Bronx and another for an assistant teacher position in Morningside Heights. I was surprised to find a full-time assistant teacher position available. Someone must have quit at the eleventh hour or died rather tragically for there to be an opening.

Excited by the possibility of staying in New York, I decided to venture out for a walk. In many ways, this day was a turning point. I was at my peak confidence and full of gratitude that I likely wouldn't have to move back to Texas.

Surely you noticed that when I first moved, all my clothes were cheap. My entire wardrobe was sourced from thrift shops and Target. On this day of good news, I showered and put on an oversized sweater dress and pleather ankle boots. I spritzed myself with some fruity spray from the Body Shop, ignorant that it was a summer scent, and inserted my contacts. Inside my canvas beach bag, I tossed my wallet and room key and decided this would be the day that I deserved the MoMA experience.

The distance was incredibly short, and I was familiar with the entrance from having passed it multiple times. Once it was in my line of vision, though, anxiety persuaded me to keep walking. In my boots, I traced almost a full rectangle around the block before I noticed the employee entrance. It was located at the back of the museum, and through the glass structure, the organs of the building could be glimpsed. Paintings graced the walls, and a complicated staircase connected various floors.

Feeling reckless, I entered through this door. I passed two receptionists at a counter who didn't glance up from their computers as I strode by with determination. It was unreal to me that I had even managed to set foot inside this great edifice, much less through illicit means. I walked toward an elevator as if I knew where I was going, but really, I had no idea.

The elevator opened, so I stepped in. Standing inside was a stunning redhead. She not only possessed perfect bone structure but was dressed in the most refined clothing I'd ever seen for everyday life. Her silk blouse was patterned with a Piet Mondrian design. It was paired with a black pleated silk skirt, which she complemented with Chanel patent leather oxfords. Being in the same space as this posh woman was beyond intimidating. I prayed her nose could not detect my discount perfume, my stamp of tackiness. I lacked the nerve to meet her eyes because in comparison, I was fraudulent. And I was breaking the law for sneaking in without paying.

Everything about me was a colossal mistake, from my appearance down to my behavior. I hadn't the faintest idea where the elevator was taking us, so when she stepped off, I trailed far behind her until I realized we had arrived in the heart of the museum. Hastily, I spun off in my own direction. Surely the woman in the elevator was going to report me, I assumed, so I hustled through room after room. My racing heart and breathlessness blurred all the art around me. Perhaps I passed a Claes Oldenburg cloth hamburger on my right. The color scheme on another wall appeared to be a Donald Judd work, but I didn't allow myself time to drink it in.

My fears became a reality when a brawny guard in a black suit stepped in front of me. His accent sounded Russian, and I was sure he was going to take me to museum jail or an interrogation room.

"Miss," he started, "are you lost? Do you need help?"

I stopped in my tracks, centimeters from his imposing frame. My breath hopscotched away from me.

I shook my head. "No help needed," I replied before sidestepping away from him and heading straight for the exit.

I'd shamed myself so completely from the get-go that I was sure my image had been captured on surveillance tape. It wasn't until months later that I realized I was overreacting. No one would remember foolish little me and my antics. At the time, if you had asked me to articulate my distress at the museum, I would've assured you that my discomfort stemmed from a lack of knowledge. Despite my degree in art history, I felt underqualified when faced with the art world in the flesh. I would not have mentioned the color of my skin. But the truth was that on that day, I'd seen the caliber and color of people who entered that space. No one there looked like me.

———✳———

Days later, on my way to interview in the Bronx, I exited the subway station and found my foot hovering above an overflowing dirty diaper stabbed with a hypodermic needle. While leaping over it, I realized this was a terrible omen and I decided I didn't want a job in this perilous neighborhood. But since two stories in *Happiness* were set in the Bronx, I followed through with the interview despite having already made up my mind.

The Morningside Heights school was posh, and I interviewed with the headmistress, a serious British schoolmarm type. We sat in an office replete with a fireplace and polished oak furniture. When she crossed her legs, I glimpsed dark stockings tucked into shiny penny loafers.

My most recent work experience had been in food service, the bakery position in Williamstown and my waitressing job in San Antonio. I was dumbfounded that I'd even been asked to interview at this elite white school.

The headmistress adjusted her thick spectacles while clearing her throat. "I see you graduated from Williams College. My niece went there as well. She's a brilliant young woman."

I nodded with too much enthusiasm. Here was the privilege, the "in" my mother had always hoped my education would afford me.

"What do you love about children?" she asked.

"Their confidence. They know what they like and follow their instincts," I said.

The headmistress leaned forward toward me. "Yes," she said. "It's truly remarkable, isn't it?"

I prayed that my face didn't betray the fact that I knew nothing about children, how honest to be with them, or even how to interact with them.

Less than a week later, I was offered both positions. Never had I been presented with so much opportunity. I knew if I accepted the job in the Bronx, I would be educating students who looked like me, Black and brown children living in less-than-ideal circumstances. The full-time assistant teacher job, though, paid better and was a shorter commute, so I accepted it without hesitation. I signed a contract that provided me with a decent salary and health insurance. It brought me immense relief because I could continue living in the city, continue being near you. The school was Episcopalian, named after a couple of saints, which elated my parents and the nuns.

"Nena, we're so proud of you," my mother said over the phone when I shared my good news.

My father took the receiver: "It was God's will, mija. All you had to do was take the first step and apply."

"Sure, Papa," I replied. It baffled me that they both accepted this as my ideal job, even though it had nothing to do with my areas of interest or study. Did I like children? I wasn't sure. I had convinced the interviewers that education was my passion. All that was left was to convince myself.

12.

I doubt you ever wondered what I was like in the classroom, but that was part of my identity too. After all, this was the job I held throughout the majority of our friendship. The rare times you asked about my work life, I avoided sharing specifics. My reticence was due partially to embarrassment. Keep in mind that I wasn't the head kindergarten teacher, so I was always working in the shadows. While she read a storybook to the children on the carpet, I prepared snack by snapping graham cracker sheets into thirds and pouring four ounces of milk into miniature plastic cups.

But let me give myself credit where it's due. Given my own reading challenges as a child, I devoted myself to the struggling beginning readers in the class. I taught frustrated children the different sounds vowels make. I pointed to pictures of apples and aliens, elephants and emails, igloos and ice cream, octopuses and ovals, umbrellas and unicorns. I helped them select books to take home and practice with their parents.

My favorite kindergarten program in the school was called Person of the Week. Each student was designated a week, and every day we learned something new about the featured student. It sounds trite to tell you this because you're a professor, but there was something magical in learning about and eating a five-year-old's favorite food each Wednesday, reading their favorite book every Thursday, and passing around their family photos on Friday afternoon. We also made a book for each Person of the Week in which we shared what we liked most about them.

Given the age group, the reasons for liking someone varied from admiring their glittery sneakers to enjoying jumping rope with them outside to being excited to see them on the 1 train on the way to school. On the days we compiled our reasons for why we liked the Person of the Week, it was my job to sit next to each child and transcribe their answer on a piece of paper they'd illustrated. Occasionally, a student would share a profound answer with me, such as "I like how Claire talks about her dog. I can tell she loves him and is a good dog mom." This ability of some children to assess other people's characters struck me as mature and emotionally astute.

Around this time, I started becoming interested in Aristotle's friendship types in hopes of understanding my dynamic with you. Surely you know to what I'm referring: (1) friendships of utility, (2) friendships of pleasure, and (3) friendships of the good. Was our bond based on utility? I didn't think so, because we weren't colleagues. For a bit, I was convinced we bonded over the pleasure of discussing books and spending time in bookstores and bars. But what I yearned for was the third type of friendship. I'd like to think you saw the good in me, namely because I recognized the good in you. It was my mortal flaw, actually, my ability to continually see the good in you.

Here are things I'll say about my work life: My coworkers were mostly single white women who lived scattered around Manhattan and Brooklyn and watched *Sex and the City*. A few times, I went to happy hour with them, but it was awkward.

Once, we all went for drinks at the Heights, a bar blocks from the school. The teacher I worked with directly was Sarabeth. The others had pony names like Gretchen and Sadie.

"My family rented a house on Fire Island," a pony shared as she sipped the froth off her Blue Moon beer.

"God, I adore Fire Island," Sarabeth offered. "It's so tranquil."

I'd never heard of Fire Island. Much like my interactions at Williams, conversations about the Hamptons or Martha's Vineyard completely shut me out. My house-sitting job on Cape Cod didn't exactly have the feel of their opulent, laughter-filled vacations.

As they waxed on about their Hamptons and Fire Island vacays, my gaze drifted elsewhere in the bar. Sitting by himself was a fine Black man I swore was Mos Def. For a full minute, I alternated between staring at my boots and stealing glances at him.

"What about you, Tatum? What's your favorite TV show right now?"

The question broke open my private fantasy of excusing myself to join Mos Def for another round of drinks.

"I actually don't *own* a TV," I said before cutting myself off. It would've been unwise to admit I loved reruns of *Star*

Trek: The Next Generation, *Twin Peaks*, and *Northern Exposure*. Nobody needed to know I lived with nuns either.

"What?" one of the drunk ponies blurted. "For real?"

Sarabeth's face became rigid. I could tell she wanted to shield me. I was her assistant, the newbie employee, this brown woman who was so unbelievably square by their standards. I was the only Latina teacher in the entire school, though two of the cafeteria workers were Dominican.

All eyes were upon me, so I shrugged as if to change the topic.

For the rest of the afternoon, they spoke about Jack Rogers they'd recently purchased, which I assumed were fruity cocktails related to Shirley Temples or Tom Arnolds. I'd never been introduced to those types of sandals before working with them.

When we were filing out of the bar, Sarabeth pulled me aside. Neither of us was drunk, but all the ponies were sloshed. We waved goodbye as they headed toward cabs in their printed Tory Burch dresses.

"Hey," Sarabeth said as she gently tugged my wrist. "That's just how they are. Don't think too much about it."

Was this a sort of apology? The cliquish-teacher version of "boys will be boys"?

I was exhausted from the socialization and saddened that the man in the bar was most definitely *not* Mos Def. Nobody was available to rescue me, so I simply nodded at Sarabeth.

"Tatum, you really need to use your words. Now, for example—and even in the classroom. How can we teach children to use their words if one of their teachers never uses her own voice?"

Her accusation landed like a hot hand across my face. How stupid of me to think she was trying to console or protect me.

"I don't fight," I said, unexpectedly in defense of myself.

"There's a difference between fighting and being passive. Sorry, but you're the latter."

My face refused to pivot to meet Sarabeth's. Instead, I stared at the hem of her blue rayon dress. Was she bullying me or speaking the truth? I couldn't tell.

"Duly noted. I'll see you tomorrow," I said before turning south on Broadway. The idea of riding the train felt too claustrophobic now that insults shadowed me.

After yet another awkward happy hour, I started receiving fewer invites from my colleagues. I figured it was for the best, and the extra time opened up my reading schedule. I spent my days off browsing bookstores for boarding school or queer novels (or both). When I wasn't at bookstores, I was strolling through PS1 alone, learning Japanese with Mayumi, or hanging out with you. I didn't have a template for career success, because as far as I could tell, I still didn't actually belong in any professional environment.

During this time, I often thought about my grandmothers. Both had been field-workers. My paternal grandmother picked cotton in West Texas while my maternal one picked cherries in Michigan. Eventually their stations in life improved: one landed a job at a textile mill, the other at a military base. Was this full-time assistant teacher job my highest achievement? Was this job fulfilling my maximum potential? Whenever I passed the city mural that reads I AM

MY ANCESTORS' WILDEST DREAM, I cringed. We'd made it out from under the sun, but as far as I could tell, this could not be anyone's wildest dream.

—⋆—

In what felt like the blink of an eye, Mayumi taught me hiragana and introduced me to katakana. Her tutelage was enhanced by the practice exercises in my workbook *Japanese for Busy People* and other texts.

"Should I fill out this page?" I asked Mayumi in English as I held the workbook open in front of me. Based on the illustrations, it looked to be a lesson on food shopping.

"Let me see," she muttered, her cinnamon Altoid breath hanging sweet in the air. We were sitting on her bed, side by side, both of us lounging in sweatshirts, leggings, and socks. Her hand brushed mine as she took the book from me. The touch of her skin sent goose bumps down my legs, and I hid my smile in the collar of my bulky sweatshirt.

From behind her glasses, Mayumi's eyes darted across the page, reading the characters rapidly and assessing the merits of the lesson. She nodded, then handed the book back to me. "And read it aloud to me. I want to hear your pronunciation."

Speaking Japanese made me self-conscious. As much as I loved expanding myself, it started to feel like the language was erasing me, that I was wearing a linguistic costume. With time, I hoped my sense of fraudulence would pass.

Together Mayumi and I made flash cards for vocabulary words, and soon my fluency improved. My newfound prowess baffled and impressed me. Little by little, Mayumi and I began joking with each other in Japanese.

"You sound so authentic. I bet you could fool Japanese people with your accent and black hair," she said to me one evening as we were wrapping up. "Wanna try next time we get a new resident from Japan here at the nunnery?"

She and I laughed ourselves into coughing fits at the prospect of this prank. Of course, I accepted the dare, and twice I introduced myself to new arrivals in Japanese, telling them that I was from Osaka. Only when they probed about specific neighborhoods, using native phrases I'd never heard, did Mayumi come to my rescue and change the topic.

I considered exchanges with Mayumi a type of incognito flirting. Each new phrase I understood brought with it a pang of excitement. Even asking her the time in Japanese and understanding her reply felt deeply intimate.

Whether she knew it or not, Mayumi was making me hers. As I was learning, my circuitries for language and desire are intertwined, which made my learning experience with Mayumi incredibly arousing. It seemed that I had the hots for teachers, or people who assumed that role. Part of me feared Mayumi was asexual. She never let slip whom she found attractive, and she treated appearance more like a spectacle than an aspect of desirability. For those reasons, things felt undefined between us. The fact remained that the richer my Japanese skills became, the less I felt like myself. I was a pulsating mind, yet something felt off.

When you weren't promoting *Happiness* and were back in the city, I loved the times you swung by my work at four and we'd go to happy hour or book shopping. It was becoming abundantly clear to me that if you'd had romantic feelings for me, they'd cooled. As much as I wanted things to materialize between us, I was worried about messing up what we had. So I convinced myself this switch to friendship was safer and permanent.

It was a late fall evening in my second year of teaching, and you and I were in a bar near my work when my book fell out of my handbag. In the tumble to the floor, the postcard wedged inside fell out. You bent down and picked up Roy Lichtenstein's *Drowning Girl*, the iconic image of a woman claiming in comic book lettering: *I DON'T CARE! I'D RATHER SINK—THAN CALL BRAD FOR HELP!*

While you recovered the postcard, I scooped up the book.

"Is this yours?" you asked as you angled it toward me.

"Yeah," I said. "My bookmark. Thanks."

I took it from you and shoved it into *The Bell Jar* and thrust both inside my bag.

"You've never read *The Bell Jar*, mi vida?"

I took a sip of my mojito and almost choked on an ice cube. "No seas necio. I read it every October. It's such a perfect fall novel."

You signaled for the bartender to get you another draft beer. "How many times have you read it?" you asked.

"Hmmm. Maybe eight or nine," I admitted. "Have you read it?"

You pushed your glasses up the bridge of your nose and nodded.

"What about her poetry? Are you familiar with it?" I asked.

Your beer arrived before you on the bar. You sipped the foam, then shrugged. "Sure. I've read a handful of her poems, but not as many as you have. *That* I can tell."

Your way of jabbing my ego was like Julissa's, both of you

toeing the line between playful and taunting. I wrote it off as banter, but I can see now that it was a type of mockery.

"It was sometimes easier as a teenager to be a nihilist about the future, but here was someone so utterly depressed who still managed to produce beautiful writing. Plath left us so much brilliant work before she departed. Can you relate to that?" I asked.

"Sure," you said before sipping more of your beer. You looked uneasy. We never spoke of your legacy, and it was clear that the idea itself was an unsettling, fraught one.

"So, Roy Lichtenstein, huh?" you asked.

"I like a ton of pop art. It's fun."

You knew about art, though you rarely shared much about it with me. As the years went on, though, it started to eat at me that perhaps your casual knowledge of art surpassed my own. But that afternoon, I smiled at you because my lifelong goal of rhapsodizing about Sylvia Plath with a close friend had just come true.

———

In some ways, it was actually convenient that what was between us had ebbed because my feelings for Mayumi were starting to crescendo.

On a train ride from my work down to Union Square, you and I split a gigantic matcha bubble tea. We kept passing the plastic cup back and forth between us like best friends with brain freezes. Then I felt something else. It was your hand on my thigh, your fingertips grazing my kneecap under my skirt.

"Mateo, I have feelings for a woman at the nunnery," I said as I grabbed the tea from you.

You immediately slid your hand back to your own leg, and for a few moments, you said nothing. You were hurt, but I had to get this confession off my chest. "Here, take the drink," I said to distract you from your shock.

Schoolchildren in uniforms shuffled off the train with juice boxes and halved apples, and women in business suits filled the empty seats.

"What's her name? What do you like about her?" you asked.

"Mayumi. She's teaching me Japanese. She's just . . ." I couldn't even buy words to explain her to you. I was embarrassed yet proud to be feeling so infatuated, so full.

"Do you want me to meet her? Do you want to introduce us?" you asked. I had never thought of introducing the two of you, but now the idea held no appeal.

"No." I shook my head. "I'm just sharing about myself. I mean, it feels exhilarating, you know?"

You slurped the rest of our tea in one drag and squinted at me. Your squint disarmed me. It distorted your features to the point that you looked like an unsympathetic stranger, like someone who had never spent a single morning volunteering at a Times Square church. You were judging me for gushing about a woman. Now I can see that's what accounted for much of the tension between us on that ride, but back then it felt like jealousy.

"Sure, I know the excitement that comes with meeting someone special," you said. Although our knees were practically banging against each other on the train, you seemed distant after my confession.

A minute later, you shared with me that you'd cheated on your girlfriend during our time at Cape Cod. I hadn't even known you were dating anyone then. Shame dizzied me, so of course I was too mortified to speak. Obviously, I was guilty of hurting your girlfriend too. You seemed relatively remorseful about your transgression, which helped me regard you as a decent person who'd made a regrettable mistake.

We moseyed down to the Strand that evening. In the fiction section, when I pulled a paperback of *Fried Green Tomatoes at the Whistle Stop Cafe* by Fannie Flagg from the shelf, your horror was apparent.

"Are you seriously interested in old southern white lady novels? Mi vida, that's basura," you argued while attempting to take the book from my grip.

"Have you seen the movie? It was a fave of mine growing up. I'm curious about the book and highly doubt it's basura. Don't be so damn judgy."

When I told you I was getting it, you mimed blowing out your brains. What you probably didn't know was that it's a lesbian love story. You could say I was doing research.

We were thumbing through art books when an Asian woman in a sweater set strolled past us. Do you remember this night? You leaned in and whispered, "Does she resemble your paramour?" Your lips grazed my earlobe.

I peered over the frame of my glasses at the unsuspecting woman. It bothered me that you assumed my type was matronly or prudish. I shook my head and flipped a page in the art book.

You were attracted to me that night. It was obvious that rendering myself unavailable had made me more alluring, a country to conquer.

As I matured, your face lost its hold over me. Your caterpillar eyebrows, pinpoint pores, the curve of your lips—

every detail was too familiar to me. The more time I spent gazing at your face, the less exciting it became. Your mind was another matter. Every so often, I browsed *The Atlantic* or *The New York Times* for op-eds or political think pieces you had written. Your political analyses were powerfully incisive, and my lust for your intellect grew as my interest in your physicality decreased.

Perhaps to prove you weren't threatened, you bought me the Sally Mann book I was thumbing through that night as well as the Fannie Flagg novel, then suggested Vietnamese food.

At Saigon Market, we spotted one of your ex-girlfriends. She was canoodling with a Gary Busey doppelgänger, an older white man with a ruddy face and a pronounced gut.

I studied you as you watched your ex caress the businessman.

"We can leave if you want," I said, sipping tea.

You shook your head. "We barely dated. She's still a stranger to me."

Based on your dating history, it was clear I wasn't your type. All your girlfriends were accomplished Latina marketing executives who dressed in clingy dresses and thigh-high boots. They all had long glossy manes and limited-edition Louis Vuitton bags. I rarely wore formfitting clothes; instead, I preferred androgynous silhouettes. Interestingly, the majority of your exes had issues acknowledging being of Latin descent and almost none could speak Spanish. I'd concluded that you liked the challenge of reforming self-hating Latinas. Being Mexican had never been advantageous to me, but this kind of self-hate wasn't one of my personal demons.

Half these flings you didn't even announce; they were blips passing so quickly that I didn't have the opportunity to feel jealous. I came to view these statuesque women as your fleeting diversions while I matured. These women would come and go, but we always boomeranged back to each other.

I allowed my eyes to drift back to your smooching ex and the businessman. The amount of fawning she displayed was over-the-top, nauseating. It struck me as degradingly submissive.

"Let me guess," I murmured. "She couldn't ask for a glass of water in Spanish if her life depended on it?"

You placed your chopsticks across the soy sauce dish as your eyes inspected the veneer of the table. You gave a quick nod before saying, "She thought cultural pride was a type of poison."

"Haven't you noticed that Latino pride is a no-win conundrum?" I asked. "You're a damn stereotype if you feel it and shout it, or an ashamed coconut if you don't."

I raised the ceramic teacup to my mouth and sipped. It was easy to diagnose strangers, but we operated as if we ourselves were free of any deleterious defects.

13.

During all my years in the city, I faithfully kept journals, week after week, month after month. But mostly the memories I'm describing for you are intact inside me because they mattered. Every day we spent together mattered to me. That's what happens when you love someone and look forward to seeing them.

This was the scene: It was an overcast July day in Central Park. You and I were sharing a wooden bench with a carton of green tea mochis resting between us.

"Why did you buy a container of six?! You're forcing us to be marranos," I said, tilting the tip of my nose up with my index finger.

"Relax, mi vida. It's summer in the city and we're both single. Might as well eat since no one is seeing us naked."

For the past hour, we'd been analyzing the many layers of Margaret Atwood's novel *The Blind Assassin*, but now my imagination was lit with images of you naked.

"Did I tell you I got a raise at work?" I asked. It was a

stupid question, but I was desperately trying to avoid thinking of us having sex.

"That's terrific," you said.

You bit into another mochi ball, sending white powder into your coarse beard.

As you chewed the remaining dessert, your eyes narrowed behind your glasses. It was the look you made while searching for the precise wording for your next statement.

"Come here," I said as I leaned over to dust the white powder out of your beard. "You made a mess of yourself."

You jutted your chin closer to me and inhaled deeply. "Are you wearing perfume, mi vida? That's a new scent on you."

"It's called Paperback, from Demeter. Aged pages," I replied with a one-shoulder shrug.

"It's interesting, but you were telling me about your raise. Why is it that you hardly ever talk about your job?"

A horse carriage clopped past us, followed by four slick cyclists with matching neon helmets.

"Writing defines you. What I do for a living doesn't define me," I said.

If pressed, I'd have answered that it was our friendship that defined me, but you didn't ask. Silence stretched out between us for a full minute or two.

"What would make you happy? Give you freedom?" you asked with sincerity.

"Ha! Less student loan debt," I blurted out.

I'd not calculated exactly how long it would take me to pay off my debt, but I knew it had to be in the ballpark of decades.

"What do you owe? Fifteen K or so?"

In the box, the last two mochis began to melt. They looked like sad puddles of green wax.

"Try more like . . . thirty-eight thousand dollars," I said as if what I was really admitting to were a hopeless cancer prognosis.

For a beat, your gaze scanned the canopy of trees above us, and I wondered if you were embarrassed for me. If you considered me irresponsible for not living up to my educational potential.

Finally, you said, "How about this: I'll pay off ten K—no, twenty K—of that amount. How many years of freedom does that afford you?"

Perhaps my face went blank with disbelief. It was a generosity my own parents could not extend. For several seconds, I remained so gobsmacked that I couldn't even swallow.

You scooted the mochi box closer to my thigh.

"What?" I whispered.

You smirked, a flirt shaping your lips. I had no idea what possessed you to make such an offer, but bathed in sunlight your skin glowed. It was like I was your philanthropy project, a dicey prospect that I welcomed.

"Do you want me to help you with your loans?" you asked. "Yeah or nah?"

Naturally, I wanted the debt canceled yesterday, but I'd never taken a handout in my life, much less one of this size. *Drowning Girl* came to mind, and I almost snorted thinking of that image. Sinking wasn't for me.

"Okay, yes," I said.

I'd seen your bare-bones apartment, and your wardrobe

wasn't exactly Armani. I had no idea on what you spent your money other than paying for New York City rent.

"I mean," I continued, full of doubt, "can you afford that sort of thing?"

"Yes, mi vida."

My acceptance perturbed me. My family had always said there was a name for a woman who accepts money from a man not related to her. This was different, or was it?

"Okay. Done," you said, and closed the mochi box. "I mean, we'll have to meet once we both collect all the information we need, but very soon, mi vida."

"A flower for your sweetheart?" a voice asked.

Standing before us was an elderly white man wearing a polo shirt, shorts, and boat shoes. A bundle of individually wrapped roses hung from a plastic sack around his shoulder.

"Yes," I said too quickly. "I'll take one for him."

The man turned to you and asked, "Do ya want to pick a color?"

"How about yellow," you answered.

Here's a fact you never knew about me: I'm something of a rose expert. My grandmother was obsessed with roses, and when I was a child, she taught me the symbolism of every color. I'm willing to believe you knew yellow stands for friendship, but the sly salesman handed you the only yellow rose with red-tipped petals. That's the one for falling in love.

———————

At the end of the summer, Mayumi and I were watching 千と千尋の神隠し in her room. In case you can't read that, the American title is *Spirited Away*. Mayumi's brother in

Japan sent her a pirated version that was captivating but shadowy. We huddled on her bed, sipping chilled rosé as the movie played on her television.

We made sounds at each other for several scenes and then something happened on the screen. The TV went blank for two full minutes. I turned to look at Mayumi during this lapse, and her quivering chin made her look so fragile, almost like she was on the brink of tears.

I leaned over to hug her and found my mouth on her bare shoulder, then roaming up her neck. It was so automatic that I only knew what was happening when she pushed me away and hopped off the bed.

"The movie is ruined," she said in a panting voice. The television screen remained a black cloud, and beyond that, I had destroyed our sense of ease.

I grabbed my empty wineglass and fled to my room.

That night I cried myself to sleep, lamenting how skilled I was at sabotaging friendships. I didn't know how I would face Mayumi the next day, but I intuited that our lessons were effectively over. What a joke that I considered myself a pulsating mind when my body had betrayed me.

I cried and shivered in shame all night, even in my sleep. In that deep haze of sadness, I dreamed I was on a dinghy in the ocean. I was terrified and drifting in and out of consciousness at sea. In retrospect, it was a little bit like *Life of Pi*.

In the dream, I wondered what would become of me, if I would starve or die from the elements. I was too fatigued to cry, but then I blinked and realized you were in the dinghy with me. You were more physically fit, and your glasses were a pair I'd never seen before. Once you appeared, the dinghy became a well-equipped boat with supplies and a radio. The dream ended with us washing ashore in the morning as if nothing tragic had happened, as if we had weathered an inclement night together but would always be safe.

14.

Days later, I was lounging on my bed, listening to Sleater-Kinney, when I heard a knock on my door. I assumed it was a nun, so imagine my surprise when I found Mayumi instead. Her mohawk rested like a limp flag on her shoulder. A trace of purple lipstick stained her mouth.

"Can I come in?" she asked.

"Yeah, sure," I said, stepping aside, allowing her to enter.

Sarabeth's comment about my passivity rushed back to me as I took a seat at my desk.

"We should talk about the other night," Mayumi said.

She'd opted not to sit on my bed. Instead, she leaned against my window, facing the Verizon Wireless parking lot.

"Okay," I said with a nod. "Go right ahead."

"Tatum," Mayumi said. "Don't you feel like you should explain yourself?"

"I thought my actions spoke for themselves," I mumbled. "I misread the situation."

The truth was, my life felt like it had more depth with Mayumi than it did with most other people. Only she obviously didn't feel the same way toward me.

Mayumi pursed her lips. "Do you think I'm gay?"

"I . . . I don't know if I thought you were queer, but I assumed you were open to more romantic possibilities than, say, Valeria or that chica that eats everyone's puddings."

"Naomi's food problems have actually gotten a lot better," Mayumi said.

It was tempting to dispute her on that point, to derail our serious talk, but I restrained myself. "Maybe I should have outright asked your sexual orientation, but isn't that intrusive? Nobody answers that question except on medical forms," I said.

"You could have asked. Or you could have realized that it isn't important to our friendship," Mayumi said.

"Listen," I said, crossing my legs, "I'm sorry about what I did in your room. Gomennasai. It made you uncomfortable. I can't take it back. I still want us to remain friends, though. Do you accept my apology?"

Mayumi smoothed the hair resting on her shoulder with her hands and nodded.

"Anything else we should discuss?" I asked.

"I do have one more question," she said weakly.

"Ask away."

"Are *you* gay?"

I chuckled. "Didn't you just say that isn't important to our friendship?"

Mayumi started to protest before saying, "No, you're right. It doesn't matter."

"I think my sexual orientation is being attracted to teachers," I said with a shrug.

"Very funny," she said as she approached my door. "Bye."

Mayumi and I were in the habit of exiting rooms in Japanese. She didn't hate me, but she'd closed the possibility of intimacy that had existed between us by switching to English to say bye.

You know that saying that if you can make it in New York, you can make it anywhere? The fallout with Mayumi was but one of a string of New York rejections, an extensive list that also included the experience at MoMA, the dynamics at work, and so much more. I became so shaped by these rejections that I started pivoting to avoid harm, to never let myself be fully vulnerable. For years, I naïvely thought I had to endure it all and never ask for much more.

I continued to avoid MoMA and gravitated to the Guggenheim, the Whitney, and the Met. While visiting their websites, I learned that Marina Abramović was going to perform consecutive nights at the Guggenheim. I immediately reserved tickets for both events. Since this was a momentous occasion, I convinced myself that a new haircut was in order.

It would've been easy to ask one of the dozens of women I lived with at the nunnery for a salon recommendation. The truth was that I didn't particularly care for anyone's style or taste other than Mayumi's, and I was definitely not interested in having my hair cut by the person who created her mohawk.

After work one afternoon, I popped into a dark-windowed salon near Columbus Circle. A tall woman named Dream with three eyebrow rings chopped my wet hair into a bob, blow-dried it, and sold me a finishing product that added sheen.

Walking out of the salon, I felt ridiculously attractive. Little by little, New York was manicuring me into a sleek woman. Consciously or not, I was inching closer to the woman in the MoMA elevator with her pleated skirt and Chanel patent leather oxfords.

My new bob readied me for the Abramović performances, and I even painted my nails a coral hue while relaxing on my bed. I was shaving my legs in the nunnery bathroom when my cell phone rang.

I answered it but continued shaving. It was you, of course.

"What are you doing this weekend, mi vida?"

"Well, as a matter of fact—" I started.

I was dying to share my joy about scoring tickets to see Marina Abramović. You were cultured enough that I wouldn't have had to explain who she was.

But instead of allowing me to continue, you interrupted.

"I'm reading in Chicago this weekend. I bought you a ticket to join me. But don't fret. You'll be back in time for work on Monday."

I placed the disposable razor on the floor, feeling flattered yet tense.

"Are you still there?" you asked. "Don't you want to join me?"

"Sure," I said. "Of course, thank you. Oh God, what do I owe you for the ticket?"

"Are you kidding, mi vida? It's on me. Pack your bag. I'll forward you the flight info."

I didn't want to be ungrateful, so I didn't mention my Abramović tickets or how much money I'd spent on my haircut. I figured you had spent as much on my airfare.

Days later when I met you at the airport, you smirked when you saw me.

"What a killer haircut," you said before hugging me. "That *is* you, right?"

"Cut it out. Don't be necio," I said.

While we waited to board at the terminal, I wondered about the optics of our relationship. Did we look like a couple? Did I look too young for you? To people who considered all brown folks a blur, did we look like siblings or cousins?

It turned out that you bought us tickets in first class, a preference that I soon learned was your thing.

In Chicago, the hotel was a deluxe suite with one king-size bed, which answered the question I was too shy to ask. I had assumed you'd get us double beds, but I was happy to be wrong.

Your reading was on Saturday afternoon, so we had Friday night all to ourselves. We ate at a Thai restaurant, my pick, which was unfortunately mediocre.

Back in our hotel room, you opened up your laptop with such a flourish that I assumed you were going to write, draft a story, or work on your novel. You'd never written in my presence, so I scooted to the perimeter of the room to disappear.

"Log in to your student loan account, mi vida," you commanded, rotating your screen toward me.

I did as you requested, all the while taking deep, erratic breaths. For a handful of minutes, you reviewed my balance, interest rate, and studied my payment history.

Without an iota of hesitation, you typed in your bank information and erased $20,000 from the balance, exactly as you'd promised. It posted as a processing payment, but nonetheless it was the greatest abracadabra of my adult life.

"Wow," I whispered.

You said there was no need to repay you in any monetary form, ever. I had never felt so pathetic yet grateful. Knowing what I know now, should I have accepted such generosity? It's hard to say. If time is money, your money bought me years. Randomly, for months afterward, I'd key into my account and remain dumbfounded by my new balance.

I'm not sure what I expected would happen next, but once you erased part of my debt, you watched a basketball game and poured yourself whiskey from the minibar. I sat on the couch next to you and waited for something to happen.

When it was time to sleep, you joined me in bed but turned to the wall, exactly as you had the night we went to Madame X. I learned not to expect physical gestures from you on these trips. It was thrilling just to be so incredibly close to you, to feel your body heat.

"Thanks again for the loan stuff," I mumbled.

I figured my voice was too muffled for you to hear me, but without skipping a beat, you replied, "No worries, mi vida. One of these days, you're going to help me out big-time. Just you wait and see."

"Of course I will," I instinctively responded, but I couldn't imagine what I possessed that you would ever need. I had almost no money to my name. You didn't appear to want sex from me. I held no power or clout in the world. All I had was my singular life.

When I woke up next to you, missing Marina Abramović's performances was the furthest thing from my mind.

CHILE: 2015

ONLY FIFTEEN MINUTES REMAINED OF MY LUNCH hour, but I ventured out on the museum grounds for a short walk. As I was looping back around, I glimpsed Rodrigo packing a box inside his office. It was such a curious sight that I rushed back indoors.

In the corridor, I ran into my colleague Sofia, who looked like she'd just seen an apparition. Her pupils were dilated, and her movements had an underwater quality to them.

"Psst!" I called out to her before asking her what had happened.

Sofia swallowed, swiveled her head to look up and down the hallway, then signaled for me to follow her into her office, where she locked the door. Anxiously, I waited for her to speak.

"Rodrigo was terminated. He'll be escorted out in a few minutes."

My eyes widened in disbelief. Among other things, Rodrigo was close friends with the renowned Colombian figurative sculptor Fernando Botero. That fact alone had convinced me that he was as permanent as the museum walls.

"Jesus," I breathed. "What happened?"

My imagination played out scenarios of Rodrigo shamelessly exhaling smoke rings in his office before skipping off to smudge ash onto white statues in the main hall.

"No details yet," Sofia said. "But the rumor is that it's about him being inappropriate with Lucia. Haven't you seen the way he always touches her shoulders and hands in meetings?"

The sound of banging in the hallway interrupted our conversation. Sofia cracked the door to look out while I remained seated on the leather ottoman, checking my watch because I was expected soon on a phone meeting.

In the hallway, our colleagues' heads peeked out of office doors, and Sofia motioned for me to join her. In shock, we watched two security guards flank Rodrigo on either side and escort him out of the building.

Some of our junior colleagues gasped as he passed by, his head bowed in humiliation. I had nothing to do with this turn of events, but for the rest of the day I was too delighted to concentrate on my work projects. My poker face revealed nothing, but inwardly I was drunk on karma's nectar.

"DURING OUR LAST CALL, you said M. became your best friend," Jamal repeated. "Do you think he would've considered you his best friend?"

Dark clouds gathered, causing the living room to become uncharacteristically dim for midday. The forecast hadn't predicted rain, but suddenly a storm felt imminent. A chill ran down my spine. I wondered if this was punishment for opening my mouth.

"At the time, I thought so, or I hoped so . . ."

Jamal waited for me to reflect some more.

"But now?" he followed up.

I fiddled with the buckle of my wristwatch before offering, "I guess I'm not sure."

Thunder boomed and all three of my cats bolted around the room with their ears bowed back in terror before scurrying under the couch.

"Can you elaborate?" he pressed.

"It felt that way at the time, but I couldn't relate much to his life then or offer career or romantic advice. I was barely out of my teens when we met."

"Why do you think you two became so close?" Jamal asked.

I recalled the conversation that Mateo and I had had in Harlem on the night we met.

"It was clear he was lonely, or at least someone who rotated through people quickly. But he didn't rotate me out of his life, so I considered that significant."

"You considered yourself the exception?" Jamal asked.

"I *was*. I was permanent," I fired back as I paced the living room, my voice a glinting switchblade.

Above the credenza hung a neon clock that Vera and I purchased in Barcelona two summers before. In zigzag neon lettering around the clockface was the phrase DALÍ PINTABA RELOJOS PARA MATAR EL TIEMPO.

Sensing that I might be hitting a wall, Jamal asked, "Should we break for a bit, or for the day?"

I allowed myself to curl up like a shrimp on my couch before answering. "I imagine you have more questions for me, but I need a talking break. I know you're the interviewer, but do you have anything to share with me?"

Jamal inhaled deeply. "Are you open to hearing María Luz's allegations?"

My throat felt parched and scratchy, as if speaking the truth had opened me up to a raging infection.

"Okay," I said, my voice shaky.

Jamal cleared his throat before playing a recording of María Luz's account. Before she began, she asked Jamal a question I couldn't make out, but I was struck by her young, street-tough voice.

> *I met M. around 2011 at the public library in Albany. To be honest, I had never heard of him. I was at the library looking for books for my little brother when I saw an event happening. Everyone in the audience looked so peaceful. I didn't know if they were rich, but their lives were comfortable enough that they could spend an hour just, you know, sitting about with no worries. Things in my own life were so stressful that I wanted to be like them. I took a seat and started listening to the man at the podium.*
>
> *The story he was reading was about a Latina like me. In school, I'd never read a story or even heard anything about Latinas, so I was surprised. I couldn't help but put closer attention. I kept thinking,* How does he understand me?
>
> *I went up to talk to him afterward. I needed to know how he knew so much about Salvadoran*

women like me. Why did he put this information in a book? Did people want to know this stuff? I had a lot of questions.

M. said people like me are important and that our stories deserve to be told. He asked what I liked to read, but I think I shrugged or mumbled something. I was in a library, but books weren't, like, my thing. Still aren't, if I'm being straight with you. I didn't know then that he was famous. He seemed nice, so when he passed me his email on a strip of paper, I just nodded and put it in my pocket.

I was bored days later, so I emailed him. His reply was real chill and, like, after a week or two, we met at a diner. I still had no idea who he was. After that lunch, I looked him up online. He was seriously on the web like white on rice. I was shocked and figured he must be like a loner, like shy or real humble and shit to hang out with me.

M. asked a lot of questions about myself and my family. He wanted to know when I learned English, when I arrived in the United States. Things no one cared about. It felt good to talk about all that, to have someone listen to how hard it was raising my brother by myself and all my worries about whether I should enroll in vocational school.

It's funny, but I never asked his age. I didn't think of him in a romantic way. He was just this guy I met by accident at the library. He was real curious about me, so we kept talking. You know, friends.

Then one day, we were eating ice cream at this

*outdoor shop when he kissed me. I didn't kiss him
back. To be real, I froze. I hadn't expected things to
go that way, you know? I should have stopped him
because that's the day things started to turn real
dark. I wasn't okay with anything that happened
after that kiss. People will say the abuse was my
fault, but I know I didn't hurt myself. It was him.*

"That's enough," I interjected as my hands tensed into
fists.

Jamal paused the recording. "That's only the beginning.
There's much more," he replied.

Rain battered the skylight windows of my house and
echoed off the metal patio furniture. I winced at how comfortable my life was compared to María Luz's.

"Does she detail what he did to her?" I murmured.

"Yes," Jamal replied.

"I don't need to hear more," I said.

"No problem. Would you be open to answering more
questions?"

I glanced at the neon Dalí clock. There were emotional
rocks I had yet to crack open, so I stretched my legs on the
couch and breathed out a resigned yes.

"According to the timeline you gave me, you and M. were
still friends in 2011, correct?"

I nodded, then exhaled a dry "Yeah."

"Did he ever mention María Luz?" Jamal probed.

"No, never. I had no idea he was traveling to Albany
either," I said. "Was he?"

"Oh, we've confirmed his time in Albany. We have ample
records."

I closed my eyes while acid ricocheted into my throat.

"Was your relationship with M. romantic?" Jamal continued.

The question hit my chest like a hammer. My eyebrows furrowed.

"I already answered this before."

"Was the relationship physical?"

"No, not really. We maintained an air of flirtation, but usually it wasn't even that. The term 'sapiosexual' was floating around at the time. Are you familiar with it?" I asked.

"Remind me," Jamal replied.

"It's when attraction to another person centers on their intelligence."

"So, you're saying . . . ," Jamal started.

"I wanted to be around him because I liked his writing and ideas."

"Did M. ever compliment your intelligence?" he asked.

I shuffled through my memories, trying to find a sterling moment in which M. verbalized our intellectual parity, but I couldn't recall one.

"He commented on my voracious reading," I said. "But we never traded IQ scores, if that's what you're asking."

Jamal chortled. "You're suggesting the two of you had comparable scores? Didn't his novel win the Man Booker Prize?" Now he laughed outright.

Silence permeated the phone line. His dig shocked me.

"I was teasing you, Tatum. You can laugh . . . or not."

My face grew hot. I reminded myself that anger was a mental formation and that I had the choice whether to react or regroup. The latter felt wiser.

A squeaky sound traveled over the phone line that I

assumed was Jamal's ergonomic chair. My heartbeat pulsed in my neck.

"Earlier you argued that your bond with M. was unique. What exactly made your relationship more meaningful?" Jamal continued.

I'd not forgotten his jab at me, but I would deal with it later.

"I suppose he had different boundaries with me because of my education or what he gauged as my intelligence. He didn't physically mistreat me."

"María Luz wants this story reported far and wide, which is why I wanted to speak to you. She's determined to be his last victim."

The word "victim" boomeranged inside my skull. His last victim. Certainly, I hadn't been a victim. He'd been so financially generous with me and never so much as shouted at me.

"How did she get in touch with you? Forgive me for being blunt, but based on her statement, she doesn't sound like someone with many resources at her disposal."

"Her younger brother was assigned a social worker at his school. María Luz asked her for help. One call led to another until she ended up sharing her story with me."

Mateo had clearly underestimated María Luz. It impressed me that this woman far removed from the ivory tower of academia was more motivated than me to hold him accountable.

15.

Whereas most books fade into obscurity, *Happiness* grew a greater readership every year. It was no surprise then that it became a mainstay on college syllabi, and your reading engagements never waned. In retrospect, I realize that part of your endless popularity had to do with the fact that no other Latino authors were being published, at least not by big publishers and especially not to critical acclaim. Sure, Isabel Allende still released novels and Roberto Bolaño was starting to be "discovered" by English-reading audiences, but for at least a decade no US-born Latinos made it, not like you. Instead, you became a sort of spokesperson. Your opinions mattered because you spoke for millions.

Your girlfriends, bound to their high-powered jobs in New York, didn't have the flexibility to travel the country. Instead, you memorized my holiday schedule and routinely surprised me with airplane tickets to join you. These jaunts aroused me, as did the fact that with you I was finally able to appreciate what it was like to live without finances dominating my every decision. All my life, I'd lived inside money's tight, cruel grip.

Once, my mother called me when I was arriving back at LaGuardia. You and I'd just spent the weekend in NOLA. I'd begged you to go to the New Orleans Museum of Art with me, but you ixnayed the idea and decided our time was better spent at a sports bar, watching a Saints game. Since you had the final say, we skipped the museum.

I answered the phone as I descended an escalator on the way to baggage claim.

"Nena, where are you? There's so much noise in the background," she said.

A TSA announcement was blaring overhead, and a Larry David type near me laughed hysterically into his phone. I thought about responding with a lie, that I was taking a stroll through Times Square.

"I'm at the airport. LGA," I confessed.

"You're in Los Angeles?" she asked, shocked.

"No, LGA. Not LAX. I'm at LaGuardia."

"Where did you *go?*" she asked as I stepped off the escalator.

"A work friend and I went to New Orleans," I replied.

"You can afford to fly around on the weekends?" she asked.

"Why did you call? What did you originally want to ask?" I said as I scanned the monitors to figure out on which carousel our luggage would appear.

"I wanted to find out if you're planning on coming to visit this year for Christmas. It would mean a lot to your father . . . and to me."

Her voice faded, and I knew she was still processing the

fact that I'd been so close without telling her. I'd been a hop, skip, and jump away from San Antonio.

"I'll let you know soon," I said. "Can you hear that honking alarm? My luggage is coming out now, so I have to go. Love to you and Papa."

Initially I shared little about you with my parents. Eventually you became a mainstay, a permanent fixture, so they pieced together more.

I guarded our relationship, and only the school librarian, Mrs. Wang—or Eve, as I called her—was aware that I knew you. She loved *Happiness*, and every year displayed the book alongside *The House on Mango Street* during National Hispanic Heritage Month. Still, Eve had no clue that you and I gallivanted around the country together. It was no one's business, and I never felt guilty. Although we always shared a hotel bed, you'll likely recall that we never so much as kissed, and most days, I believed what existed between us was pure. When I applied Aristotle's categorization to our relationship, I was positive we had a friendship of the good.

It was raining the night I met you in San Francisco. During the long flight, I reviewed several graduate school brochures. For months, I'd been contemplating transitioning from teaching kindergarten to teaching Spanish. Learning Japanese with Mayumi had awakened my love for linguistics, and I wondered whether teaching Spanish might be my life's purpose. Until I was officially accepted into a program, however, I decided to keep my academic aspirations to myself. The prospect of telling you I'd been rejected would be too crushing, and I feared it would color your opinion of me.

Our hotel suite was on the nineteenth floor of the Omni, and when I entered the room, you were shaving in the bathroom with the door open.

I wheeled my suitcase to the bed, where I took a seat, dividing my stare between the panoramic view of the foggy city and you. Half your face remained covered with white foam.

"Mi vida," you called out, "how was your flight?"

"First class is always good. Thanks," I said, lying down on the bed.

"De nada," you replied.

I fanned my arms across the bed like a snow angel, excited to be at yet another hotel in another city. I was addicted to the traveling, the tidal wave of applause, fans trembling upon meeting you for the first time, particularly because my life in New York was becoming stagnant. At every reading, there were at least two or three people who confessed to you that your book made them proud to be Boricua, Dominicano, Chicana, Cuban, even the blanket Latino/a. These impromptu moments of honesty, I suspected, fueled you.

"Is there anywhere you want to go before dinner?" you mumbled.

"Yeah, Green Apple Books," I hollered, "to get that graphic novel *Persepolis*!"

You rinsed your razor, then met me on the bed. Your face was more angular than the last time I'd seen you, and it had a woodsy aroma. Your scent had recently shifted from figs to forest.

Lying down, you extended your body parallel to mine. I always played off our closeness like it was no big deal. But the truth was that inhaling you made me high, and feeling your energy inches, centimeters, from my skin, quickened my pulse.

"I've hated myself all day," you stated. "I'm so glad you're finally here."

I knew I was supposed to ask why you hated yourself, but throughout the years, I'd become versed in every possible explanation. Later after dinner, I would ask, but in that moment, I listened to your quiet, dejected voice, inches from my black hair. I closed my eyes and remembered our early phone calls when I was in college and your voice first captivated me.

"How do you tolerate me?" you asked.

I faced you and noticed a white hair growing amid your black eyebrows.

"Because you love me"—I shrugged—"and I guess the feeling is mutual." My mouth parted in a lopsided smile. "I'm totally pendeja, right?"

You draped an arm around my waist. Beneath my clothes, a wave of euphoria spread through my body. I tried to recall if you were dating or had recently ended things with a marketing executive, but all I could conjure was a revolving door. It's likely we both wanted the same thing, but terror prevented me from undressing. Instead, we lay on the bed, posed like two people photographed in a moment of deep contemplation.

Two or three exhales later, you were asleep. I'd never known you to take naps, but you knocked out so quickly that soon your eyelids twitched. The flight had exhausted you, and it hit me that you were aging. Instead of going to Green Apple Books, I left you undisturbed on the bed and wandered over to the panoramic window. I set an alarm to wake you up before your event, sufficient time for you to dress and do a few push-ups to get your blood flowing.

We didn't end up at the bookstore that trip. It turned out like the New Orleans weekend getaway, but by that point, I'd resigned myself. This was how it would be with you: You decided our agendas, and who was I to question them?

16.

etween all the traveling, I occasionally attempted my hand at a normal life, one that afforded me other joys. Once Mayumi moved out of the nunnery with one of our housemates, I grew to outright loathe the nuns. One of the greatest mysteries of all time is how I managed to live with them for so long. It might amuse you to know that I carved an inverted pentagram into a pew in their chapel.

Allow me to fast-forward to an important day that offered me a better path. During parent-teacher conference week, I had a forty-minute break to grab dinner. I knew the healthiest option would be to grab a hand-tossed salad at Nussbaum & Wu, several blocks away, but I couldn't risk long lines, so I turned the corner on Broadway and entered Morning to Midnight, an Asian convenience store. You and I had slurped bubble teas from there together more than a few times.

In front of the food-to-go refrigerators, I scanned the

shelves for my usual fare. While I was grabbing the last tuna onigiri, a tall Japanese man with ravine-like cheekbones and chin-length black hair placed his hand on the same item.

He relinquished the onigiri and chuckled. "Go ahead. You can have it."

I was pressed for time and hungry, but I felt rude. He was also the most stunning specimen of man I had ever encountered.

"Are you sure?" I asked, drunk on his presence. The next set of parents could wait. No one was going to die if I arrived a couple of minutes late. Plus, the head teacher formally conducted the conference, while I was there merely to provide specific examples of how each child was performing.

"Yeah," the man said, nodding. "Take it. Next time we grab the same item, though, it's mine, okay?"

I wanted to admit he could have anything he wanted and that I would never forget his billboard-beautiful face.

"Deal," I said. "I've never seen you before. I work at the school around the corner."

The door chimed, signaling the exit of another customer. I had to leave, but I couldn't pull myself away. The possibility of actually having time to wolf down the onigiri was becoming slim, and the draft issuing from the refrigerated case made me shiver.

"You're cold," he said. "Let's move to another aisle. By the way, I'm Hiroshi," he said with a llama-like smile.

I followed him to the cracker aisle, where he selected two packets of senbei and a box of strawberry-flavored Pocky sticks.

"I'm Tatum," I said as he scanned the shelves for other items.

"Tatum?" he repeated. "That's an unusual name."

Out of nervousness, I removed a box of wasabi crackers from the shelf. I guess I was buying this item as well. The idea of committing a misstep in front of Hiroshi seemed fatal.

"Oh, those are my favorite," he said, nodding toward my cracker selection.

"Really?"

My mouth was slightly ajar, and I hoped my teeth were sufficiently white. My imagination transported Hiroshi and me to a sky-rise apartment in Tribeca. On a black leather couch, I imagined us feeding each other wasabi crackers. My face, I figured, had to be betraying my fantasy to him, but Hiroshi's expression remained unchanged.

The door chimed again, interrupting my daydream. I turned to my watch and realized I had three minutes before my next parent-teacher conference.

Hiroshi was examining the ingredients on a bag of chips, and in an adjacent aisle I could hear a mother reprimanding her child in Japanese. Yes, I could still understand the language.

"Listen, I have to go," I said.

"Well, we should definitely go out sometime and duke it out over plates of food," he said.

Although I received my share of stares and occasional nods from men, I had not been asked out on a date in New York. I was momentarily speechless.

". . . Unless you don't eat off plates," Hiroshi said, trying to bridge the silence between us. "In which case—"

"No," I said. "I mean, yes, we should grab a proper dinner sometime."

Although I had no experience with this sort of flirtatious

situation, I knew this was the exact moment when I was supposed to volunteer my phone number.

"Here," I said. "Let me give you my number."

I hastily shoved the onigiri and crackers onto a shelf and fished my phone from my pocket.

Hiroshi recited his phone number, which I quickly pecked into my keypad.

In the text box, I typed: Sorry about the onigiri. ☺

The screen of Hiroshi's phone glowed blue with the new text. He nodded, and the beginning of a smile tilted his bottom lip.

I grabbed my two items from the shelf and hurried out the door, the door chiming this time for me. Only halfway down the block did I realize I had unwittingly shoplifted.

After my romantic faux pas with Mayumi, I became cautious about what I shared with you. I intentionally never told you about Hiroshi until our relationship was well established. It was easy to keep it to myself because you went incognito for almost a month. I assumed you were neck-deep in your writing, though knowing what I know now, that probably was not the case. You were likely keeping company with a bevy of women.

For our first date, Hiroshi took me to a Yankees game. It was a clear spring Thursday, ideal for a night at the ballpark. Up until then, you were the only person I'd routinely spent time with after work. With Hiroshi, falling in love seemed inevitable. All the excitement made me feel like a teenager in a John Hughes movie.

The scene was this: He met me in the driveway of my

work wearing a Derek Jeter jersey, fitted dark-wash jeans, and neon-orange Adidas sneakers. His black hair was wind-blown, perhaps a result of running up the train steps to ground level, and it fluttered above his shoulders. Happiness tensed his cheeks, and when I laid eyes on him, he giddily threw his arms around me without reservation. This gesture shocked me, but I immediately reciprocated the hug.

Once we pulled apart, he handed me a white gift bag. "You'll probably want to go back inside and change into that," Hiroshi said, nodding toward the bag.

I had been raised never to open a gift in front of the giver, but Hiroshi seemed to expect it. Folded inside was a blue T-shirt.

"I'll go inside and change," I said. "Be right back."

The school's closest women's bathroom was at the end of a long corridor. I rushed down the hallway, a leap in my step. Inside a stall, I pulled the T-shirt out of the bag. It was a Hideki Matsui shirt with 55 printed on the back. At the time, I was unfamiliar with the player, but I slipped into the gift and sprinted back to Hiroshi.

"Thanks for the shirt. How do I look?" I asked as we began walking toward the train.

A gentle breeze whirled around us, and out of the corner of my eye I caught one of my coworkers ducking into Morning to Midnight.

Hiroshi smirked. For the first time, I noticed a tiny mole above his lip. "You look like you're ready for Yankee Stadium," he replied.

The train ride to the Bronx buzzed with hundreds of people wearing Yankees gear. Several people were already intoxicated, and throughout the halting ride, Hiroshi and I were awkwardly thrust into each other. Each time, we just shrugged or raised our eyebrows at the other in amusement.

Between our run-in at Morning to Midnight and our first date, Hiroshi and I had talked and texted multiple times. I'd learned he was a model, his family lived in New Jersey, and he loved baseball and raves. I'd admitted to him that I'd never been to a rave, but he assured me their poor reputation was largely undeserved. Over the phone, I'd told him that I read a lot and had learned hiragana years ago from a friend. He admitted his Japanese was fairly good but joked that I should correct him if he erred.

The crowds inside Yankee Stadium resembled a massive riot. Hundreds of heads and arms pushed in opposing directions. Hiroshi secured my hand in his and navigated the way to our seats.

The view of the diamond from our row was picturesque, but I couldn't help wondering if I was one of a dozen girls Hiroshi had brought to a Yankees game—if he, too, had a revolving door like you. Perhaps oodles of ladies had placed their rumps in these seats and worn versions of the T-shirt I had on. I inhaled a shallow breath, eyeing Hiroshi with brief suspicion.

"These seats are incredible," I said despite myself.

Hiroshi scanned the field momentarily, then returned his gaze to me with a nod. "I figured we'd have a good time here," he said. "Are you hungry? I can get us hot dogs, pretzels, or whatever you want."

It took time adjusting to being in the company of a man who was not you. I was unsure of how to accept his outward affection, his concern. How naturally he seemed to expect me to make decisions. I closed my eyes and let the experience wash over me.

"I'm not hungry, but feel free to get something. I'll be here," I replied.

Within a month of our first date, Hiroshi and I moved in together. His friend's father owned a rent-stabilized apartment building in Hell's Kitchen. Mr. Simmons offered us a railroad-style two-bedroom place for a price we would have had to be mad to turn down. In no time, Hiroshi purchased us eclectic one-of-a-kind furniture from boutiques in Chelsea. Soon we had a dining table and chairs from Peru and an ottoman from Norway. Hiroshi's aesthetic was flawless and everything he paired together made our home chic. In the evenings after work, we shopped for bedsheets and towels at Bloomingdale's and arranged the apartment to our liking.

As you might imagine, it was a relief to leave the nunnery and embark on this new adventure. I had hardly any belongings in my rented bedroom with the nuns, so it took less than half an hour to pack up. Yet it was bittersweet, saying goodbye to my first home in New York. For the most part, I'd abided by a 1950s curfew as a grown woman in the twenty-first century, and I'd even fallen into the habit of eating the three-course meals the nuns prepared each night: pea soup (which always made me think of *The Exorcist*), iceberg lettuce salad with shredded carrots and ranch dressing, and an entrée of roasted chicken and potatoes or meat loaf.

The stringent nunnery life now struck me as basic training for an extraordinary life with my new boyfriend. The next phase awaited me eight streets south, in the apartment Hiroshi and I leased. Whereas I hadn't been allowed to invite you to the nunnery, now I had no desire to invite you to my apartment. My heart was slowly learning to keep a few things sacred and shielded from you.

All these details are proof that I almost had a normal relationship. With Hiroshi, my life was more secure and for the first time it felt stable and healthy. It was hard for me to truly grapple with the fact that Hiroshi was mine, especially because my attraction to you two worked in reverse. With you, I found your writing and your mind so brilliant that you became beautiful to me. With Hiroshi, he was so physically beautiful that the attraction started there, and I worked to find things I admired about him. Until Hiroshi, I had never considered every centimeter of a person so physically perfect. My high school boyfriends had been smart, somewhat nerdy, with style ranging from nonexistent to meh. I had enjoyed distinct aspects of their appearance—their smile, eyes, dimples—but never had I stared at any one of them in utter fascination.

Within weeks of dating, I snapped a few digital photographs of Hiroshi, and while he was out buying groceries or meeting up with a buddy for a drink, I studied them. It was one of the greatest mysteries of the cosmos how we happened to be single at the same moment in time, to say nothing of our chance encounter at Morning to Midnight.

The last photo I'd studied so intently was your author photo on the back cover of *Happiness*. Surely it's unkind to admit as much, but had someone asked me to compare your appearance to his, I'd have scored yours lower. Hiroshi's various modeling campaigns proved he was internationally and indisputably attractive. Men and women the world over agreed on the merits of his face, his build, his everything.

Before moving in together, Hiroshi and I briefly discussed our exes. His last relationship ended four months before we met. Her name was Yoo-jin, which she spelled as Eugene. The story was that they'd met through friends at a party and dated for almost two years. She was an economics student at NYU and eventually she began micromanaging his life until he decided to end things with her. I didn't mention you as an ex, because we never dated, and I didn't want to arouse suspicion if I ever spent time with you. Instead, I told Hiroshi about my college experience with Adam and mentioned that my closest friendship was with a famed writer. When Hiroshi inquired if I'd dated the writer, I shook my head. It wasn't a lie. We'd had sex once—which I never divulged— but our relationship maintained itself in a nebulous limbo between distraction and soulmates.

"I gotta admit that I'm a bit surprised more guys haven't flocked to you," Hiroshi noted.

We were eating brunch alfresco at a bistro not far from the nunnery. I chewed a bite of my eggs Benedict and eyed him as he sipped coffee.

You periodically voiced the same sentiment, but the fact remained that men rarely approached me. Around New York, I occasionally caught men studying me on the train or in a café, but I chalked this up to people-watching, not necessarily a romantic or sexual interest. I people-watched too. It was my second-favorite pastime in the city after jay-walking.

"Yeah, well, reading books in the privacy of the nunnery

never exactly situated me in the company of many bachelors," I said with a shrug.

Since nothing had materialized with Mayumi, I didn't mention my infatuation with her or my apparent teacher fetish. These weren't purposeful omissions. I was still figuring myself out.

———————

Our nightly routine rarely deviated. Teaching required me to go to bed early, whereas Hiroshi's schedule allowed for more flexibility. He fell asleep well after midnight, but I always found my way to bed by eleven. Usually, he watched *Dog Whisperer with Cesar Millan* in the living room while I prepared for bed. Once fatigue began to close my eyes, I'd call him to the bedroom and within moments he'd appear at my bedside.

"Oyasumi, nena," he said, wishing me good night in a mix of Japanese and Spanish.

"Please put my socks on me," I said.

From beneath my pillow, I pulled out a balled-up pair of sand-colored cashmere socks, my only material indulgence beyond books.

Methodically, Hiroshi straightened out the socks over his knee, carefully removing the wrinkles. He pushed the duvet aside. With unspoken affection, he slipped the plush socks over my feet. This act never failed to make me feel safe and loved.

"Domo," I replied. "Oyasumi, neno."

"Neno" was the diminutive term I created for him. As you know, nena means "baby girl" in Spanish, but neno is technically not a real word. Nevertheless, Hiroshi understood.

Before drifting off to sleep, I closed my eyes and mentally thanked the universe for him. I had lucked out.

⸺⸺·⸺⸺

You called me a couple of times within the first month that Hiroshi and I were dating. The first time, Hiroshi and I were at the Whitney enjoying an Isamu Noguchi exhibit when I ignored the vibrating phone in my handbag. For once in my life, I had more pressing priorities than talking to you. My new relationship was so upbeat compared to your general malaise that I started to view life through a brighter lens. Hiroshi's outlook was largely positive, and when something unfortunate happened, his face momentarily dropped to reflect his disappointment. Usually, he marked these occurrences with a comment like "That sucks" or "Maybe next time will be different," before moving on. Having been friends with you for years, I was accustomed to ruminating on the negative for days, if not weeks or months.

Being puritanical now that I was involved in a relationship wasn't my goal, but I also didn't feel it imperative to see you as often as you wanted. Over email, I informed you that I was seeing someone, a Japanese model, and that we shared an apartment together in Hell's Kitchen. Given this was my first legitimate boyfriend since meeting you, I'm positive you were at a loss for how to incorporate this information into the puzzle that was our friendship.

"Emotional pillow" was a term I'd heard used before as a derogatory way to describe people like us, who refused to label what we had as a full-fledged relationship. I no longer required you to be my emotional pillow. My relationship with Hiroshi encompassed both emotional and physical aspects. It only dawned on me much later that the reason you remained leeched on to me was because you never grew emotionally close to any of the mujeres in your life. All you sought from them was sex, various forms of sex, and every visual marker society associates with femininity.

Still, your response to hearing that I had a boyfriend was the most uncomfortable exchange of our then four-year friendship:

> *mi vida, well this news is muy unexpected! congrats. it was a matter of time before some fulano dug you and your brilliant brain. tell me he's at least a smart model, uno que lee derrida or žižek. also, have you become a japanophile?*
>
> *first that girlie who taught you the language and now this dude. dios mío. if you want to go to japan tell me and i'll take you. did this fascination all begin with your love for haruki murakami and specifically* sputnik sweetheart? *anywho, things are good with me.* happiness *is officially in its fourth printing, so my publisher is feliz. the reading engagement schedule has no end in sight. more hotels across the country! not looking forward to braving them alone but as you mexicans like to say ni modo. next saturday i'll be reading at the brooklyn public library. it'd be dope to see you there. how long has it been since we've browsed the strand juntos or ate phở? i can't keep track but i imagine you have the details in your mental diary, that paperless book that forgets nothing, ever.*
>
> *besos,*
>
> *m*

Besos? Abrazos had spontaneously graduated to besos. Undoubtedly, you felt threatened. In the context of the email, Japanophile felt like a slur, perhaps the only insult you'd ever slung at me. Definitely you aimed to hurt me. My eyes began to scan the email again but halfway through rereading it, I stopped and logged out of my account.

What you didn't know was that I'd been planning to screw up my courage to go see a movie at MoMA the same Saturday as your reading. Believe it or not, I'd not returned to MoMA since my earlier snafu. Since Hiroshi had to work, I figured I'd go alone. But once I had your invitation, I convinced myself that MoMA would be packed with tourists on a weekend, and I could catch the movie during the week, after work.

CHILE: 2015

THE SECOND FLOOR OF MY NEIGHBORHOOD LIBRARY was one I could navigate in my sleep. Cream-colored walls and pale wood furniture created a welcoming, well-lit space in which to think. The two sections I frequented the most were memoirs and spiritual books, particularly meditation guides.

This evening, nothing on the shelves caught my attention, but often walking up and down the aisles was calming all on its own. It was my own personal version of supreme holiness, but my last conversation with Jamal had robbed me of peace. I hadn't even heard the worst of María Luz's account, but a heavy nausea had taken up residence inside me.

As I was descending the stairs, I glimpsed a reader on the ground floor engrossed in a book. It was a woman in her twenties, rail thin, her eyes feathered in outrageous aqua mascara. Her hands gripped the sides of a book like she was driving herself deep into another dimension.

Casually I crossed in front of her table to catch the

book's title, but instead my gaze fell on the author's name: M. Domínguez. Coincidentally, it was the Spanish version of *Emulations of Us*. It was my first time seeing it in translation, but here it was, a reminder of the life I'd worked hard to forget.

Without breaking my stride, I continued toward the exit. The crisp outdoor air bristled my skin, and I felt something akin to an electric shock. My gaze fixed on the snowcapped Andes in the distance, and it struck me as surreal that the novel had followed me into this hemisphere, into my own public library.

I recall my father throwing his copy of *Dianetics* across the living room when I was a child. The book had been ubiquitous in the 1980s, with volcanic commercials gracing our television every night. My father had been intrigued by the advertisements, but after hours of reading the book, he'd come to the conclusion that it was malarkey, fit for the trash.

Seeing *Emulations of Us* in the wild pierced a film within me that I hadn't known existed. As I approached my car, I felt something cold oozing inside me. It was like ink was spilling over my organs, timidly writing a new story, one to challenge this critically acclaimed novel.

Luckily, the streets leading me home were empty. I drove in a trance, ruminating on the power of storytelling. *Emulations of Us* had reduced the library patron to a pulsating mind, an enviable state, but it was hard not to feel like it was at my own expense.

My cats, Lispector, Bolaño, and Allende, greeted me at the door with a chorus of meows. Their furry little faces and open mouths melted my heart.

I served them kibble in metal bowls and refilled their

water. They gobbled away with gusto, their heads ducked down in the food bowls.

In the hallway, I rubbed the petals of our succulents. I was lost in thought when Vera wandered out of the bathroom.

"¿Cómo te fue hoy?" I asked before telling her that I'd fed the cats.

Vera told me about her patients; one was a regular, a little boy aged ten. For lunch, she'd tried a new restaurant with a coworker, a Lebanese taverna. Then she asked about my day.

I continued rubbing the cactus leaves.

"I went to the library after work," I started in English. "I saw Mateo's book . . . the novel."

Vera leaned against the long window, blocking a sunray with her body.

"Anyhow, I'm thinking of writing to him. *Not* an olive branch email," I said.

Vera rolled her eyes before storming off toward the living room. I peered at her as she started flipping through our vinyl collection. She'd quit smoking cigarettes a month before we met, but the tension in her body told me she was craving a nicotine stick.

She placed a record on the turntable, and Natalia Lafourcade's sweet voice filled the anterior part of the house. The old me wanted to return to the bedroom and fall face down on the duvet. A nap would be a delicious way to evade the talk we needed to have.

I carefully walked over to one of our couches and collapsed with a sigh. Through the windows I observed the pink sun beginning to set, and I realized I wasn't the least bit hungry for once.

"Vera," I said in my steadiest voice, "please come join me. Talk to me."

She was standing near the neon Dalí clock. "We always forget to dust this thing when we clean," she noted before joining me.

"I want you to know that I don't want to be Mateo's friend again," I said.

"Well, then don't write to him. Problem solved!"

"That's just it. My problem won't be solved if I ignore him forever," I replied. "I wish ignoring him were a viable solution. If it were, then I wouldn't be in this position three years later, but here I am."

Vera removed her earrings and placed them on the coffee table. She rolled her head around her shoulders. I was stressing her out, but all of this had to be said.

"So what's your plan, then? You think you can talk shit about him to a reporter but then send him a nice email, and he won't know?"

Lispector trotted into the living room, her pointy ears startled by the tone of Vera's voice. The cat studied my face, then pivoted toward Vera, a little judge.

"When you became an adult, did you confront your uncle?"

"Which uncle?" Vera asked as the corner of her mouth twitched.

"Renato. The one who hurt you," I replied tenderly.

As a tear began to roll down Vera's cheek, Lispector jumped onto her lap.

"I didn't . . . I *wanted* to confront him, but by the time I was old enough, he was dying. I couldn't live with the idea of causing him a heart attack. I'm not evil. I didn't want him to suffer in his last days."

"I'm sorry, Vera. Do you feel like you have closure with what he did?"

It was a question I knew I should have asked years ago but hadn't.

Vera inhaled as she petted Lispector's head. Her chest heaved. "Yes, I have some peace now. You know I've undergone a lot of therapy, but I wish the timing had worked out. I wish I could have confronted a younger version of Tío Renato."

I ran my hands down the length of my pants. "That's the chance I have now. I have to seize this opportunity to confront Mateo."

Vera eyed me with uncertainty. "But you said Mateo didn't abuse you, right?" she asked. "Have you changed your mind? I don't mean to sound unsupportive; I'm just confused."

I curled my legs under me and tried to picture myself in her position. I sounded all over the place, so I couldn't blame her for being lost.

"He didn't beat me or scream at me, but the relationship, the dynamic—"

For the life of me, I couldn't finish my thought. I tried again.

"He was in a position of power. The scales were tipped in his favor and he took advantage of that. I want to be the person who doesn't cower in silence."

"Excuse you! I didn't cower," Vera said with spite in her voice.

"No, not you. That wasn't a judgment on you. I swear. I need to tell Mateo what it was like for me. How he hurt me. Tell him the whole story as I experienced it. I was still a student when we met, for Christ's sake. Some people would argue that he groomed me."

Lispector hopped off Vera's lap and approached me. She sniffed my socked feet.

"Would you agree? Do you think he groomed you?" Vera asked, shocked.

"To tell you the truth, I'm beginning to see it."

Lispector stretched out on the floor, and Natalia Lafourcade's dulcet voice again blanketed us like a mist.

"What will you do if he writes you back? What if he figures out where you live or calls us like Jamal did? Then what? If you write to him, you'll need a plan. It's not just about you anymore, Tatum. This will likely affect me too."

As I stood, dizziness greeted me. I was thirsty and I could feel my heart rate climbing.

"I'm getting a glass of water. Do you want one?" I asked Vera.

She nodded. At the sink, I ran water into two glasses and plopped in a few ice cubes.

Vera was supine on the couch when I handed her a glass. She sipped, then placed it on the floor.

"I'll come up with a plan. He's not going to interfere with our lives. I promise you that. I'll find a way to say what I need to share, then excuse myself. I'll make it clear that I'm not interested in a friendship, and I'll even tell him I spoke to a reporter."

Vera elbowed her way into a sitting position and drank from her glass again.

"Do you see how important this is to me?" I asked.

Again, Vera nodded. "We're important too—me and these naughty cats. Take care of us too."

17.

While Hiroshi slept in, I slipped out of the apartment and took the train to the Brooklyn Public Library to find out if hearing you read in your melodic pitch still soothed me. For years, your readings served as meditative spells, and they were the closest experience I had to being in a quiet church. All the chaos of my daily life dropped away when you read, and for twenty minutes I focused solely on your short story, the world you'd created, which already existed fully developed inside me after multiple readings of *Happiness*.

The reading was held in the library's auditorium. By the time I arrived, the space had almost reached capacity. Since I hadn't notified you that I was attending, you hadn't reserved me a spot. Instead, I meandered the crowded aisles until I found an empty corner seat, two rows from the back.

The composition of the audience was mostly brown and Black women, chatting and laughing in high pitches. Many clasped a copy of *Happiness* against their ribs or had a copy on their laps. Several full-bodied women were adorned in colorful Caribbean-inspired floral blouses or dresses paired with deep purple or magenta lipstick. In an attempt to settle my anxiety, I inhaled deeply. A trace aroma of coconut oil lined my nasal passages. Rather than feeling calm, I felt like an outsider around Caribbean culture. My assumption that you were family now struck me as incredibly silly and reductive. We were both of Latin American origins, but our cultures were distinct.

Before walking out of my Hell's Kitchen apartment, I had spritzed myself with Paperback perfume and grabbed my battered copy of *Happiness*. Methodically, I ran my palms over the soft vellum cover. For so many years, this book had served as my worry stone, my therapist, my mirror.

An exuberant hum bounced off the auditorium walls, causing me to feel jittery motion sickness. Sitting near the back removed me from the commotion. Even though the stage was clearly in sight, I felt dwarfed by your ever-growing fame. I reminded myself that sitting this far from the stage was my choice. I could have notified you that I was planning to attend, but I'd deliberately kept quiet. Being with Hiroshi was worth this trade-off, I told myself. I vowed to cook a seafood dinner for him back at home. I'd surprise him with a bottle of his favorite white wine too. Still, my left leg bounced beneath me in anticipation of hearing you read again.

A moderator climbed the stairs to the stage and thanked the audience for coming before reading a short bio. I'd heard a dozen variations of this script: *Born in San Juan, Puerto Rico, M. Domínguez moved with his family to New York at the age of fourteen. As an undergraduate, he attended City College of New York before pursuing his MFA at Brown University. Individual short stories from his collection* Happiness *have been anthologized in three editions of Best American Short Stories, and the collection was awarded the Story Prize. He is a writer-in-residence at Columbia University.*

You took the stage, thanked the moderator, and greeted the audience before asking if anyone was from the islands. Hoots erupted from the floor, as did applause. You nodded, then explained you were going to read an excerpt of your short story "Listening." Do 90 percent of your literary events still consist of you reading "Listening"?

Despite having heard the story countless times, I was hypnotized by your cadence. Within six words, I was transported to rural Puerto Rico, where a teenage nun carries out a hunger strike. The audience remained captivated in silence as the plot unfolded. The only discernible sound was of women fetching tissues from handbags to absorb their free-flowing tears.

At the end of the reading, you signed books at a table stationed outside the auditorium. The line was so tremendous that I considered peacing out. But after all these years, my copy of *Happiness* remained unsigned, and I wanted a justifiable excuse to see you and comment on the crowd.

I decided to endure—*aguantar* in Spanish. It was a term my grandmother ingrained in me. I stood and waited and waited and smiled at the enthusiastic women who surrounded me. Their excitement was both infectious and overwhelming. Looking back now, I wonder how many of these women you mistreated or abused. Did you leverage their culture against them? Reel them in with talk about how you were family?

After twenty minutes, your signing table was in my line of vision. In your typical animated fashion, you chatted with your readers, smiling for phone pictures and addressing books to women, their children, their nieces and nephews, relatives back in the Caribbean. Every signing was a party, a fucking pachanga. Sweat creased my armpits as I inched half a foot closer to you.

Directly in front of me stood a reed-thin woman in a bright canary jumpsuit, her Afro an iridescent shade of rose gold. It was unlikely you could see beyond this lady's mountain of curls, and I remained thankful for the shield.

The woman's name was Shelia. She offered to spell it, but you insisted you knew how to write it. As you scribbled inside her book, Shelia explained that she had read your book while visiting her grandmother in Haiti and that she planned to read it again once she graduated from City College. Shelia's words exited her mouth at rapid-fire speed as if she were aware of an invisible timer, seeing as how more than fifty women still followed her. From beneath the arm of her jumpsuit, I watched as you pushed her signed book back across the table to her. She lingered in her own monologue before retrieving the book and moving off the assembly line.

"Oh my fucking gawd," you said as I appeared before you. Delight caused your eyes to nearly disappear as a smile overtook your face. You shot up from your chair, walked around the table, and embraced me. It had been months since we last saw each other, since before Hiroshi and I had moved into our Hell's Kitchen apartment together. Until the hug,

I had not realized how much I truly missed you, the heat of your chest, your full forest scent.

We carried on in front of the table as if we were catching up in a bar instead of a library. People in line craned their necks to investigate what was taking so long. The signing rhythm had been broken without explanation.

"Don't tell me you fucking stood in line for an autograph?" you asked.

"Sure, why not?" I said with a shrug. "It's been such a long time that I thought I'd come hear you read. Go ahead and sign my book."

You studied me with newfound curiosity, then shook your head. "You've matured since I last saw you, mi vida. You look above the age of fifteen now. It's probably porque estas viviendo con un hombre. You look feliz."

Your speculation that regular sex was changing my appearance bothered me. Were you implying that my hips were widening? Regardless, your comment seemed a reflection of your insecurity. I knew an invisible timer existed for our interaction too. It made no sense to start a disagreement in the Brooklyn Public Library.

"Yeah, well, you've successfully warded off the viejito look for another few months," I replied with a wink. Passive aggression was best suited for these sorts of quick encounters.

You resumed your seat at the table and opened my copy of *Happiness*. For a moment, I considered asking you *not* to sign it. I knew whatever you wrote would last a lifetime, and I feared you'd ruin it with a careless tontería written on the fly. Especially because you were giving me such a hard time for having a boyfriend. As you jotted a sentiment across the page, I turned and glanced at the line behind me.

So many people impatiently waited for me to scoot along. The desire to give you a gift in exchange struck me, and for a second I hesitated before retrieving my wallet from my handbag. You pushed the book toward me, and I grabbed it just as Shelia had.

Instead of walking away, I tapped your wrist from across the table and deposited a two-dollar bill in your palm.

"What is this, mi vida?" you asked, perplexed.

"My papa gave it to me the morning he had brain surgery," I said. "It's got *c/s* written on it—con safos—so you can't give it back."

"I can't take it," you said. "You never told me your father had brain surgery."

"No, I want you to have it," I insisted. "His surgery happened way before I met you. And if I tell you to take it, you take it. ¿Entiendes, Mendez? It's good luck, and I don't know when I'll see you again. We live sorta separate lives now." I choked back tears but cleared my throat as if battling allergies instead of love.

You tilted your head back in minor exasperation. "Don't say that, mi vida . . . ," you nearly whispered.

"Why?" I asked, brushing fallen hair behind my ear. "It's true."

Whether I admitted it or not, I had run out of courtesy for people in line waiting to have their books signed. This was my earned time.

You winced before holding up the crumpled bill. "Thank you," you finally said. "This has been touched by two special Chicanos, so it's clearly good luck."

You opened your wallet, slid the folded bill into a secure compartment, then tucked the wallet into your back pocket.

"Take care of it and it'll take care of you," I said as I walked off down a long carpeted corridor.

Ten feet from the door, I heard a booming voice shout, "Mi vida, I love you!" This public announcement was for me alone.

Without missing a beat, I shouted back, "I know!" My voice ricocheted off the walls and ceiling as I let the door flap behind me. Our unbreakable connection remained safely protected inside the library, where it belonged.

On the train platform, nausea overwhelmed me. Was it the overflowing trash cans or front-row access to rat culture? I was sure I was inured to both, but my stomach felt queasy. The idea of buying fresh fish in Chinatown was enough to cause me to dry heave.

I glanced up to see when the next train was arriving: 17 MINUTES. I was reminded of why I always avoided traveling to the boroughs on the weekend. Hauling fish from Chinatown wasn't going to happen. As I watched the sign update from seventeen minutes to twenty-eight minutes, I realized wine was probably not going to happen either. Good thing I hadn't told Hiroshi about my dinner ambitions.

Maintaining a friendship with you left almost no room for anything else in my life, including my relationship with Hiroshi. I gave myself away to you. I couldn't see it, so I couldn't stop it. Our dynamic had been set when I was still in college, and I knew no other way.

18.

And then another year rolled by, a year of the same in terms of my job and romantic life. You probably don't remember it well, but we were a bit distanced circa 2006, you and me. I was happy enough in my relationship and you were speaking at practically every university with a Latino Studies program. It's likely you were also avoiding your novel because you stopped mentioning it altogether.

Before meeting Hiroshi, I was certain the next big event in my life would be enrolling in graduate school. I'd hoped academic immersion would thrust me into a classroom or library with a love interest. Now that I had Hiroshi, I was no longer searching, and much of my graduate school motivation vanished. Finally connected to another person, I dared not change any variables.

The university brochures, however, kept rolling in with the mail.

One Saturday morning, Hiroshi entered the bathroom

while I was showering. Through the clouded Plexiglas, I noticed his outline leaning against the sink.

"Are you going back to school, nena?" he asked.

"Why? Did I get more junk mail?" I shouted over the blast of water.

"Is it junk mail if you're actually applying? Some of these colleges aren't even in New York." The panic in his voice was palpable.

"I'm just looking at programs and prices right now. I've not applied to anything," I replied because it was the truth.

Before meeting Hiroshi, I'd been searching for someone mind-blowingly brilliant who would understand me and support my aspirations. But as time passed, I wondered if what I labeled as my own intelligence was merely an ordinary level of knowledge, analytical skills, and curiosity. It was possible I had overinflated my own mental resources.

I'll admit I wasted too much time trying to figure out my attachment to you. Ours was the one relationship that had endured all else. It worked because I didn't expect you to be charming or particularly nice, just honest and stable. You were an intelligent man who showed an interest in me but who didn't need me—which made the moments when it seemed like you did all the more thrilling.

Sometimes it seemed obvious that Hiroshi was not my type. I couldn't picture myself with him forever, but neither did I want to end things with him. I couldn't bear the thought of being alone. Even while I was with him, I kept finding myself imagining what a romantic relationship with you would look like. I wondered what would have happened had you been interested in me. What if it were you, and not Hiroshi, sharing the Hell's Kitchen apartment with me? Would that relationship have been fulfilling?

— ❧ —

Instead of applying to local universities, I completed an application for the master's program in Spanish at Middlebury College in Vermont. The application required me to write two essays and provide transcripts with evidence of my proficiency in Spanish. The irony of my life was that all my grades in Spanish were mediocre—a series of Cs and Bs. As a child, I'd been fully bilingual, but my transcript told a more complicated story.

I held on to the completed application in anticipation of submitting it closer to the deadline. Middlebury's MA in Spanish required that students spend a semester abroad in Madrid. But leaving Hiroshi for a few months was something I knew I couldn't do, even though I daydreamed of seeing *Guernica* in person. A voice within me warned that we'd grow apart if I ventured that far.

And yet something still pulled me toward the program. I was aching to be a full person, away from the men in my life. I was eager to see who I was in a new country. Two nights before the application deadline, positive that I would be rejected, I uploaded all my documents. Hiroshi was still at work, so I convinced myself that none of this counted. What I was doing wasn't real—being sleepy and dressed in pajamas helped with the delusion.

I clicked past several screens asking if I was a veteran or disabled, and one that asked me to identify my race and ethnicity. Finally, I came to the last page and its blue SUBMIT button. Going to grad school wasn't really what I wanted, and I doubted my application materials were strong enough to admit me, which is probably why I went ahead and clicked SUBMIT. Seconds later, I received a confirmation email and promptly deleted it.

Those years of fumbling and half-made choices taught me a lot. Back then, I was certain that you were intellectually superior to me—in part because I loved your book, in part because of your fame. That fascinating person I so desperately wanted to meet in grad school or New York? Well, Mateo, I finally became her.

CHILE: 2015

AT SIX O'CLOCK, PARQUE DE LOS REYES was still bathed in predawn shadows. A primordial energy buzzed through the greenery.

I stretched my hamstrings while craning my neck to look for Don Lázaro. On Saturday mornings, the elderly man appeared in white overalls to feed the local birds. He often asked me philosophical questions, but he must have slept in and taken the birds with him, because I was the lone soul in the park.

Saturdays were perfect for long runs. My route often began in Parque de los Reyes before transitioning into Parque Forestal, then Parque Balmaceda, and beyond. I was on my phone, trying to decide on a playlist, when a booming voice rattled me.

"Muchacha!" Don Lázaro called out.

Copal, his signature scent, greeted me when I looked up. "Buenos días, Don Lázaro."

Four thrushes circled the elderly man's peeling boots. "Are you running to American music today?" he inquired in Spanish. "La Madonna or Michael Jackson?" He laughed sourly.

It was endearing that he was stuck in the 1980s. I wondered if he had children my age, if they had moved to other countries and traded places with me.

"My dad and I used to love watching Michael Jackson dance on TV," I volunteered with a smirk. I used the word "dance" because I had no idea how to say "moonwalk" in Spanish.

Don Lázaro's eyes watered, either from allergens or emotion. My comment seemed to have transported him into a distant memory. His wrinkled hands dipped into his burlap grain bag and he turned around to find his winged creatures.

None of my playlists included 1980s music. Hip-hop it was: Biggie, Foxy Brown, Kendrick Lamar, Kid Cudi, Missy Elliott, and the Roots. I hit SHUFFLE, and when the beats dropped, my feet took off.

Three kilometers on, I felt a tightening sensation in the bridge of my left foot. I tried to flex my muscles within my sneaker without breaking stride. *It feels better already*, I told myself, trying to will away the discomfort.

Cicadas screeched. The irritating chorus reminded me of Jamal's jab at my intelligence. Where had that come from? Wasn't he supposedly a women's advocate? The article hadn't even been published, yet I could feel my disappointment snowballing already. Stories of this nature always flattened women into caricatures, portraying us as naïve victims for believing that any man could be decent.

As if flipping through catastrophic channels, I speculated about the reception of the *New York Times* piece. How many women were contributing to the story? How harsh would the indictment be in the court of public opinion?

My Garmin watch vibrated on my wrist, indicating that I had reached five kilometers. In the last couple of weeks, I had stopped defending Mateo's abusive behavior. So many of his actions repulsed me, and yet I couldn't find it in me to hate him. Hating him would've been a relief, but my feelings were more complicated. I knew that in order to remain close, I had learned to minimize Mateo's objectionable behavior. It was a habit, an unwitting reflex. Forgive and forget. I diminished all incidents in which he was controlling or dismissive, in which he failed to act with care. But here I was, years later, out of practice with forgiving and forgetting, free to act differently.

Up ahead, the paved path was lined with lampposts, and a red kite had snagged around one of the poles. Passing directly underneath it, I leaped up to tug at it, but the string remained out of reach.

According to my watch, I was approaching eight kilometers, roughly the halfway point of my run. Did my foot still ache? I couldn't tell, which likely meant that it was fine.

Pieces of my conversation with Vera about my need to write my own account floated back to me. The prospect of writing it intimidated me, but I would have no peace if Jamal had the final word. As much as I knew the journalist's intentions were sincere, it was likely he would paint all the interviewees with the same brush until we blurred into a shapeless, pathetic Latina. If I wanted to avoid being reduced to a few sentences, I'd have to write my own story—one in which I was the subject, not the object, a complete person.

I knew how my account would begin: with the train ride the night our relationship disintegrated into dust.

19.

What was the consequence of my being in a relationship and growing distant from you? Punishment, of course. In the middle of the spring, you texted me a photo of a woman's left hand sporting a gigantic diamond. Beneath the photo were the words: She said yes!

Because your love life was a conduit for chaos, I couldn't even take an educated guess at the *she* referred to in the text. Based on the tan, immaculately manicured hand and the tennis bracelet peeping out from the corner of the screen, I surmised that this woman was a hotshot marketing executive of some Latin American persuasion.

When the text arrived, I was in a yoga class, but I glimpsed the message forty minutes later, as I rolled my mat. Chispas! Congrats! I replied, though my inner skeptic wondered if this was a hoax to test my gullibility.

While awaiting your reply, I fired off more texts: When did this happen? Forgive me for asking, but cómo se llama and do you have a date set?

Your bizarre engagement news robbed me of any tranquility the meditation had imparted. Love happens, and my relationship with Hiroshi was prime proof of Cupid's serendipity. My initial thought, though, wasn't that you'd fallen in love. I knew I was likely overthinking it, but it felt like the Babylonian law: an eye for an eye. Once I plunged into a committed relationship, you one-upped me and raised the stakes.

In six years of friendship, I had never known your relationships to have the stamina to make it to the altar. Not once had you even expressed an interest in marriage.

As I walked out onto 9th Avenue and back to my apartment, I wondered if one day I'd send you a text with a ring photograph of my own. I doubted you would be capable of feeling genuine joy for me in any scenario where you weren't the recipient of my adoration. It seemed unlikely that I was in love with you, and I sincerely doubted we'd even function well in a romantic relationship. But the idea of that door closing was earth-shattering. Your news kicked up dust around a topic I purposely avoided—my priorities.

Your reply texts lit up my screen:

It happened earlier today.
Her name is Denise and you need to meet her.
Quién sabe the date.
It's up to her.

Absent from the flurry of replies was your term of affection for me: mi vida. Perhaps I'd stopped being your life when things got serious with Denise. Worse was your insistence that I needed to meet this chica. I wasn't sure I could bear it.

A block from my apartment, I slipped my phone into my hoodie pocket. Given the good news you'd shared, an unspoken pressure existed for me to text back in an upbeat tone and agree to meet Denise, but I didn't have it in me. My breathing had become labored and noise warped around me. I couldn't tell how close I was to other people or objects, and twice I inadvertently bumped into pedestrians sharing the curb.

Once I had time to absorb this unexpected reality in my apartment lobby, I reread our exchange and went numb.

Inside my apartment, I stormed straight to my bedroom, closed the door behind me, and lit a pomegranate candle. On better days, it ruffled me a bit that New York had turned me into a bourgeois Jo Malone candle owner. Once the air was suffused with sweetness, I splayed out on my bed. Instead of climbing beneath the duvet, I wrapped it around me. Although I'd kicked off my sneakers, I remained in my yoga clothes and hoodie. In my pocket, my phone vibrated. I retrieved it and glanced at the screen. It was a text from you. It read: I think I have your papa's lucky dinero to thank for my engagement. When you talk to him next, send him mis saludos!!

I flung the phone across the room and watched it sail by the lit candle, missing it by mere centimeters.

I drifted off to sleep, the flame still flickering on my dresser. When I awoke, I wondered where Hiroshi was, before remembering that he had flown to London on a modeling shoot for Topshop's men's line. I hadn't heard from him, and whenever he was out of the apartment, even if he was only picking up takeout for us, I felt strangely single, unbound to anyone or anything.

Next to my candle, in a red Lucite frame, was a photograph of Hiroshi and me in Trafalgar Square. In it, Hiroshi's left arm was draped over my shoulders while I stared at him in admiration, my hand on the hip of my gray knit dress. Although the photograph was less than a year old, I noticed how dewy and hopeful we appeared, vines full of green life.

In the kitchen, I uncorked a bottle of Juan Gil, my favorite tempranillo, and poured myself a generous glass. A cautionary inner voice led me back to the bedroom to extinguish the candle before I got soused.

On my bed again, I opened my laptop while sipping wine. The last thing I wanted was to accidentally encounter mention of you. I searched Salon.com. To my knowledge, you hadn't written for *Salon* in over a year.

On the landing page, I found a review for the film *Half Nelson*, an article about NASA's mission to Pluto, analysis regarding North Korea's missiles, and then an essay titled "Fearing Fatherhood." I clicked on the last link and gulped a mouthful of wine.

The essay was a candid portrait of a decent man experiencing problems with romantic relationships due to his fear of fatherhood. He discussed the failure rate of condoms and how the margin of error made it almost impossible for him to enjoy what should be the most intimate experience possible with a lover. By far the most impressive aspect of the essay was its tone. The opening few sentences seemed deliberately cavalier, leading the reader to believe that the author was a sleaze. But as the narrative unfolded, it became clear that the writer, a Chilean living in Miami, was remarkably sensitive and self-aware. The essay ended with him philosophizing on whether his decade-long fear was a long-term fixation requiring therapy or part of his core identity.

After finishing the article, I abandoned the laptop on the bed and ventured to the kitchen for more wine. From a detached perch in my consciousness, I watched my hand wobble as I refilled my glass. Usually, it took more to get me buzzed, but it dawned on me that I had bypassed dinner. The last thing I'd eaten was a Granny Smith apple around four o'clock. I grabbed a handful of candied pecans from the pantry and popped them into my mouth.

By the time I'd polished off my third glass of wine, I decided to contact the writer of the fatherhood essay. It was clear we had much in common. I intimately understood his parenthood fear because I'd been struggling with a similar phobia since learning about your engagement hours before. I didn't want to become a mother, but it seemed you might want to become a father, so I finished the bottle of Juan Gil.

My life was blessed. Yet things felt off, like a scale that refused to balance. That night I would've pointed to your engagement as the root of my discomfort, but that was only one-third of it. My heavy head started to spin, but luckily, I was already horizontal on my bed. I scrolled to the writer's bio at end of the *Salon* essay: *Alejandro Vega is an editor at large for Salon.com. Contact him at AlejandroVega@Salon.com.*

Remarkably, we shared the same last name. This was too easy. Contacting you years before had required substantially more effort. Without so much as a second thought, I logged in to my email account and shot off a praise-filled message. Sleep was beginning to shut my eyelids, but I typed with fervor. Several times I forgot that what I was composing would actually be read by someone. The act of writing felt cathartic and necessary. Before I had a chance to second-guess myself or even reread my email for typos, I hit SEND.

Seven hours later, the sound of garbage trucks woke me. Sunrays slipped through the silver velveteen curtains of my bedroom, landing on my forehead, my nose, the equidistant part of my lips. The time on my phone read 6:54 a.m. Fuck! I'd forgotten to set my alarm the night before. I leaped out of bed and started dressing. There was no time for a shower. I had to teach in an hour, and the morning rush was intense at this time.

Once I was out the door and sprinting to the train stop in my ballet flats, I checked my sent box. Had it been a bad dream that I wrote to a random writer whose article I read on *Salon* the night before? My last sent email was time-stamped 11:50 p.m. The subject: *Fearing*. The fact that I'd not received a delivery error message sank in, but I didn't have the luxury to care until after work.

I scrambled down the steps leading to the 1 train. The subway platform was crowded with mothers holding hands with their backpacked children.

I stood near the tiled subway wall and watched as a boy wearing a Yankees shirt in a stroller picked his nose and smeared a bubbly trail of snot onto his mother's Coach handbag. She was engrossed in a paperback that I immediately recognized as *Happiness*. When the train arrived, she pushed her stroller onto the train, none the wiser about her snot-streaked bag because as soon as she found a seat and positioned the stroller between her heels, she went back to reading.

———❦———

Who knows if Alejandro at *Salon* ever read my late-night email? What's important is that he didn't engage with me. Whatever he felt about the fan letter—flattered, creeped out, indifferent—still lives within his private realm. He had better boundaries than you, the writer who apparently befriended all his female fans. I wonder who I would've become if you'd tossed my letter in the trash can, if you had let me be.

———❦———

I decided to text you back during my lunch break. My head was spinning with possible responses as I walked to Morning to Midnight. I typed: Hey, Mateo. I'd love to meet Denise. You tell me when. Besos, Tatum

You were the one to introduce "besos" into our friendship, and I planned to roll with it until kingdom come. But even typing the word made me think about how you and I had lost our chance to ever kiss each other again. You were Denise's now, and you had picked her, not me, for the remainder of your life. I'd been so certain that we would have more time. That we could waste time in reams, for years, until we chose each other.

As I turned the corner on Broadway toward Morning to Midnight, I tried not to hate myself. The doorbell chimed when I walked in, and the woman at the counter raised a hand to greet me.

Your text arrived while I was selecting a container of sea-weed salad and a tuna onigiri: Hey, T. Yeah, having a rooftop bbq next Saturday @ 5:30 p.m. Bring your novio. It isn't pot-luck so don't bring nada. For real!

As much as I adored Hiroshi, the idea of marrying him petrified me. Rationally, I knew the security of having the devotion of a beautiful, decent man would be virtually any sane woman's dream, but it didn't feel like *my* dream. That afternoon I was starting to fear the possibility that something in the design of my personality didn't allow me to pair off with long-term success. The flaw wasn't Hiroshi's; it was mine.

As I left the store and started back down the sidewalk toward my work, I wondered how you could possibly be more capable than I of loving another person and binding yourself to them.

A light drizzle started to fall as I turned the corner on Broadway toward 116th Street, so I began to sprint. You and I had spent over six years together in a symbiotic relationship, and it was a hard pill to swallow that I was, in fact, the defective one. That I was now the one left alone.

※

Days before the barbecue, I invited Mayumi to meet up after work at Kinokuniya. A few times a year, we'd text each other updates, so I knew she was still living in Williamsburg with one of our former housemates. Mayumi worked and danced in midtown, so meeting at the bookstore was convenient for her.

Our Kinokuniya routine had formed on the first day of our acquaintance, and now whenever we met up, we had an unspoken understanding to meet in the aisle containing instructional Japanese workbooks. When I arrived, I found Mayumi flipping through a turquoise handbook. She was decked out in a psychedelic jumpsuit and floral-printed boots. Her hair was still styled into a mohawk, but only the tips were ash blond—the rest was black, and her frames were a mismatched circle and square.

The first thing that flashed through my mind when I saw her thumbing through workbooks was that she was teaching Japanese to a new Tatum.

Mayumi turned and smiled. Her face had thinned a tad since the last time we hung out. Quietly she placed the book back on the shelf.

"こんにちは," she said. "How's your day?"

"Are you teaching someone else Japanese?" I asked in Japanese.

"No," she scoffed, and gave a half laugh. "We always meet in this aisle, weirdo."

The truth was that I hardly spoke complete sentences in Japanese anymore. Hiroshi was a code-switcher with Japanese the way I was with Spanish.

Mayumi and I wandered to the bookstore café. We sat at a glass bar hugging a window facing 6th Avenue. As we watched the evening crowd bustle by in suits and trench coats, Mayumi discussed her grueling rehearsal schedule and invited me to her next performance. I made a mental note and promised to attend.

Mayumi sucked on her tea through a pink straw.

"Do you have plans for this Saturday?" I asked. "My friend got engaged and he and his fiancée are having a rooftop barbecue."

Inviting her in English shamed me. My words sounded so stark and desperate.

"What time?"

"It starts at five-thirty," I said. "It's in Harlem. We can meet beforehand and take the train together."

A man with thick glasses and a manga encyclopedia abruptly hopped on the wooden stool next to Mayumi. She scooted closer to me to avoid banging against his elbow. I swished my bubble tea, realizing I had never considered the possibility that she would say no.

"Don't worry about taking food or anything," I added.

"Okay, sure," she said with a shrug. "What else is new with you?"

"I'm starting to think I might be bisexual," I said, lacking control over my mouth.

"No way! I would have *never* guessed," Mayumi said with a knowing smirk. It was the first time I'd seen her employ sarcasm. "Does this change your relationship with Hiroshi?"

"No," I said, shaking my head. "There's nothing to change. It's an unproven hypothesis. Probably it's malaise veiled as an identity crisis."

"Speaking of Hiroshi, how is he?" she asked in Japanese. "Is he coming with us?"

My focus was toward Bryant Park, where a red event tent was being erected. Six men hoisted up pole tents with breathtaking synchrony.

"He's well. He's flying back from Italy today," I said. "He's been modeling for Topshop and Prada. He's busy the day of the barbecue."

"I've still never met him," Mayumi said with a frown. Clearly, she was hinting at another invitation. She'd seen pictures of Hiroshi and me together on my phone, the Trafalgar Square photo, and a handful of others. She could dispel the theory that he was a figment of my imagination. However, they would never meet if I could help it. The way I loved people was by making them the nucleus of my world.

⟶✦⟵

Obviously, I never told Hiroshi more about you, so he had no idea you were engaged or having a party, and he certainly was in the city that evening.

Once Mayumi and I arrived at your building, I texted to let you know we were outside. You had asked me not to bring anything, but I bought Denise blue roses, a symbol of attaining the impossible. The front door buzzed open and your text instructed us to take the elevator to the eleventh floor. It had been years since I visited your place, so I was curious to see if you were still decorating from the Goodwill aisles.

The apartment lobby was well maintained but humid. As Mayumi and I waited for the elevator, I figured it would be best to give her background info. I explained that you were my longtime friend, a writer, and this engagement was a bigger deal than most because your relationships were nearly all short-lived.

"This chica Denise must be world-class," I said with wide eyes.

When the elevator arrived at the eleventh floor, we knocked on your apartment door. After a full minute, the door swung open.

The entire place smelled of figs, causing me to smile.

"Hey, Tatum," you said with open arms. You were wearing a white guayabera, white linen pants, and flip-flops patterned with the Puerto Rican flag.

"Hey, congrats," I said as I walked into your hug. "You're so *Miami Vice*," I chided before stepping back to admire your wardrobe makeover.

"This is my friend Mayumi," I continued. "And these flowers are for Denise."

No doubt you had been expecting to meet Hiroshi—this much I knew, but it thrilled me to subvert your expectations. You shook hands with Mayumi while she congratulated you on your engagement. Did you consider her my "almost" girlfriend? She was an enigma you'd heard about years ago, but whom I'd withheld until now.

As you two spoke, I scanned the apartment. It was still modestly furnished, but it had been upgraded. A woman— Denise, I was sure—had insisted on a sofa and a glass coffee table with a rug beneath it.

"Is everyone else on the roof?" I asked.

"Yeah, I came down to greet you. Ready to go up?" you asked as you dunked the flowers into a pitcher of water.

Surely you remember your engagement party. I didn't let on that afternoon, but I found it all so high-class. The rooftop was stunningly arranged, with round tables covered in white linens, a glass vase containing red geraniums at the center of each. To the left of the tables were two open grills and massive speakers. A Control Machete song blasted across the rooftop in aggressive Spanish. A few feet from the speakers, a man and a woman flipped meat at each grill station, laughing about something we were too far away to hear. Facing Frederick Douglass Boulevard was an enclave of four wicker couches arranged in the shape of a cube. A dozen guests chatted on the couches, many sipping wine or beer.

"This is wow," Mayumi whispered as we made our way across the roof.

The setup was clearly the work of professional decorators. If Denise was in marketing, and I put money on the fact that she was, she could have afforded this display, but my gut told me you had footed the bill. You were, by all exterior measures, straight up in love with this woman.

"Introduce me to Denise," I said, placing a hand on your arm.

"She really wants to meet you," you said. "I've told her so much about you."

It turned out Denise was the woman flipping burgers. By woman, I mean gazelle. Like Mayumi and me, Denise wore shorts, but hers were minis that served to highlight the fact that she was nearly six feet tall, with a lithe figure and tousled pecan-colored hair.

"Denise," you said as the three of us approached.

Denise was laughing with the man at the other grill when she looked over her shoulder and saw us.

I wanted to be anywhere else, but I steeled myself internally and managed what I hoped passed for an authentic smile.

"You don't even have to tell me," Denise blurted out. "This is your little friend Tatum, right?"

We were now standing inches from the grill, smoke billowing in a wormlike pattern up to the clouds. I wanted to know what you had said about me that she was able to identify me sans introduction. Little, as in little girl? Perhaps you still had photos of us from Cape Cod, but I couldn't imagine you showing them to her. We looked loved up in those pictures.

"Yes," I said, stepping forward to shake her hand. "I'm Tatum. Un placer, Denise."

New York had taught me its games too well. I could have made small talk with Ann Coulter if the occasion called for it. But I wanted to like Denise. It was essential for my emotional well-being that you be in good hands, that you two be equals. The unspoken understanding that you and I had that we would forever belong to each other was being broken for this person.

"Mateo says you're his oldest friend," Denise chirped, then rolled her eyes. "I mean, you're not old, but your friendship with him is, like, so impressive!"

Behind her, the meat sizzled loudly. "Sorry, give me a second," she said, turning to attend to the fire. When she turned back to us, I introduced Mayumi.

"Your hair is incredible," Denise cooed at Mayumi. "And your glasses!"

Mayumi gave a modest smile and thanked her. Her days were one long parade of people complimenting her.

"Listen, darling," you said to Denise, "I'm gonna get them set up with some drinks and then we can eat. Everyone has arrived, right? Or is your friend Lorena still on her way?"

While you and Denise discussed Lorena, Mayumi and I meandered a few feet away to admire the skyline. The Control Machete song had faded, and now a remixed version of "Eres Para Mí" by Julieta Venegas played across the open space. You'd replaced your monotonous reggaeton and long-running Calle 13 playlist with my Mexican jams. You were grafting the soundtrack of my life onto your happiness. The blatant thievery was equal parts flattering and offensive. But this day belonged to you and Denise, so I stifled my quibbles and acted pleasant.

"We have lots of beer and some white wine. What speaks to you?" you asked as you crouched in front of a cooler. You squinted at us from your squat. Something about your pose struck me as tender and I could feel my love for you swell up in my chest.

"I'll take a Yuengling," Mayumi said.

You dug your hand into the ice and tossed her a green bottle.

"Y tú ¿qué quieres, mi vida?" you asked, still squinting and looking up at me from your squat. There it was again—mi vida. My heartbeat quickened. The affection had not been retired or buried in your lexicon cemetery.

"Dame lo que salga," I said. "I'll take a Stella Artois si hay."

As you searched for a beer for me, I noticed a trickle of sweat run from your neck down your back and into your pristine guayabera. You didn't like Stella Artois, but the cooler was full of it. It was clear you had stocked it because it had become my beer of choice over the past few years.

With drinks in hand, Mayumi and I moseyed over to the couch area. We smiled casually at the other people deep in conversation, then sat alone on one couch. For several minutes, Mayumi and I sipped our beers in silence, enjoying the breeze, the music, the view. It pleased me that Mayumi had agreed to come with me.

Soon after, the barbecue was ready, and you invited us to help ourselves to grilled chicken and burgers. Denise's friend Lorena showed up with a Caesar salad, and a fruit salad appeared in a huge bowl atop a bed of ice.

Out of my periphery, I noticed you approaching me, and I was grateful Mayumi was now talking to another guest. You collapsed in a wicker couch next to me, our arms mere inches apart.

"Hey, mi vida," you said.

"Hey," I replied, suddenly sad that in about six years, I had somehow failed to give you a nickname, a term of affection that would've made you all mine. Denise deserved you, whereas I had been too careless. But I didn't want to marry you, a voice inside me insisted.

"Congratulations," I said numbly.

"Mi vida, you've congratulated me more than anyone else here," you said.

I shrugged, momentarily unable to speak. It was of no consequence if Denise was a self-hating Latina. She was on the verge of having everything I maybe wanted.

"Is your sister here?" I mumbled.

You shook your head and explained her absence. "Why didn't you bring your novio?" you asked.

I shrugged again. It had been a long time since I felt so childlike and confused. All I did was make mistakes.

"Are you happy?" I asked. "Can you see yourself with Denise forever?" The words exiting my mouth surprised me. They sounded almost like a dare.

You nodded. "I'm a good man with her." Your eyes shut from behind your glasses. It appeared your admiration for her was so all-powerful that your face was short-circuiting with love for her.

"I'm glad." I nodded, bringing the bottle of beer to my lips again. "You deserve happiness."

In my chest, a twirling pain begged me to ask you if we would remain friends, close friends after you married. It was unfair to ask you to peer into a crystal ball, to reassure me on a day that was yours, not mine. We had slept in our last hotel together and I hadn't even known it. At the time, it had struck me as just another night in an endless stream of hotel nights with you. Nights where you sipped whiskey and we discussed books, played hangman, or watched baseball games on TV. All I wanted from life was to hang out with you and, perhaps, one day be immortalized as a formidable woman in your books. I obviously had no idea what was to come and how you would pervert my dream.

"Send me an invitation to the wedding," I said.

You rubbed your forehead with your hand and nodded some more. "The date is up to Denise. I'll let you know."

A strong gust of wind swept over the roof, so I pulled my knees to my chest. You watched as I rubbed my hands over my legs to keep them warm. This was when, in other circumstances, you would have offered me your hoodie. I locked eyes with you and mentally implored you to offer me a blanket from your apartment, anything. Instead, you stood up and returned to the huddle formed by your other friends.

20.

You know what happened next. A handful of months after your engagement party, you fell off the map. You texted me a few random messages that year, so I knew you were alive, but you seemed uninterested in divulging much.

And then the text that simply read: Engagement is off. Can't talk. Am broken rn.

I was on the first floor of Book Culture, flipping through *Last Evenings on Earth* by Roberto Bolaño, when the message arrived. My pulse made itself known in my throat as I reread your text. It's awful to admit, but I was elated to hear you or Denise, or both of you, had come to your senses. But something pulled at my heart because I was certain you were suffering. I'd seen the look on your face at the barbecue. You'd believed in whatever you had with that woman. It had thoroughly convinced you.

I closed the Bolaño book and replied: Lo siento. I know

you said u can't talk, but if you change your mind and want to share, let me know. I'm here for u.

Your broken engagement was a curveball I wasn't expecting. I now wondered what this meant for Hiroshi and me. The fact that you were unattached again marbled my feelings.

Weeks went by. Even a month passed with no word from you. Then randomly you sent me an email that said you were miserable, unable to write, focus, or sleep. In the last line, you begged me not to reply, so I respected your request and left it unanswered in my inbox.

In a few online photos I saw of you with fans, you looked gaunt and pale. I'm no psychiatrist, but it was obvious you were depressed. Then, unexpectedly, you resurfaced.

It was eleven o'clock on a Thursday night, my exact bedtime, when my computer pinged with the delicate chime signaling an online chat. I'd been in bed reading *Epileptic*, a French graphic novel translated into English.

An hour before, Hiroshi had run to the corner store for cigarettes but still hadn't returned. The monitor pinged again. I stood and moved the laptop to the bed, crisscrossing my legs. Typed across my screen, I saw: *are you still up? i feel like an owl. no one seems to be up.*

You were on Gchat.

yeah, i'm still up, I typed. *you still there?*

My cursor blinked in place, then followed your script.

TATUM! mi vida. you're awake. what's new with you?

The latest news with me was that I suspected Hiroshi was hiding something. It wasn't that I suspected he was cheating, but he seemed to be living a double life. I was beginning to feel that we might be doomed as a couple.

> *have I told you i've been taking advanced Spanish language and literature courses at Instituto Cervantes in midtown?*

What I didn't share was that years before, I'd applied to and been rejected by the master's in Spanish program at Middlebury College. Somehow my modus operandi with you had shifted from vulnerable honesty to veiled secrecy and omission. Surely we'd spent sufficient time together for you to detect the change, but at this point, you were too depressed to care.

why? you responded. *You're fluent or at least proficient.*

> *yeah, but dude the subjunctive makes an idiot of me.*

Three minutes lapsed. You'd either lost interest in the topic or real life had distracted you. I typed: *i read your Atlantic article about undocumented workers in new mexico. It was terrific. how's the novel?*

You replied: *it's been weeks since I've written a fucking sentence for my novel. I'm a mess.*

The more distance I had from you, the more my mind split you into two distinct people: the renowned author and my friend Mateo. It was hard to reconcile both identities into one person. Although we shared a history, I often read your interviews and learned something new about you, like that you loved Oreos or tried to visit Japan every summer.

For years, my relationship with Hiroshi had distanced us,

but now that Hiroshi was almost in the past tense, a gnaw ate at me. I hated myself for limiting our time together, especially now that you were a shell of yourself. If anyone could help restore you to a better state, it was me, right?

> You: writing isn't that important to me right now

> Me: i read you're almost done with the novel. It was in The Village Voice.

> You: i was talking out of my ass in that interview. not the first time I've done that.

> Me: wanna meet at Yaffa Cafe this weekend?? i'll treat you to coffee or lunch. we could veg out and read on a blanket in Central Park

> You: it's okay, mi vida. i'm sorry to burden you like this. this is a job for me to fix.

> Me: i want to help you, though.

> You: sorry, gotta go. talk soon.

You signed off, leaving me to stare at our exchange.

You were a hurricane and its aftermath—a wreck that perpetuated itself—one that frequently left me second-guessing myself. Instead of returning to the graphic novel, I decided to reread *Happiness*. It was my first time opening it in two years, and I stopped at the note you had written in the front:

Para La Tatum, who's been there from the start . . .
Love, Mateo

———※———

Hiroshi spent four hours allegedly buying cigarettes at our corner bodega. By the time he returned, it was after 2:15 a.m. Although he entered the bedroom stealthily, I sensed movement and parted my eyelids. My alarm was set to ring in four hours, and exhaustion urged me to ignore him and fall back asleep.

In the coal darkness, Hiroshi's movements resembled jerky pantomimes. Through cracked eyelids, I watched as he stepped out of his jeans and folded them over a chair next to the bed. He vaguely smelled of cigarettes, but I couldn't tell what else lingered on him. Was he seeing someone else? The very idea caused me to turn to the wall.

"Where did you go?" I murmured.

"To buy cigarettes," he muttered.

The bodega was a two-minute walk from our apartment. His deliberate obtuseness infuriated me, but I wasn't interested in picking a fight. We could discuss his whereabouts in the morning. Although my initial impulse was jealousy and suspicion, I now wondered why I cared so much. A critical voice inside me concluded that I could find a more intelligent partner. If he wasn't focused on me, what could I do? I let sleep crawl over me like a colony of invisible ants. I didn't balk or fight.

———※———

The end was actually a string of events. The night of the smokes was one incident, but then weeks later, Hiroshi texted me from Prague. He was decompressing at a bar after back-to-back modeling projects. The text was an image—a black-and-white drawing I was acquainted with from my adolescence.

The text read: I went to a museum today and learned about this incredible artist.

The sketch was a Kafka doodle—a well-known one, at that.

I replied: ¡¡¡Franz Kafka!!!

Hiroshi was surprised I could identify an artist he'd assumed was obscure. I knew a good girlfriend would feel happy that Hiroshi had stumbled across the Kafka Museum. But I wasn't that girlfriend, because what I felt was envy—such an excursion would have been better enjoyed by a Kafka reader like myself.

I replied: Didn't you read the roach story in high school?

As soon as I hit SEND, I realized I didn't care if he'd read *The Metamorphosis*, because obviously he hadn't remembered the author. Literature didn't speak to him; it didn't illustrate the world to him in the way that it did for me.

Traffic chugged outside our bedroom window, and my eyes drifted toward the horizon. Even after having lived in New York for years, my geography was elementary, but I presumed I was gazing at New Jersey.

Hiroshi's reply arrived in my hands: Roach story? Whhaatt??

My reply: Oh nvmd. How's the rest of Prague?

For twenty minutes we chatted about food and weather and mundane things that couples compare notes on, but I observed our exchange from a distance, and it was more than continents dividing us. It occurred to me there was no better person to talk to about food and weather, no better person to order a pizza with than Hiroshi. But life was so much more than shooting the breeze about Wiener schnitzel. Hiroshi had nothing interesting to say about the Kafka drawing. It was simply cool to him. Full stop.

When he returned from Prague, Hiroshi came bearing gifts. That's the kind of guy he was and probably still is—considerate. He brought his mother soaps and a silk paisley kerchief. For me, he brought a pair of shoulder duster earrings, which I wrote off at first as not my style. They weren't European but Tibetan, actually, with dollops of turquoise and coral.

That night, we sat on the floor of our living room as he dug out items from his leather backpack. The earrings were encased in a plastic zip bag, and when he placed them in my palm, I must've tensed my eyebrows or revealed my lack of interest.

"You think they aren't you. But try them on. I promise they *are* you."

I slipped the earrings on and walked to the bathroom to view myself in the mirror. Oddly enough, Hiroshi was right. The earrings were quite me. I've always loved dangling stones, and the turquoise complemented my olive skin.

"Neno," I said, bounding back into the living room, "I adore them!"

"See, nena," he said before telling me more about the Franz Kafka Museum.

Mateo, I loved Hiroshi. I really did, but as he recounted what he saw in the museum, I pictured you and me there instead. What a thrill it would have been to roam that space with you, with a writer, or anyone brilliant who appreciated literature. Of course, I had tremendous guilt, thinking all of this in front of Hiroshi while wearing the gorgeous Tibetan earrings.

My list of his petty flaws would seem trivial not even a week later, when I found cocaine in our bedroom. The plastic baggies were in Hiroshi's cedar box, a gift his father had given him for his seventeenth birthday. It's where he stored all his beloved belongings: his Cartier watch, his kidskin wallet, and spare keys to his parents' house. I did my best to respect his privacy and rarely peeked in the box. But that day, the lid was off, and the inside called me forward.

I should have been shocked by the full pouches of coke stashed next to a rolled twenty-dollar bill, but I wasn't, not as much as I was strangely relieved. By this time, I knew Hiroshi and I weren't going to end up together for life. Now I had something concrete to point to as the reason. I squished the bags between my thumb and index finger as if they were water balloons. This was, in the grand scheme of things, better (for me) than if I'd found out he was cheating. That would have hurt. Revise that—it would've been humiliating. Instead, I was disappointed, but I decided to let the relationship ride itself out. I knew how to step out of the way once the first domino tipped the next.

In my estimation, we had a handful of months left. But instead, everything happened in the bat of an eye. One evening, I came home from work to find Hiroshi lying on the floor, a syringe protruding from his arm. The last time I'd seen a needle up close was the day I interviewed in the Bronx and almost stepped on an overstuffed dirty diaper.

Hiroshi's eyes fluttered, so I knew he was alive, but still I panicked.

"Neno," I said, dropping down to my knees. "Wake up," I said, touching his cheek. I pulled the needle from his arm and peered into his barely responsive face.

"Wake up," I said over and over. "I'm gonna have to call 911 if you can't wake up."

Strangely enough, I thought about the drug party I'd escaped as a kid. Remember how I told you I called my parents to rescue me when I was thirteen? I couldn't believe my apartment was becoming a drug den. All you need to know is that Hiroshi survived. He vomited his guts out for almost a day, and I begged him to seek help. My pleas had no effect, so a week or two later, while we were eating at a Burmese restaurant and both of us were sober, I told him the truth.

"This isn't working anymore," I said as I pointed to him and then back to me.

"What do you mean?" he asked, a bit baffled.

A votive candle flickered between us and our plates. Sade was crooning "By Your Side." I recall this so vividly because he and I were both big fans of that song, and I couldn't believe I was corrupting it for us forever.

"Go to treatment or we're over."

And just like that, Hiroshi and I were over.

21.

After my breakup with Hiroshi, I moved into the first apartment share I could find in my price range. It was a fully furnished bedroom and bathroom in Morningside Heights, walking distance from my teaching job.

The first Saturday after moving in, I allowed myself to wallow in bed like an angsty teenager. What if the problem was not Hiroshi or any love interest, but how I loved people? For hours, I stared at the ceiling while listening to "The Moon" by Cat Power on loop. Eventually, I texted you: Things with Hiroshi are over and I might've made a mistake. I don't know yet. I can't think straight.

Through the open bedroom window facing West End Avenue, I heard a fire truck zoom down the street. Its approaching siren echoed an intensely personal song.

Less than a minute later, I received your reply: mi vida. Sorry to hear it. Why do u think u made a mistake? Do u want to come over to my place & talk?

You rarely invited me over, and for a second I wondered if this was a best friend invite or a holding/sex invite. For days, I'd been too dispirited to leave my neighborhood, much less venture to your barrio, but here was a chance for us to reunite again.

I replied: say what?

I hit SEND, rotated onto my side, and reread the invitation. It wasn't a figment of my imagination. I anxiously awaited your reply.

Finally, your text arrived: Come over. To my place.

It sounded like a command, a command I wanted to obey, but one I feared.

I typed: come here instead.

The rest, well, I'm sure you remember the rest. Within fifteen minutes, a cab deposited you at my new apartment and you were in my bed. For the first hour, we did nothing but kiss. Were we both shy or afraid to ruin our relationship? It'd been a lifetime since we were physical, so it took time for us to approach the edge.

Then you let me lead. First, I removed our eyeglasses and placed them on my nightstand as if this were our routine. Without your glasses, you looked older and defenseless. You'd been so young when we met, though it had been hard for me to see your youth then. When I smiled at you, through the blurriness that separated us, I felt like I was seeing all the versions of you throughout the years, refracted in my bedroom. My astigmatism is terrible, but I'm certain you winked at me, as drunk with anticipation as I was of what was to come.

I called all the shots that night and left you naked for my admiration before I even removed my blouse.

Touching you for the first time again was kinetic. Eventually desire overtook me, and I was saying things I had no control over.

When we finished, I wanted to know only one thing. In your ear, I whispered, "Who else do you call mi vida?"

We were intertwined under my duvet, both of us still undressed. The room smelled of sex, figs, sweat. You reached for your glasses, placed them on your face, but left mine on the nightstand.

"You are the only person who has ever earned that title."

"Promise?" I asked, blinking away my doubt.

You nodded before stating, "You're my family, more so than my blood family."

I'd waited for this moment for what felt like my whole life, certainly my entire adult life. My eternal patience had finally paid off. Our life together could now begin. Little did I know how rapidly we were approaching the end.

In retrospect, this conversation must have made you feel too vulnerable because you switched topics. You asked if we should take a trip together and named a few options. Brazil? Chile? Argentina?

All our trips until then had been domestic, but we had just proven we were graduating to the next level. It seemed entirely plausible that my life's purpose was traveling the world with you.

I replied, "Chile!"

Somewhere I'd read that Chile was the astronomy capital of the world, a fact that intrigued me. One of my fantasies included sharing a telescope with you as we beheld the cosmos. While in Santiago, we could visit Roberto Bolaño's birthplace and browse bookstores.

Now seems as good a time as any to tell you I'm writing to you from Chile. That's right. I made it here without you, Mateo.

CHILE: 2015

EARLY SUNDAY, I DRANK MY MORNING COFFEE while pacing the living room. Though I longed to be sleeping next to Vera, a restlessness overtook me. In my bones, I knew I had procrastinated enough.

With my laptop tucked under my arm, I headed to the most forgotten part of our house. Even though attics are relatively uncommon in Chile, I had insisted on one when we were eyeing real estate. Perhaps Vera had chalked it up to American nostalgia. When I told her, "We need an attic and I'm going to furnish it," her response had been, "Okay. Let's do it." And while we had modestly styled it, until today it had otherwise gone untouched.

Inside the attic, the sun drenched my abandoned desk in citrine light. I placed my computer on top of it and closed my eyes. A fluttering in my chest rippled my breathing. Thousands of thoughts flooded my mind. Did Mateo think of me often? What did he look like now? Was he working on a new book? Was he still serially dating marketing executives? Was he balding? Was he miserable?

Thinking about him generated a strange endorphin rush. It was shockingly similar to a runner's high. Shame immediately slackened the corners of my smile.

I'd told Vera I was going to confront Mateo, but as I sat staring at the blank screen, the task felt overwhelming. A line from an Alejandro Zambra book came to me: "To read is to cover one's face. And to write is to show it." Quite true, but that revelation didn't embolden me. Was my aim to tell Mateo how horrible he'd been? Or was it to tell him that he'd been important to me? Was the truth a kaleidoscopic mix? I didn't have an answer, but perhaps the sentences would sort themselves out.

In the park, I had decided to start with the scene on the train. In a blink, I was back on the subway in my oxblood wool dress and suede boots. I could smell notes of my ylang-ylang perfume, and "Billie Jean" lyrics synced with my heartbeat.

My eyes roved the attic, landing on a beanbag chair next to my desk and a stack of boxes packed with my New York belongings. I was obviously no longer on the train, but I felt just as vulnerable as I had that day. Tears weighed down my lower eyelids, blurring the room into sizzling zigzags.

In a feverish state, I typed, aiming to recapture every detail of our last evening as if the sights and sounds hung suspended in the air around me. I wrote until my mind grew calm and clear enough to recognize my own hunger pangs. I saved the document, emailed it to myself, then shut my laptop.

My phone vibrated. It was an email from Jamal, requesting one last phone call to finalize the interview. I enthusiastically welcomed ending that chapter of my life. I quickly pecked back: Sure. Talk to you a week from today.

All that remained was for me to shape my account to Mateo. The task of unburdening myself felt daunting, but now that I was excising it from my body, my commitment was unwavering.

When I opened the attic door, a potted spiral aloe rested at my feet. Neither one of us had ever used this room until today, but Vera had intuited my whereabouts.

I crouched down to scoop up her present and marveled at our connected type of love.

22.

The hardest part of becoming re-infatuated with you was that nothing about our day-to-day lives changed. We still hung out sporadically, relying mostly on text messages to connect us. It was so laissez-faire that I began to doubt whether you'd actually spent the night at my new place and professed such loving things to me. Had it been a dream?

After that night, I'd idiotically purchased a guidebook and hiking boots that I was sure we'd break in somewhere in Patagonia. What I never told you was that I'd been saving money. Once you shrank my student loan debt, I started to save a few hundred dollars a month. The hiking boots purchase was the first time I touched that stash.

Splurging on another luxury item struck me as a potential way to deal with your aloofness. Rationally, I knew an extravagant purchase was pointless, but better ideas eluded me, so I took the 1 train to the Barneys Co-op in Chelsea. Years before, I'd bought myself heavily discounted French designer sandals during a Barneys warehouse sale, and twice I'd purchased graphic T-shirts for Hiroshi there. It seemed like the right store, a retail solution to an emotional conundrum.

The train deposited me on the corner of 7th Avenue and 18th Street. As I was making my way toward the store, I realized that none other than Hiroshi himself was headed toward me. He wasn't alone either. He was hooked arm in arm with a blond woman in theatrical makeup. Where he had crossed paths with a New York City Ballet performer or an actress was beyond me, unless she was also a model. Her head of slicked-back hair bowed a little as she laughed at something humorous Hiroshi said. *He's not that funny*, I almost announced. My stride slowed, and I considered crossing the street, but it was too late. He and I had seen each other. My jaw tightened, and from behind my eyeglasses I carried out the equivalent of a drive-by shooting minus the bullets.

The sidewalk was wide enough for us to pass without any of us having to scoot aside. Still, the thought occurred to me to cut between them, to rupture their link as my body slid between theirs like a knife.

Once they passed, against my better judgment, my head swung back, and I studied the backs of their bodies to see if they leaned into each other. Had our bodies turned toward each other in a similar fashion, a pair of quotation marks with nothing left to state? Her legs were leaner than mine, whiter, more muscular. Her rayon skirt swished as she hurried down the street with her lover. Legs full of confidence and joy. With the ballerina, Hiroshi had climbed to a higher echelon in society. His tastes had turned prim and immaculate. My head remained turned and I tripped into a punk dog-walker managing two huskies.

"Whoa," he said as we collided.

"Sorry," I said. "My bad."

The worst thing about seeing Hiroshi was that it was further proof I was no one's true type. Seeing him with a white woman reminded me that the world knew me as a brown woman, a fact that sometimes slipped my mind. Hiroshi didn't typically date women who looked like me. But then again, neither did you. Adding to my confusion was the sneaking suspicion that perhaps pursuing men was merely a learned habit for me.

When I returned to my apartment that afternoon, you texted me. It was my first time hearing from you since you'd been in my bed three weeks before.

Hey, mi vida? How's your sabado?

What happened to Chile? I replied.

In my windowpane, I caught a glimpse of myself. My wavy hair was unruly, and I appeared anemically pale.

My novel's waaaayy past due! I can't leave the country. I have to buckle down otherwise my name will be mierda.

I was tempted to guilt-trip you and question your commitment to our relationship. I'd been fantasizing about us and scrutinizing images of you on the web, of which there were now millions.

What's your novel about? I replied.

That's exactly what my editor and I were arguing
about early today. I'm sorry if I've been absent. Once
the novel is out, we'll go to Chile. I'll have money for
lots of trips, ok?

Your promises were so fucking empty. You knew you
were about to betray me. That I would never recover from
the humiliation. You knew.

I'm happy to report back that I've made good use of those
boots while exploring Parque Nacional Torres del Paine
with my partner, Vera. It's truly the most majestic vista in
the world. In fact, it doesn't remind me of any book or film.
It has no facsimile.

23.

While you and your editor "figured out" what your novel was about, I enrolled in more Spanish courses at Instituto Cervantes in midtown. On Saturday mornings, I plugged through class after class until my language skills reached native level. Don't tell me I kept this a secret from you, because I didn't. I told you about these classes circa 2008 on Gchat. After class, I dropped by the Strand or Three Lives & Co. and continued my sexuality research. I stumbled across Patricia Highsmith's *The Price of Salt*, which convinced me that life-changing adventures still awaited me.

During this time, you and I stayed in close contact. We texted, called, emailed throughout the week and hung out about three times a month. You told me you were growing more confident about your novel, and I recall congratulating you over wine at Riposo 46, that cozy bar in Hell's Kitchen that I heard no longer exists. We split a cheese plate that afternoon with toasted baguettes and raw figs. You claimed to dislike figs that evening, but who chooses to smell like something they hate?

During the wine date, I imbibed enough to become unfettered. You had just finished telling me about your publication schedule when I asked, "Doesn't it strike you as odd that there haven't been any popular Latino authors since you? Latinas must be writing books, too, right? Who's vaporizing all the literary Latinas?"

You fumbled with a fig stalk and avoided eye contact. Obviously, you'd given the idea of tokenism consideration, but perhaps never questioned why you were appointed to be the only one.

"It's all random," you said with a flippant shrug. "None of it makes sense."

After our date, I wandered south on the island for quite a while. Eventually, the sun set, and SoHo glowed ultraviolet. The evening mood made me think of Cape Cod and Chile. What was South America like?

When I reached the Prada boutique on Broadway, the store lights were off, but spotlights shone on the window display. I studied three mannequins positioned in a semicircle, two sitting on wooden trunks and one facing the street. Each was dressed in a sequined wool sweater and taffeta skirt. On their sloped plastic feet hung striped grosgrain heels. Silver confetti was strategically arranged, as if to give the impression of an impromptu party.

This was a modern-day Florine Stettheimer painting. New York's riches abounded, and as if through osmosis I'd learned the names of fabrics and trends associated with the elite. A pang of jealousy quivered inside me as I admired the mannequins and coveted their lack of emotion. A near lifetime ago, I'd been a human database of art facts, an amateur historian with an ill-defined dream that I'd forgotten to pursue.

24.

It kills me now when I think about it, but another year rolled by without any change. You still had no novel to show the world, and I remained directionless and solitary as I turned thirty.

Every day at 9:15 a.m., my students sat cross-legged on the rug for morning meeting. While the head teacher prepared materials for language arts, I led a discussion with the children about the day of the week, the month, the season, the weather. We recognized anyone in the class celebrating a birthday with a round of applause. Our routine was both charming and dulling. The repetition helped seal information into their base of knowledge while the monotony of it deadened me a little more each day.

At night, I followed along with tai chi DVDs in my bedroom. Sometimes I felt weightless and magical while working through a sequence of movements. But within an hour of finishing a DVD, the malaise returned.

One afternoon, I was organizing the cubby area of my

classroom when you called with exciting news. For the first time in your career, you had a reading in San Antonio, my hometown.

"I'm excited to see your calles," you joked over the phone, presumably referring to my old neighborhood streets.

"Are you inviting me to go with you or just telling me about the reading?" I asked, gently kicking a blue crayon across the linoleum floor.

"Of course you're invited, mi vida. That goes without saying," you said with a sigh.

For once there was no background noise on your end. Instead of walking through Little Italy or Clinton in search of a good macchiato, you might have been stretched out across your futon.

"I'm eager to see my parents," I admitted. "It's been years since I visited."

"Pack a bag, mami."

So I did, for the *n*th time, packing my hopes as well.

———⋄———

Our flight departed New York at 6:00 a.m., but in first class we managed to doze off intermittently. Do you remember this trip? It was our last, our Gethsemane.

Mid-flight, I informed you that my mother would meet us at the reading. Afterward, the three of us would eat dinner together; then I'd return to my parents' house for the night. You didn't like the idea of sleeping alone and tried to dissuade me. I wanted us to be together again, but the idea of making you yearn for me also thrilled me.

"My parents are über-Catholic," I explained. "We're not married, and it'll be good for me to spend time at their house."

"Tatum, you're thirty years old," you said. "I understand your parents are Catholic, but come on! You're your own mujer."

Your mother was Catholic, too, but there were no rules for men. You had to have known that the expectations were different, but your tone conveyed disappointment. If need be, you would've sacrificed a hand not to be alone. It took substantial generosity on my part not to point out that thirty-eight years was sufficient time for you to overcome your fear of solitude. Such a response would've been too cruel, particularly because you'd financially afforded me the opportunity to see my parents. And, yes, looking panoramically at our relationship, you were always materially generous with me, much more so than you were with María Luz.

"This is a moot point," I said, then shut my eyes. To be honest, it felt good turning you down, calling the shots.

At the airport, we hopped into a taxi that took us to the Hyatt Regency on the River Walk downtown. Our spacious fourth-floor room contained a brown leather couch, a mahogany desk, and a super-king-size bed.

I tossed my bags on the couch and flung myself onto the bed with open arms. By far, this was the largest bed we'd had in any of our hotels.

"This bed is its own fucking country," you said, sitting down and pressing the mattress with your palm.

I suppressed the urge to holler, *Everything is bigger in Texas!* Instead, I rubbed my face against the white pillow and attempted to get cozy.

"Take off my shoes, please," I mumbled.

This was something I would've asked of Hiroshi. I couldn't believe I was asking it of you, but now I curiously awaited your reaction. With the bedspread clutched in my hands, I turned to look at you.

"Will you take off my shoes?" I repeated.

You adjusted your glasses with both hands, blinked, and considered my request.

"Take off your *own* shoes," you said, and snickered before scooting off the bed and retreating into the bathroom.

This was your revenge on me for not keeping you company that night. As you stalked away, I realized almost half your hair was gray. For a split second, I considered myself too young and attractive for you. As you locked the bathroom door, I had one thought: *There's a man in there, kind of an older man.*

While you showered, I called my parents. My mother said she was afraid to embarrass me and asked me what she should wear to the reading. She feared appearing under- or overdressed. The last literary event she attended had been fifteen years before, when she took me to hear Sandra Cisneros read.

"I don't remember what I wore to see La Sandra," my mother admitted. "It was so long ago."

"People wear different things. Some go in T-shirts and jeans, but since it'll be at Trinity, I suspect the dress code will be slightly more formal," I said. "Don't worry too much about your outfit. Mateo is excited to meet you."

"Afterward we're going to Mi Tierra to eat?" she asked.

I placed the phone on the bed and hit the SPEAKER button as you crossed the room and stepped onto the balcony.

"Yeah, that's the plan. Let Mateo pay. Don't take out your wallet," I explained while slipping a blouse over my head. Through the window, I watched you on the balcony. You were reading on your phone, probably *The New York Times* or email, I assumed. Now I'm certain you were texting with other women.

After we hung up, I brushed my hair and fished my jewelry bag out of my suitcase. I slipped on the Tibetan earrings Hiroshi had bought me in Prague and spritzed myself with Paperback perfume.

I heard the balcony door slide open as I was applying maroon lip gloss. You stood behind me in the mirror, wearing a white-and-green embroidered guayabera, black pants, and black New Balance sneakers. This was your standard reading ensemble. I'll admit it: you looked striking.

"Mi vida, we should head out in the next ten minutes or so," you said.

I nodded at your reflection behind me. "Ya mero," I mumbled.

I rifled through my suitcase. As I picked through my garments for what I'd need at my parents', you sat on the leather couch. I shoved a pair of black jeans and panties into my handbag and a toothbrush.

"Lista," I said.

<hr>

The auditorium was packed and the reading a success. According to Trinity staff, the only other time the space had been that full was when Yo-Yo Ma performed years before to a sold-out audience. The English faculty, particularly a spindly white lady with spiral curls, insisted on taking you to dinner, but you gracefully declined, citing prior plans. You were careful not to label me your girlfriend or friend. Instead, you had a prior family commitment. *Family.* The syllables diffused themselves through my nervous system like an intoxicant. The readings, I assured myself, would never end. I was family. End of story. *Let's go eat*, I thought.

My mother and I were walking a foot ahead of you in the parking lot when a heavyset man caught up with us.

"Mr. Domínguez! Sorry to interrupt, I mean, disturb you."

The man's breathing was labored, and when we turned I noticed he was hardly more than a teenager.

"Sorry, sir," he continued, his T-shirt wet with sweat patches. "I work with the radio station here at Trinity and I was wondering if you could record a station announcement for us. It won't take more than five minutes, sir."

You tilted your head, a sign that you were considering his request. You were hungry, probably ravenous at this point, and I had warned you that my mom couldn't stay out too much longer. She had to work early the next morning.

"Can we record this announcement from a restaurant?" you asked.

The radio guy nodded. "Um, yeah, I can bring the device I need. Where should I meet you?"

Our footsteps continued toward my mother's silver Toyota Corolla in the distance.

"Where are we eating, Tatum? The name?" you asked.

"Mi Tierra," I said to the radio guy. "Meet us there?"

He nodded with vigor.

You might recall that Mi Tierra is a huge, bustling multi-room restaurant downtown that's open 24/7. I wasn't sure how my fellow Chicano would find us there, but that wasn't my concern. He had practically invited himself.

My mother clicked open the doors to her car. You motioned for me to sit in front with her. Following such a

hugely successful night, it felt strange for you to sit in the
back. Back seats were for car seats, children, and oversized
dogs, not literary celebrities. I climbed into the passenger's
side and buckled up.

"Señora," you said to my mother once we were backing
out of the parking lot, "forgive me for not shaking your hand
and introducing myself properly. Mucho gusto."

"Igualmente," Mama said.

"Mateo, the reading went very well," I interjected.

I craned my neck back and saw your outline in the dark.
Your profile was turned toward the window. I wondered if
you assumed these were my exact calles. In fact, this was a
middle-class neighborhood, a decent twenty-minute drive
from where I'd grown up. It was unlikely we'd have reason
to take a spin through the vatos locos barrio where I'd been
raised.

"I've really been struck by how many types of Chicanos
I've met tonight. I've seen cowboy Chicanos, who actually
speak with a Texas twang. I've seen husky nerds like home-
boy who's meeting us at the restaurant and southern belle
Chicanas who look like they walked off the set of *Dallas*
or *Dynasty* with hair out to here," you said, extending your
hands above you. "I've also seen Chicanas who look Asian,
the Tatum types who give off serious Japonesa or Filipina
vibes, and others who look straight-up Indigenous. Need-
less to say, I feel like I've been given a thorough introduction
to Tejano culture."

"Oh yeah," Mama said. "Almost everyone's Mexican
here. Some speak Spanish. Others don't. It's a mix."

The headlights of other cars occasionally lit up our faces

with unexpected theatrics, but for the most part, traffic around us was sparse. We glided into downtown on quiet streets.

Mi Tierra's trademark décor has always echoed a Yucatán holiday. From the ceiling hung hot pink and aqua piñatas shaped like donkeys, stars, and wrestlers, interspersed with metallic green and orange papel picados.

"Wow," you announced as we strolled in.

"Chévere décor, right?" I asked.

A regular at the restaurant, Mama drew a paper number and rejoined us. According to the flashing screen, seven people were ahead of us in line.

"Is the food good here?" you asked as you shoved your hands into the pockets of your jeans.

"Do you like comida mexicana?" my mom asked.

She was growing bolder as she got more comfortable around you. It made me happy to witness your interactions because I was certain there would be more.

"Claro, señora," you said.

My mom was midfifties but could have passed for forty-three. She was a far cry from old lady territory, and I hoped you were taking note and drawing the parallel that I would age well too.

"Then you'll like the food," my mom said with a nod. "Hopefully they'll seat the people before us rápidamente."

Children weaved between us, giggling and passing sections of what looked like a ripped-apart chocolate doughnut.

"You'd never know it's almost ten at night. This place is where the party's at tonight," you said.

Overhead, a woman's voice called number 104 in English, then in Spanish. The crowd shifted to allow a family through. Ten minutes later, we were seated, but the radio guy was still nowhere to be seen.

"Maybe the chamaco from the radio forgot or got lost," my mom said, verbalizing what we all must've been thinking. Her eyes widened as if to say ni modo, whatever.

You disappointed us by ordering a chicken sandwich. When you closed the menu and handed it to our server, I locked eyes with my mother. So much for Mexican food.

"You better eat an empanada for dessert," I said after the server left.

"Sure," you said. "I'm down for an empanada and café."

I looked up and saw the lumbering outline of the radio guy approaching us. Strapped across his chest was a satchel that I presumed contained the recording equipment.

"I'm glad I caught you. I got so lost downtown that I was sure you'd be gone by the time I found parking. Gracias a Dios you're still here."

I'd forgotten the implicit religiosity of my own city, the assumption that everyone believed the same fricking dogmas, the laws of the Sacred Heart of Jesus.

"Take a seat," you said, pointing to the one empty chair at our table.

"I'm Luis," the radio guy said, extending his hand toward you. "I'm really grateful you agreed to this recording. I'm a big fan of yours. I've read *Happiness* so many times. I read it to my little sister years ago and now she wants to be a writer."

Our waitress returned with our beverages and was surprised to find another person at our table. My heart melted a little for sweaty Luis and his faceless *hermanita*. I knew what it meant to find a home in *Happiness*.

"I won't be here long," Luis explained to the waitress. He was unpacking his equipment and surely noticed the raucous volume of the restaurant. It would be impossible to get a clear recording at our table.

A chill overcame me, and I noticed a whirling ceiling fan above our heads. I pulled a pashmina from my handbag and draped it around my shoulders.

"¿Tienes frio, mija?" Mama asked.

I nodded and watched as your face remained neutral through the outpour of Luis's praise. It was something you'd heard nearly every day for the past decade, how important your book was to people, their friends, or their relatives. Years before, my letter had moved you, but time was making you almost stoic, or so it appeared to my observant eye. Stupidly, I didn't realize then that you were becoming indifferent to me too.

"Okay," Luis said, brushing aside his wavy comb-over. "Ya mero."

My lips tensed into a quarter smile. Only in San Antonio did I hear others use "ya mero" like I did.

"Luis, my friend," you said. "It's loud in here, hermano. Are you sure you'll be able to record this thing of yours?"

A trickle of sweat dribbled down Luis's neck into the scoop of his T-shirt. He nodded vigorously, sending his wavy hair into a slight bounce. He now held a metal microphone in his hands.

"All I need you to say into this is 'This is M. Domínguez,

and you're listening to KRTU 91.7 in stereo,'" Luis said. "Didja get that?" he asked before repeating the exact wording.

You placed your elbows on the table and exhaled. I could tell you were hungry and losing patience. You and my mother had exchanged only a dozen words, and the ceiling fan was spinning cold air over us all.

"I got it!" you snapped, leaning over to reach for the microphone.

"Okay, okay, let me turn it on," Luis said. His fingers fumbled with the device. You lowered it below your chin and spoke in a level voice, enunciating each word with maximum clarity. That night I found it remarkable how you instantly memorized the phrase and repeated it into the device. It makes me cringe now how easily you impressed me.

Luis removed jumbo noise-canceling headphones from his satchel, placed them over his ears, and listened to the recording.

As he inspected the clip, the waitress returned with our dinner. My mother's chalupa plate was placed before her first, then I got my nachos.

You relaxed back into your chair, and the waitress slid the chicken sandwich over to you. You bit into it and winked at me.

"So, this sounds okay, but I'm wondering if you have time for one more recording?" Luis said with the headphones still on.

You lowered the sandwich onto your plate with a whiff of impatience. It was obvious you were exercising as much restraint as possible. That's when you pulled your phone from your pocket and glanced at the time.

"Coño, gordo—it's ten fifty-one p.m., and I'm just now eating dinner—" you started, but stopped mid-thought. Out of the corner of my eye, I witnessed my mom's jaw drop. In your impatience, you'd barked at Luis, publicly calling him a fatty. Immediately, you recognized your misstep and said, "Listen, you're already here, so let's record one more and then you can do your editing magic and mix them together or whatever works for you, okay?"

For the first time that night, Luis's attention shifted to my mother and me. Until then, our presence had not registered in his animated brown eyes. It now dawned on him that we were witnessing your exchange, though he still failed to greet us or even smile.

The second recording sounded to me far inferior than the first, mainly because halfway through, mariachis started serenading a teenage girl two tables away.

Time was up, though, as were all reservoirs of patience. Luis packed his belongings, shook your hand, and glanced at my mother. He was several steps across the room when he rushed back, his shoelaces untied and fresh sweat coming down his neck in rivulets.

"I almost forgot to ask you if you could sign my sister's copy of *Happiness*." The copy he placed in front of you could easily have been mine. The paperback cover was creased, the pages browning and crisp like autumn leaves.

"Do you have a pen?" you asked between bites. You wiped your hands on the cloth napkin draped across your lap, took a blue ballpoint from Luis, and hastily scribbled a line that looked nothing like your signature. If the sister looked it up online, she would be convinced her autograph had been forged. A muscle in my chest convulsed for a fellow reader. None the wiser, Luis thanked you and bowed away.

We ordered empanadas to go. My mother made sure your bag contained one pumpkin and one pineapple. For my dad, she ordered a variety of pumpkin, sweet potato, apple, pineapple, and cream. You paid the tab and tacked on a fifty-dollar tip for a meal that cost thirty-five, then excused yourself to the bathroom.

Watching your back disappear through the crowd, I regretted my decision to go home with my mom. After witnessing how Luis idolized and commodified you, it was clear you needed me more than my parents did. For a second, I considered renegotiating the plans, but it was after eleven now, and my mother had to wake up at six the next day.

"I'll be right back, Mama," I said. I left my handbag hooked around my chair and followed your path toward the restrooms. I did my best to forget how you'd insulted Luis's size. My own dad was heavy, and picturing the two of you interacting made me uneasy.

You were checking your phone in the alcove by the bathroom when I placed my hand on your side. Beneath your shirt I felt striated muscle definition. It'd been months since I'd touched you in that particular spot, but a current passed between us. Suddenly my pulse made itself known between my thighs. Surely for at least a second, you, too, entertained the idea of resuming what we'd started in my bed in New York.

"Hey," you said, an element of playfulness in your voice.

The moment overcame me, and I wrapped my arms around your torso, angling my face up at yours. You draped your arm around my back. We stood gazing at each other for almost a full minute. Neither of us spoke but our inhalations and exhalations synced.

"I wasn't lying. I really have to go to the bathroom," you finally said.

"Go," I said, laughing. "See you back at the table."

———— ❧ ————

It was disorienting, waking up in my teenage bedroom and staring at a map of Manhattan, an island as familiar to me as my own voice. My hand felt for my phone. It was 7:54 a.m. At 1:54 a.m., you had texted me: no sleep. te extraño too much!

I typed back: Buenos días, Mateo! Are you awake? When no reply came after several minutes, hurt flickered inside me, but I pretended I didn't feel it. Instead, I showered, dressed, then found my father drinking coffee in the kitchen.

"Good morning," I said as I poured myself a cup.

"How'd you sleep? What's the plan with your friend? When do you fly back?"

I took a seat next to my father and realized I had, as usual, left my parents in the dark about this trip. A lifetime of being an only child had fashioned me into a lone creature who reported to no one.

"We fly back today," I said with genuine sadness. "Around four-thirty in the afternoon."

My father rubbed his tired eyes before asking if I wanted to go out for breakfast tacos. His favorite taquería had a special on Fridays.

"You don't have to work today?" I asked.

"I took the day off," he said. "It's not every day that I get to spend time with my lovely daughter."

The entire waitstaff at Taquería Jalisco #3 waved to my father as we walked in. A buxom woman quickly seated us at a front booth facing Fredricksburg Road.

"You're like a minor celebrity here," I joked.

"Minor?" my father huffed. "More like el rey."

Together we laughed and it occurred to me how much I missed being in my parents' company when they weren't talking about Jesus.

"Your mother tried to get the day off, but her boss wouldn't approve it. They have an audit this week at the bank."

A waitress with a rose chest tattoo, a Spurs tank top, and tight jeans came to take our order. In Spanish, my father ordered five potato-and-egg tacos with avocado, our usual since I was a child.

"How are things in New York?" my father asked. "How's work?"

I sipped my black coffee and shrugged. This was my least favorite topic ever. "Todo bien."

My parents knew that when I answered in Spanish, it was my own version of con safos, the end of a discussion.

Over the phone, they occasionally probed about whether I was applying for museum jobs, employment tied to art or art history, my supposed specialty. Lately, those questions had all but vanished, but they seemed satisfied knowing I was nearing the end of my student loan payments. I never told them that you paid off twenty thousand dollars of my debt. They'd have urged me to return the money if they'd known.

"Are you happy, mija?" my father asked.

"Más o menos," I said because my life flirted with happiness.

"You turned thirty this year," my father stated. "You've been hanging out with this writer for, what, almost ten years now. What kind of relationship is it? Are you two serious?"

The waitress returned to refill our coffees, and I was grateful for the momentary break from the conversation. It was the second time during this trip that a man had referred to my age as if it were a medical emergency.

"Do you have lots of friends in New York? Don't you want to settle down at some point?"

Every time my dad mentioned friends, I flashed back to waiting for my parents' car outside in the dark, waiting like an orphan to be rescued from a drug party. No doubt if I'd stayed at that party and acted like everything was copacetic, I'd have developed into a completely different adult.

"Papa, Mateo and I are . . . really close," I finally managed. "I'm not dying to get married right now . . . to anyone."

The waitress brought us our tacos in two plastic baskets.

"Gracias," my father said as she nodded and walked away.

Mention of you made me check my phone to see if you'd answered. No reply. You'd probably crashed at two or three in the morning and were still sleeping. Next to someone. I'll admit now that I wondered if you were out chasing women or if you knew a mujer in the area. Who had you been texting by the bathroom? Don't make me laugh by saying your editor.

"Mija," Papa said, unwrapping the foil from his taco, "have you ever considered whether Mateo is the devil?"

My throat constricted. How could I have forgotten my

parents' obsession with souls and damnation? Here was the true reason my father hadn't gone to the reading.

"What are you even saying?" I said, my voice a heathered whisper.

"Everyone adores this man. He sells out everywhere. Has tons of money, I'm sure. What if what you have with him is only a false promise? The devil plays people like that. The devil will make you think you want to marry him, or at least spend eternity with him in sin."

You know I don't believe any of that Bible talk, but what my father said struck a chord. He saw that ours was a straw house that could be blown away. And he was right that I was waiting, always waiting, for a full-fledged relationship to materialize between us. But there was no way I was going to admit that to him, or to myself.

"Well, then I've definitely not met the devil," I responded. "Because I don't want to spend eternity doing anything except reading or traveling."

I tried to force an audible laugh from my gut, but my insides felt like dried-out clay. My appetite was gone, though I busied my hands as if I were hungry and about to dig in.

As a child, I loved playing Mexican bingo with my family. Whenever I drew the Lotería card for El Diablo, a mischievous smirk overtook my face and I shouted his name and waved the card like I was the winner. The taboo was still thrilling, even though I considered it all a ridiculous fairy tale.

My father drizzled picante over the contents of his taco and pushed the jar closer to me. In my childhood, he'd trained me to eat picante on everything, and now my tolerance for spice exceeded his. I poured and poured until his eyes grew huge with incredulity.

"Híjole, mija. Don't hurt yourself," he said.

I knew he was talking about the picante, but also about you.

25.

On the flight back to New York from San Antonio, you held my hand. "Promise me you'll stay with me at the next hotel?" you asked. "It was so boring and lonely without you, mi vida."

"Sure," I said. "In five years, if we don't hate each other, we should consider moving in together, don't you think?"

You jerked your head as if given an electric shock. "Hate each other?" you asked, focusing on the least important part of my question. "I'm incapable of hating you."

"Imagine how much we could save in rent!" I mumbled before falling asleep on your shoulder.

We were so skilled at avoiding discussions about what mattered. In that sense, we were made for each other.

26.

Although you were still reading from *Happiness* at different universities from time to time, you had finally finished your novel, which you obliquely told me was slated for release the following year. Whenever I asked about the novel's title or premise, you changed the subject. In not so many words, you informed me you'd become superstitious—the process had been so tedious and never-ending that your main objective, until its release, was to discuss it as little as possible, to treat it as a nonentity.

It was a Thursday evening when you called. I was lounging on my couch in sweatpants when my phone rang.

"Let's go away somewhere far," you suggested. "Once the novel drops, my schedule is going to drive us crazy again."

Your voice wavered with an energy I couldn't pinpoint. It was as if mention of your own novel made you sick with doubt.

"Are you afraid it won't be as well received as *Happiness*?" I asked.

You sighed, and for a moment I wondered if you were about to divulge details. "No, I think it's actually better than *Happiness*. If I'm allowed to say so, it's a tragic page-turner, but enough about this fucking libro. We deserve a vacation, Tatum. The last trip we took involved seeing your family."

"Where do you have in mind?" I asked.

You knew spring break was around the corner, so your timing couldn't have been more perfect.

"Wherever you want to go! Haven't you been talking about Chile for all eternity?"

In that moment, I think you knew the terms of our relationship were about to change. Maybe you even intuited that our end was near. You began to catalog everything I said or did, probably because you wanted to remember me.

When I told you earlier that I'm in Chile, I didn't mean to imply I'm here on vacation. I landed a museum job. All those Spanish classes on Saturday mornings have come in handy, particularly when I'm preserving work for the museum's archives.

After our relationship ended, I realized I'd saved enough cash to do something major. I moved first to Valparaíso, though I've spent quite a bit of time exploring Patagonia, Easter Island, Santiago, and Vicuña. In retrospect, I'm grateful we didn't travel here together and taint this paradise. For the longest time, I felt like everything would remind me of you—that I was doomed to relive our story and never regain my footing. What I've shared with you is proof that I still remember, but in writing this, I find that my memories are releasing their hold on me.

Several months after moving here, I was staring through

a telescope at the Observatorio del Pangue. All the stars in the night sky spangled like flecks of platinum, and only then did I realize how much of the world remains unchartered for me.

27.

I'm sure you recall that *The New York Times Book Review* devoted two full pages to the release of your long-awaited novel—*Emulations of Us*. In her review, Michiko Kakutani described it as a modern masterpiece, a literary hybrid of Carlos Fuentes meets Jay-Z meets Man Ray. The comparisons were an impressive testosterone sandwich. The review summarized the novel as a poignantly rendered narrative about ambition and the lack thereof, celebrity, and lost identity.

The day of the release, I came down with the flu and couldn't make it to the book launch. I was so disappointed, but you promised to sign my copy when I recovered. Days later, when I was well enough to leave my apartment, my hands were practically shaking when I purchased a copy. Since we'd met, you'd been chipping away at this novel, and now it was a real object in the world. At nearly five hundred pages, it was a tome, and as I carried it home, I beamed with pride at all your painstaking work.

In my apartment, I cozied up on my couch, sipping cup after cup of hot tea as I read the opening chapters about an aging Mick Jagger–type musician. Though I normally wouldn't have been interested in such a protagonist, your command of language and your syntax were hypnotic. Your authorial control was such that I trusted you to take me anywhere with the narrative. But as I turned the pages, my breathing became labored.

In the novel, a naïve young woman named Penelope writes a fan letter to the musician, praising his early albums. My eyes widened as I read what was almost verbatim the letter I'd sent to you over a decade before, now printed on the page. Although you had substituted musical terms for literary ones, I dropped the book on the couch in utter disbelief. You hadn't mentioned your intention to use my words or admiration in this way. Was this a mockery of me?

An ice-pick headache spread at my temple as these thoughts swirled inside me. I wanted to give you the benefit of the doubt, so I continued reading while ignoring the deep quiver in my limbs.

With each chapter, Penelope's portrayal crumbled. You depicted her as an obsessed fan possessing middling intelligence and no ambition. After the musician she devotes her adult life to touring with succumbs to a chronic disease, she is left purposeless. As I read on, I was disturbed by Penelope's subservience. Was this what you thought of me? That I was nothing more than a pathetic groupie? In what seemed like a sick coincidence, the novel contained thirty-one chapters—one for each year of my life.

You had used the very basis of our relationship—my fan letter—as the catalyst for your novel. But that was only the beginning. Penelope is a day care worker her whole life, and her signature aroma is none other than my Paperback perfume. Naturally, Penelope straddles the same socioeconomic class as me. She is college-educated but in debt from student loans (which, of course, the musician graciously pays off). But you saved the dagger for the end. As the musician's health fades, a distraught Penelope gifts him the prized two-dollar bill that her own ailing father had given her. It was a plot point that one reviewer called a unique and tender nod to Chicano culture.

I couldn't believe what I was reading. Had I been nothing more than source material for you? A chill ran through me and I wondered how much of our relationship had been lived for us and how much had been lived for your novel. As I shut the book, I remembered what you told me in Chicago: that one day I'd help you out.

The memory enraged me, because I wasn't even truly your muse. A muse is exalted and admired, or at the very least respected. Your disdain for Penelope was laced into every paragraph. But your disrespect for me was most evident at the novel's end. Your acknowledgments were quite possibly the longest I'd ever read. You thanked several of your elementary school teachers, a number of your undergrad and grad classmates and professors, your colleagues at Columbia, the foundation that awarded you the grant in Spain, Nathan Englander, Janet Malcolm, Haruki Murakami, obscure philosophers, your friends all over the world, your nieces, cousins, sister, and mother. For fuck's sake, you even shouted out OutKast, two ridiculous reggaeton bands, and a Japanese company that manufactures specialized pens. You thanked everyone but me. My DNA, or a distortion of it, was smudged all over your novel, but I hadn't even warranted a simple thanks. I just wasn't significant enough to you.

When I closed the book, my face went numb. My eyes blinked like mechanical gadgets, and I was certain I was relapsing with the flu. A glutton for punishment, I felt compelled to reread the last four chapters as I chugged more tea.

Of course, I'd always secretly hoped that you would immortalize me in literature, but I had never expected that the depiction would be so degrading. It was impossible for anyone to identify me as Penelope, because I was the opposite of well-known. Somehow this struck me as even more wretched, that I could have served as inspiration yet still remain so anonymous. It felt in many ways like you had discarded me in an unmarked grave. I had been rendered a caricature. Whether I wanted to be portrayed in literature was no longer up for debate. It was a fact that couldn't be undone, and something horrible in me howled out in anguish.

I picked up my phone and typed: I read your novel. Just finished it.

I fought the urge to text more, to indict you for your portrayal of me. It was enough to let you know that I'd consumed your analysis of us, this supposed work of fiction. So much had been lifted directly from our lives that I couldn't consider this anything but a thinly veiled memoir.

What I wasn't expecting was an instantaneous reply. Tears spilled down my cheeks as I read: Gracias, mi vida.

Your reply did not invite more. Though I was vibrating with the urge to lash out, I couldn't compose myself or my thoughts. Anger overlaid self-hate overlaid defeat inside me. I flipped my phone face down on the couch, placed a decorative pillow over my face, and screamed.

28.

Not long after I finished your novel, you invited me to your NYU reading, and despite everything, I felt hopeful. I told myself that you were apologetic, that you wanted to make things up to me. Maybe, I thought giddily, you would even give me a special shout-out at the reading in front of the admiring crowd. To top it off, you had specifically used the word "date."

I often wonder what would have happened if, at the last minute, I'd decided to skip your reading. If I'd not gotten off the train and trudged in the cold to NYU. Of course, we'll never know. I was looking forward to confronting you afterward at the bar. As we threw back martinis, I planned to wow you in my oxblood wrap dress and suede boots while making you answer for yourself.

Which brings us back to where we began.

The scene was exactly this: As the train thundered down the track toward the Astor Place station, my fingertips grazed the hardcover of *Emulations of Us* snug inside my leather handbag. Unlike *Happiness*, I'd read it only once, though I'd returned to certain chapters multiple times, particularly the first characterization of Penelope. No fiction went into Penelope's physicality. She was my mirror image, waving to me with my own raised hand. The passage gave me goose bumps, as if a magnifying glass were set upon my skin, grading the quality of my hair, the odor of my breath, the circumference of my wrists.

On a blank page following the acknowledgments, I'd committed several notes as if presenting a counterargument against the novel's conclusion.

- Beauty and purpose can be found in devoting yourself to another person.
- Individuality is overrated. Not everything special is unique.
- Protagonist has an Übermensch complex / disconcerting ego

After finishing the book, I had searched my email account for your name. Within seconds, Gmail tabulated our electronic communication over the past ten years: 4,525 emails, a yearly average of almost 453 emails. It was a never-ending ping-pong match with unabated intensity.

In numerous psychology textbooks I consulted, it seemed impossible for limerence to last this long. What we traded electronically and in person had to be love. A new breed of love. Who sends thousands of emails just to toy with someone? For the sake of a plot? Who invests that much time, so much heart?

The evidence was in the kilobytes, megabytes, and

gigabytes. We amassed so much historical memory in phones and laptops, but mostly in our brown bodies.

Back in 2000, when I first wrote you a fan letter, it was the equivalent of two hands waving in the air for attention. What I'm writing here is my final gesture to you—my goodbye wave. Do me the favor of deleting it once you read it. I hope you can give me that. Let there be no trace left of us.

That night on the train, I kept reminding myself, *Mateo proposed a date tonight, so the sentiments in the novel are purely fictional, and an apology and explanation are forthcoming*. Cognitively, I knew the danger of conflating fact with fiction, but as my boots carried me out of the station, my facial muscles involuntarily tensed into expressions of severe disappointment and extreme joy, a spectrum I slid along without anchor.

⸻ ✦ ⸻

There were easily five hundred people snaking the perimeter of the building. It was an unprecedented turnout for a reading. You always attracted a crowd, but the release of your critically acclaimed novel had established you as *the* face of literature. Even old white readers had opinions about your work, generations who hadn't engaged with literature since the Johns: Cheever, Updike, and Irving.

"Hi," I said to the bulldog security guard controlling the crowd. "I have a reserved seat to the event."

"There are no reserved seats," the man replied, holding up a hand to prevent me from passing.

Several people in line turned and snickered at me. Ever

since someone stole Jonathan Franzen's specs, I'd become aware of your extreme vulnerability in public. All the people in line around me struck me as uptight, insufferable assholes who would have gladly pulled a similar prank on you just to make the headlines.

"I'm a friend of the author's," I said. "Can you call upstairs and check? Trust me. I know I have a reserved seat."

The guard hiked his shoulders, then shook his head. "Listen, lady. This ain't Cipriani. If you want to get in, you best get to the end of the line. The event begins in less than ten minutes."

Leaning back, I gazed up at the building towering above. In my excitement, I'd forgotten to ask on which floor the reading would be held. These logistical obstacles aggravated me, and the idea of joining the line was maddening. But the prospect of not seeing you and jeopardizing our date moved my feet. When I finally reached the end of the line, I shifted my weight from my left heel to my right. It occurred to me that I was the most invisible I had been in ages: a brown woman without my usual *I'm with the author* power, without any leverage to get in. In front of me stood hundreds of taller, warmer bodies.

The line edged forward a few steps. My watch read 7:25, and the reading started in five minutes. A voice inside me urged me to go home. This was pointless. My breath materialized into a thin white paragraph, then dissipated. In my mind, I was already fast-forwarding to after the reading, to after drinks, to our long-postponed confessions.

From my snug coat pocket, I removed my phone and scrolled through the contacts. I selected your number, then held the phone to my ear. It rang twice before I heard a young woman laughing in the background. *Wrong number*, I assumed, but I hung on.

"Oops, I answered your phone," the woman cooed near the mouthpiece.

"Patricia, mi vida. What're you doing? Didja say hello?" your voice echoed in the background.

I froze. *Mi vida?* How many lives did you have? A sharp pain radiated from my ribs, as if I'd been speared. In my very bed, you'd promised me that I was the only person with whom you used the term. Me alone. But here was the truth: I was interchangeable. Although many scenes from your novel seemed directly lifted from our time together, others didn't. It occurred to me that Penelope might have been based on Patricia or a collage of dozens of us. Every woman in your life was a mannequin to you.

I hung up. For a moment, I was certain this scenario was a lucid nightmare until I reached for my earlobes to check for my earrings. This habit of mine, which vanished the night we first met, immediately resurfaced. Both earrings were in place. This hell was indeed real.

I dialed your number again. This time a new rage boiled within me. I shuffled forward on the pavement, almost tripping over my own heels. As soon as you answered or your voice mail began, I planned to scream, *I'm not yours anymore!* The phone rang three times before a recording announced that the caller's voice mail box was full, and the line disconnected.

The security guard informed the crowd that the event had reached capacity and shouted at us to go home. As the dial tone blared in my ear, I stepped out of line. Once again, I was my thirteen-year-old self, standing outside in the pitch-black night, waiting to be rescued after things had gone horribly wrong. That night in Washington Square Park, no one was going to rescue me, and I knew it.

29.

I didn't see you at first. It was the Monday after your reading, and I had no reason to believe you'd come to the school and wait for me at the end of the day. It was days before Christmas break, so all my students were dashing out to their caregivers with tinsel wreaths and Styrofoam Santas with cotton ball beards.

My colleague, the head teacher, had left an hour earlier for a dental appointment, so I was overwhelmed and alone at dismissal. Among the crowd of parents and nannies, there you were, your eyes downcast as if shame had pulled you into my radius. The moment I recognized you, so did a parent.

While her son clung to her calf and his holiday crafts, she praised your novel. "I finished it the other night and immediately gave it to my best friend. She's hooked."

You politely nodded in acknowledgment.

"If I may ask, what're you doing here?" the parent asked. "Do you have a child in this classroom?"

"I'm waiting for a friend," you mumbled, then signaled toward me with your eyes.

The parent, a wealthy Upper West Side woman, examined me with disbelief. The word "friend" made me bristle. After all that had happened, it was audacious of you to refer to us as friends.

"Can we go, Mommy?" her son begged.

You understood that just as you had obligations to your fans, I had responsibilities to my students. Patiently, you waited for me to send off every last one of them. After almost twenty minutes of zipping children into their jackets and brief conversations with nannies, we were alone.

I quivered with nervousness at what we would say. Nothing could be tender enough to repair us.

"Let's go outside," I said. "Around the corner. I don't want to talk here at the school." I grabbed my coat and scarf off a hook in the cubby room.

As I bundled up, we walked in silence. You followed me because this was my territory. The security guard at the front entrance glanced at you, then nodded to me as you and I exited the building.

Drizzle began to fall, though it had not been forecast. Heavy snow was expected, not rain.

I tried to feel nothing as we wandered outside. My anguish from the other night had been so intense that I'd been on the verge of a mental collapse. I feared breaking further, especially in front of you. I had no idea what my body was capable of, and I didn't want to find out.

Rain streaked our eyewear, and out of nowhere I was disassociating, remembering the final scenes of *A Farewell to Arms.* Rain and suffering were still married in my mind. Your novel intruded into my thoughts, this lauded masterpiece that rendered me as utterly pathetic.

"Hey," you said when we reached the corner of 115th and Broadway.

Instead of answering, I trained my eyes on you. You, my betrayer, who had canceled much of my financial debt only for me to incur an even greater emotional debt to you, you who had distorted my persona for fame.

"There was some confusion the other night—" you started.

"Yeah, you forgot we had a date," I said. "Probably because you had another date, an overlapping one with another woman you call mi vida."

"She's not my girlfriend. I've never hidden my novias from you," you shot back.

Although there was truth to what you said, the weight of what was transpiring between us hit me like an infection. A heat originating in my stomach radiated up my torso and neck until it bloomed across my face.

"Oh, fuck your terms—girlfriend, novia. Leave your semantics and equivocating for *The New Yorker.* You lied to me about being the only one you called mi vida."

Thunder startled us overhead, as if nature were co-signing my anger. Within seconds, we were drenched in a downpour.

"The misunderstanding," I continued, "was that I thought I meant something to you, but it turns out that I don't. Your novel . . . all these years . . ."

I couldn't even finish my sentence, so I turned my back to you in humiliation. An image of us sitting across from each other in that first Harlem bakery flickered across my mind, both of us sipping coffee and embarking on this journey together.

The incessant rain and your cruelty were hollowing me out.

"Tatum," you said.

In your mouth, my name sounded like an indistinguishable riddle. When I didn't respond, you touched my shoulder to turn me around. Everything in me demanded I shout at you, tell you never to touch me, but I was vanishing and couldn't muster the will.

"Of course you matter to me"—your voice was cracking—"I paid for your—"

"Don't talk to me about money!" I finally managed to shout. "I'm talking about my very existence."

Your faux gentleness struck me as another facet of your indifference.

"No one is special to you. Not me, not anyone."

"Tatum."

"This *mattered* to me, Mateo. For a decade, I've lived a muted life, waiting for you to realize my importance. You were the nucleus of my world, and I was sure I would eventually be central to yours."

That's when I started hyperventilating. I turned, scurrying back like a maimed animal to hide in my classroom among the wooden blocks, Crayola markers, the boxes of dress-up clothes. If teaching kindergarten taught me one thing, it was that adult matters made me so sad. In my classroom, I could suspend my feelings for a bit among all the safe familiar objects.

I knew you wouldn't follow me that afternoon or ever again.

It took only a matter of hours for me to hate myself for saying the quiet part aloud. Toxic relationships are like ticking bombs. Once I pulled the pin and acknowledged your disregard, your disingenuousness, your betrayal, we could never rewind and begin again.

THE DALÍ CLOCK APPEARED TO BE MELTING. I shook my head and remembered that was the intended illusion. Jamal's voice echoed in my ear.

"I know when you agreed to this interview, you were hesitant," Jamal said.

"Honestly, had I known how much time this would take, I would've declined the request," I replied with a chuckle.

Over the past week, I had begun questioning my cooperation. A thought kept itching at the edges of my mind: In his own way, wasn't Jamal also using me for his own self-aggrandizement? This breaking story was sure to catapult his journalistic career.

"Well, I appreciate your participation in this investigation," Jamal said, his tone far friendlier than before. "You contributed to the public good, but I hope you got something out of this for yourself as well."

Out my living room window, I watched Vera's strawberry

guava shrub bend in the wind, then straighten itself. The tiny berries rattled before becoming still again.

"I probably did," I added coyly.

"Do you want to elaborate? Off the record?" Jamal asked.

"Not particularly," I answered honestly. "I'm fairly talked out on the subject."

My duty to the investigation was over, and Jamal wasn't entitled to a slideshow of my soul. Writing to Mateo, I was discovering, was doing more to pinpoint and neutralize my feelings than exposing my memories to Jamal ever could.

Days before, I had shared with Vera that what remained in my heart for Mateo was a tainted fondness. He was like a spoiled wine that I kept around because it had once been my favorite. What I hadn't shared, what was still forming, was the hope that soon I wouldn't need the corroded bottle or any echo of him.

Jamal allowed for a respectful silence to follow before continuing. "Thank you for all your time, Ms. Vega. You've been generous. Anything else I can assist you with?"

I twisted an agate ring around my index finger before speaking. "In fact, yes. Next time, think twice before cutting a woman down."

Jamal knew what I was referring to and murmured something that sounded apologetic.

"Will you notify me before the article goes live?"

"Absolutely. I can certainly do that," he said.

30.

The last question the journalist asked me was whether he could use my name. I said yes.

For the record, I believe the accusations brought against you. I haven't wanted you in my life for years, and now even less so. I can't read *Happiness* anymore. The first story I loved was "La Mónica," but now I wonder about the girl or woman who inspired it. What happened to her?

As a lifetime reader, I've learned to cultivate empathy even for villains. Despite everything that transpired between us, I don't hate you. We shared too much for me to hate you. You were the first person in the world to make me feel seen when I so needed a spotlight on me. That can never be undone.

Do you want to know my most formative memory of us? Before I sign off for good, I'll share it with you.

Kalmus Beach on Cape Cod was windy that May evening. You and I trudged side by side over small hills of corn-colored sand. I hated sand, but I didn't want to sound sour or unappreciative of nature, so I kept the pet peeve to myself.

You intertwined your fingers with mine, our palms clasped together, as we neared the lapping waves. The coast-line was part of a private beach from which we could make out indistinct moving figures we assumed to be other people. None of the shapes bore names and we were still intoxicated with each other from the night before when our bodies had become one. You flashed me a sweeping smile as we trudged over a peak of sand.

The wind picked up and crushed us together until I felt at home in your shadow. My own silhouette had been swallowed by your outline, and on the sand, I disappeared.

"Mateo," I whispered. "Don't ever move."

Acknowledgments

You wouldn't be reading this book were it not for my agent extraordinaire, Ashley Lopez. Big thanks to the entire Waxman Literary Agency. Special thanks to Cecily van Buren-Freedman for having smart ideas and for telling me when it was necessary to try again. I am so grateful to Randi Kramer and Celadon for welcoming me into the family.

This book was mostly drafted from 5:30 a.m. to 7:20 a.m. at Local Coffee in the Medical Center of San Antonio. Every barista who served me coffee and interacted with me on those mornings was a gift. Thank you for powering my brain with caffeine and being real friends through it all: Don Tran, Kyu Lee, Katie Well, Michael Alejandre, Elnuh, Johnny White, Jacob Bonetta, and Levi Travieso.

Super thanks to Alexandra Ford, who read the story version of *Like Happiness* and asked me a million questions. Answering those questions turned this into a full-bodied novel. Big thanks also to T Kira Madden, N. Michelle

AuBuchon, and Mona Awad for reading an earlier version of this novel. For their friendship and support, thank you to Nicole Dennis-Benn, Denne Michele Norris, Justine Champine, and Sebastián Páramo. I'm so grateful for my Sarah Lawrence experience and for my time with Mary LaChapelle, Mary Morris (who saw me cry so much), and Brian Morton (my second dad).

I have a battalion of excellent friends whose support has been invaluable. Big thanks to them all: Miriam Elman, Marques Brooks, Suleman Hussain, Kaustubh Thakur, Micaela Rios, Lilly Gonzalez, Robert James Russell, Chris Hoffman, Evan Mallon, Jenny Irish, David Hicks, Pam Kingsbury, Alejandro Varela, Kimberly Garza, Rheaclare Frasier-Spears, Keith Spears, Jiordan Castle, Moira Mackay, Gloria Mackay, Shannon McLeod, Steve Edwards, Jennifer Schooley, Eleanor Henderson, Nicolas Duron, DeMisty Bellinger, Melissa Kozak, Aaron Burch, James Brubaker, Elizabeth James Gonzalez, Fernando A. Flores, Rubén Degollado, Megan Giddings, Barry Duncan, Noah Bloem, and Zachary Bond.

This is a book about loving books. I have a lot of authors to thank for helping me become a pulsating mind. Big love to LaTanya McQueen, Sigrid Nunez, Melissa Broder, Fernanda Melchor, Olga Tokarczuk, Muriel Spark, Roberto Bolaño, Fannie Flagg, Barrett Swanson, Mary H.K. Choi, Brit Bennett, Kiese Laymon, Tommy Orange, Evie Wyld, Sylvia Plath, Julio Cortázar, Jason Mott, Junji Ito, Chris Ware, Adrian Tomine, Rutu Modan, Cathy Park Hong, Cristina Rivera Garza, Janet Malcolm, Karl Taro Greenfeld, Eman Quotah, Stephen Graham Jones, and Silvia Moreno-Garcia.

Who knows if I would be a writer today were it not for my middle school English teacher, Mrs. Suzanne Elizondo. She told me I was a born writer when I was only eleven years old. I believed her and good things followed.

All my love and gratitude go to my family, including Paulo, Loles, Cecilia, Ana, Bob, my brilliant munks, and Seleni. Thanks to my aunt Virginia for taking me to bookstores all throughout my childhood and cultivating my thirst for knowledge. Enormous thanks to my parents, Manuel and Sylvia, for never trying to convince me to be anything other than what I wanted to be—a writer.

My heart belongs to my husband, Fernando, for carving out a life with me that allows me to create books, revise them, hate them, perfect them, and send them out into the world.

ABOUT THE AUTHOR

Ursula Villarreal-Moura was born and raised in San Antonio, Texas. She is the author of *Math for the Self-Crippling*, a flash-fiction collection. *Like Happiness* is her first novel.

CELADON
BOOKS

Founded in 2017, Celadon Books, a division of
Macmillan Publishers, publishes a highly curated list
of twenty to twenty-five new titles a year. The list of
both fiction and nonfiction is eclectic and focuses
on publishing commercial and literary books and
discovering and nurturing talent.